Strictl

Jason could've been any one of those young punks standing on the corner of Sunset Boulevard, daring people to start a fight with him. That wasn't what Dahlia had in mind at all. She wrapped her wrists in the silver links of his wallet chain.

'You're playing,' he said. 'But I'm not.'

There it was again – that hot liquid look, as if he knew something about her – something she hadn't come to terms with yet herself.

As Jason pulled her into the car, his hand tight on the silver chain, she mentally asked herself her favourite question: who am I tonight? Her identity kept slipping, changing. In the bar, with her admirers, she'd been on top. Out here, on the back seat of Jason's car, she was on the bottom – and she loved every minute of it.

Strictly Confidential

ALISON TYLER

BLACK
lace

Black Lace novels contain sexual fantasies.
In real life, make sure you practise safe sex.

First published in 2001 by
Black Lace
Thames Wharf Studios,
Rainville Road, London W6 9HA

Typeset by SetSystems Ltd, Saffron Walden, Essex
Printed and bound by Mackays of Chatham PLC

ISBN 0 352 33624 2

To VK,
for everything.

To SAM,
for ever.

I am a DJ. I am what I play.

David Bowie

Prologue

'*P*ut your mouth on it, Dahlia.'
  'Like this?'
 'Just like that.'
 'Or this.' Bed sheets rustled. There was the unmistakable sound of skin on skin, followed by a palpable wetness in the dark. Almost like a kiss, but different.
 'That. Oh, God, *that*. That is so fucking good.'
 'Should I move down a little?' Her voice was perky, but every time she spoke, it stopped her from doing the one thing he wanted and took her pretty lips away from him.
 'I don't know, Dahlia. Don't ask me questions. I can't think.' He reached out to pull her to him, but wound up with his hands full of her thick, auburn hair. When she moved her head, the glossy strands slipped free from his fingers, leaving him holding on to nothing but air.
 'Please, baby,' he said next, trying a different tactic. 'Please.'
 Dahlia looked up at him, her green eyes flashing in the candlelight. 'Do you like that?' she asked. Her breath felt hot against his skin, dangerous yet sexy.
 He nodded and stared at her, seeing white teeth shining in a perfect smile, full lips that were wet and

1

slick. Dahlia was obviously in a playful mood. He wasn't. When he spoke again, his voice sounded husky, raw with need.

'Just don't stop,' he said softly. 'Don't ever, ever stop.'

Part I

'I've been a bad, bad girl.'
Fiona Apple, 'Criminal'

Chapter One

*F*riday was date night for Dahlia. She'd scheduled a double-header, meeting Harry for drinks at the Formica Cafe before dining in Beverly Hills with her newest fan. Having Martinis with Harry didn't actually count as a date. He liked the boys. Still, he always looked to Dahlia for help with his problematic love life. She had an innate sense about matchmaking.

Carolyn sat perched on the edge of Dahlia's white satin duvet, watching her roommate complete the final stages of her meticulous beauty rituals. First, Dahlia outlined her deep-set eyes using a kohl pencil, expertly smudging the line with the ball of her thumb. Mascara followed. She opened her mouth in a circle as she dragged the brush over her long, pre-curled eyelashes. Dahlia knew all the little tricks, the type featured in ten-step beauty articles about turning the everyday you into a better you. In the mirror, Dahlia nodded to the new-and-improved version of herself, then raised her expertly arched eyebrows at Carolyn.

'Going out tonight?' Dahlia asked the question in a sympathetic voice, obviously knowing the answer ahead of time. Carolyn shook her head. In the mirror, her own reflection was blurred, the lenses of her heavy black-framed glasses shining in the light. Unlike Dahlia, who was exquisitely decked out in a navy wrap-around dress, Carolyn had on her standard uniform: a long-sleeved white T-shirt, beat-up boots, and a pair of frayed jeans with holes ripped in the knees. She ran her hands along her slender arms as if for warmth, even though it was a balmy mid-September evening. Just another one of her nervous habits.

'Are you sure?' Dahlia asked. 'I'll bet Harry would be up for something.'

Carolyn shook her head again, more violently this time, her dark brown ponytail whipping back and forth. Instantly, Dahlia quit probing. She always knew just how far she could push this line of questioning.

'Then you can entertain Terrie?'

'No problem,' Carolyn said, meaning it.

'Don't know what I'd do without you.' Dahlia flashed her 200-watt super-smile. 'You're an angel.'

Dahlia was no angel. A positive fiend, she snaked one hand into Jason's lap as he manoeuvred his sleek red convertible along the twisting roads of the Hollywood Hills. At each intersection, Dahlia gave specific directions, knowing exactly where she wanted to go. She'd done this sort of thing before.

Jason listened carefully, but he had a difficult time concentrating on her words, especially when she unzipped his neatly pressed khakis and slipped her delicate fingers into the opening. Easily, her hand reached into the slit of his striped boxers, finding his straining hard-on, working it within her fist. She stroked him in perfect rhythm to the music on the radio, a Roxy Music classic. Bryan Ferry crooned from the speakers about catching that buzz. Love was the drug he was thinking of.

It was the drug that Jason was thinking of, too.

Or, if not exactly 'love', then certainly lust. Because, even after only one date, he had definitely fallen head over heels in lust with Dahlia. The girl was out of control, turning the evening into one unlike any he'd

6

previously experienced. Sure, he'd been with his share of sexy women before, but none who were so intensely focused on setting an erotic mood. None like Dahlia.

Jason wanted to look down and watch her fingers as they milked him, and he had to work to keep his eyes on the road. When she finally said, 'Here,' pointing to a spot where she wanted him to pull over, he sighed with relief.

But where exactly was 'here'?

He looked around as he parked his convertible on the lip of the road, then got out, walking to Dahlia's side of the car to hold open her door. She stood and gracefully turned to lean back against him, her body aligned with his. Jason's fly was still open, his cock striving forward, pressing hard against her ass. She was the one to sigh now, grinding backwards so that she could feel his erection, the promise of it making her squirm.

'What next?' Jason asked.

There really wasn't enough room in his foreign two-seater to fuck. Did she want him to bend her over the back of the car, lift up her dress, pull down her panties? He could do that. He was ready for anything. Since the moment her stockinged foot had probed under his pants cuff at dinner, tricking its way up his calf, he had been ready. Now, his hand slid along her firm thigh, dragging the silky material of her dress upwards with the movement.

'Wait,' Dahlia said softly. 'I want to look.'

From the edge of the road, they could see all of Hollywood, the lights of the city spread out like a magic carpet of shimmering jewels. A few paces from the convertible stood a metal chain-link fence, intended to keep graffiti artists spraying-distance away from the famous towering white letters of the Hollywood sign. Dahlia started down the sloping hill, and Jason followed her, understanding immediately. She wanted him to fuck her right here, where she could stare out at the lights, feeling the cooling night air on her skin, his warm body on hers from behind. She didn't even look over

7

her shoulder to see if he was following her. Such confidence. He liked that; liked her accepting the fact that he would come after her. It made him wonder what other things she might expect of him in the future.

Dahlia reached the fence first, then turned towards her date. Her eyes glowed at him, issuing a challenge. Jason moved quickly into action, undoing the tie at her waist that let her dress fall open. Then he hesitated a moment, and Dahlia, a half-smile on her face, took pity on him and helped, lifting her arms so that the dark cloth fell away from her body. She waited silently, hip cocked in a model's stance. Her cherry-red lingerie stood out boldly against her tanned skin. Jason stared at her, his body tense with anticipation.

'You are so fucking beautiful,' he said hungrily, wishing the words could equal his filthy thoughts. The way Dahlia looked against the fence was pure porno fantasy come to life. Her soft curves displayed on the background of hard steel made Jason's cock throb, ready for action. He wanted to take her right then, press her against the metal and fuck her. Yet he also didn't want to rush things, didn't want to let her down.

Dahlia's expression was one of patient understanding, and Jason longed to change it. He intended to make her as excited as she was making him, and this meant that he had to stop staring and start acting. With trembling fingers, he undid the clasp on her bra and slid it off. An idea blossomed in his mind, and without telling Dahlia what he was going to do, he turned her so that she faced the city again.

'You look out at the lights,' he said, lifting her arms over her head, using the bra to bind her wrists together, pinning them to the fence. Dahlia sighed, letting him know that he'd made the right decision and had guessed correctly that her fantasies might meld with his own.

In one swift motion, he slid her panties down her thighs and let her step out of them. She still had on her high-heeled sandals, but that only added to the vision. Naked against the fence, the moonlight bounced off her skin. Jason hesitated for another moment, just watching. He could smell the scent of her arousal, a perfume all around them. The fragrance was rich and heady, and it made him feel as if he'd drunk much more than just the one glass of red wine at dinner. He slid two fingers between her legs and came away with the liquid of her sex. She was dripping already, and he licked his fingers clean.

'So sweet,' he said, wishing for a moment that she was facing him so that he could lose himself in her body; seal his mouth against the split and drink from her. He could imagine it exactly – the sticky nectar smeared over his lips, melting away on his tongue. Then she whispered something that erased those candy-sweet images. Two words that made his heart race even faster than when she'd played footsie with him at the restaurant or even when she'd given him the hand job in the car.

'Spank me.'

Yes, she was his perfect match. But even though he'd wanted to play this way from the moment he'd first spotted her, he never would have allowed himself to hope that she would actually be into the games that he liked. Spanking games. The spark of pain that intensified pleasure for him. Worked through his body just like a drug.

Bryan Ferry was so right about that.

Pacing himself, he took a breath, preparing for his next move. With Dahlia's body captured by her wrists, he couldn't take her over his lap, but that truly didn't matter. They could try it that way later; could try it so many different ways. For now, he slapped her naked ass and then watched the rose-coloured handprint as it formed on her right cheek. He spanked the left side just as hard, and listened to her make that happy sighing noise again. He kept on spanking her while using one hand to wank himself because he couldn't wait any longer. His cock felt heavy in his hand, and he worked himself faster than when he was alone. Tugging on it, the need for relief overwhelming him, he envisioned coming on her reddened ass, but no ... that would be such a waste. He had to be inside her, to feel her wetness surrounding him, enveloping him.

Still he spanked her harder, longer, so that she ground her hips up against the cold metal fence. He watched as the pain flowed through her, making her back straighten, making her toss her hair away from her lovely, heart-shaped face. When she turned her head, he could see crystalline tears sparkling in the corners of her eyes, and he knew that the picture-postcard view before her had become blurred, an impressionist's vision of the lights of the city. He was pleased that she didn't tell him to stop, and seemed to draw strength from accepting what he gave her. To him, this meant that she would be willing to go deeper, to play rougher.

In the future, he would introduce her to all of his favourite activities. Now that he knew she would be a willing partner, he could open the dark toy chest of his mind and show her who he really was. Break out the tools, the implements, paddles and belts, cuffs and crops, blindfolds and ball gags. For now, he would be satisfied with spanking her lovely ass and listening to her breath as it sped up, excited, catching in her throat.

As his fingers played over her body, Jason felt a sudden need to be naked, too. Urgently, he pulled his light grey V-neck sweater over his head, then kicked off his shoes, slacks and boxers. Then he took her, slammed her up against the fence, the cool metal in her fingers, his hot body entering hers from behind.

His cock parted the lips of her pussy, thrusting forward, meeting the creamy wetness that awaited him. She gripped on to him as tightly as her fingers were hooked into the metal openings of the fence, and the power behind her contractions made him groan. Neither said a word, although he felt that she spoke to him with her body; told him how to fuck her, how hard to ride her, how deep to plunge. He used his cock with finesse, letting her feel the length of it, the whole rod, before teasing her with only the head, rocking that in the mouth of her pussy. Even revved up to the point of desperation, he held himself back.

'You like that, baby?' he murmured, the tension in his voice giving away how difficult it was for him to stay so contained. 'You like that, don't you?'

She didn't reply, didn't formulate the words. Instead, when Dahlia came, she leaned her body against his, her soft ginger-coloured hair cascading over his chest, her back arched. Startling Jason, she suddenly screamed into the night. Howled, like some wild animal, a creature unleashed. To look at her, one would think that she'd never let loose. Never got dirty. But now Jason realised that this image couldn't have been further from the truth. Pure on the outside, maybe, but wicked on the inside. She was his favourite type of girl, one whose mixture of sweetness and sin was both rare and special.

Then he finally had to stop thinking, stop categorising her, watching her reactions. Because Dahlia's screams made Jason come with her, pumping once again and then reaching the place of release that he had yearned for all evening.

It was like a dream.

But it was real.

Terrie and Carolyn went for a starlit walk to the park. At least, it might have been starlit had they lived in a location less populated than Los Angeles. Here, the Big Dipper was obscured by millions of city lights. To see constellations, Los Angelenos had to drive to the Griffith Observatory and watch a glittering light show on a make-believe sky. LA was never entirely dark, but Carolyn didn't mind. The light was comforting.

As was her mace.

When she walked solo she was armed with a canister, carried in her right hand, ready at all times. 'That's the only way mace works,' her self-defence instructor had explained to the class. 'If you have to search for it in your jacket pocket, you'll either find it too late or end up gripping a can of breath freshener, which just isn't as

11

effective. Not even spearmint.' With Terrie at her side, Carolyn was able to let her guard down – not much, but slightly.

This evening, the duo walked a bit later than usual, heading to the stretch of green grass near the famous CBS studios on Fairfax. After looping several times through the park, they strolled the long way home along Beverly Boulevard, past a line of casually dressed people standing outside of Sammy's Mango Hut, a cult favourite restaurant. Couples mingled outdoors while waiting for the best tables on the tiny patio. The tinkling of Margarita glasses carried on the breeze, and Carolyn could almost taste the lime and salt, the sweet and sour.

Within a block of Melrose, the neighbourhood took on a slightly seedier edge. Collages of colourful flyers, like works of modern art, were affixed to telephone poles. A brown-eyed teenager smiled down from one poster. Above her photo was the word 'LOST' in bold, black letters. Carolyn had seen the recent news reports – the girl had been missing for several weeks – and she felt her body tense as she passed by the picture. There was still hope that she was simply a runaway, that she would wander back to her family on her own. Still, Carolyn swallowed hard, trying to erase the wash of fear that had so quickly come over her.

No need to worry – she and Terrie were almost home. Turning one more corner, the two could see their four-plex apartment, where a rectangular 'For Rent' sign stood amidst several plastic pink flamingos in the centre of the building's well-manicured front lawn. Carolyn felt her heart rate return to normal as she slipped her mace back into her pocket. Safe home again, she and Terrie bounded into the living room from the landing. As usual, Terrie reclined on the cream-coloured suede sofa while Carolyn headed to the kitchen to get them each a drink. Hers in a wine goblet, his in a large blue plastic bowl. Her standing Friday night date was with the sweetest-faced, golden-furred mutt in Southern California.

'Come on, baby doll,' Carolyn heard when she reached the kitchen. She spun around wildly, looking for the source of the voice. A man was speaking, his tone low and cajoling, and it sounded as if he were standing directly behind her. A quick inspection of the small kitchen confirmed that it was empty. Standing still, Carolyn waited to hear the voice speak again and solve the mystery. She wouldn't accept that her kitchen had suddenly become haunted.

'You *know* you want to.'

There. From the metal grate low down on the wall. Without thinking, she bent on her knees on the black and white linoleum squares, getting in close to the bronzed curlicues. The metal was covered with a light layer of dust, so she didn't breathe in.

'Do you like the way that feels, Dahlia?'

The grate, which led to Dahlia's closet, was an old-fashioned remnant from a time before central heating. From the kitchen, it appeared to be a modern artist's version of a very fancy cat door. From Dahlia's room, Carolyn knew that the grate was invisible unless you went into the closet and moved aside her impressive collection of high-heeled shoes, marabou slippers and zippered vinyl boots.

'What a pretty baby you are.'

Carolyn put it together that the man speaking was Jason, Dahlia's date, but she couldn't figure out where they were. Did they decide that making out amidst Dahlia's clothes would be exciting? Or were they pressed against the wall opposite the kitchen, putting on a live porno show for her personal listening pleasure?

Terrie barked from the other room, growing impatient for his drink. If the lovers hadn't known she was home before, they did now. Terrie had made that clear to everyone in the building. Carolyn quietly filled his bowl with cold tap water and took it to him. He lapped contentedly, and she returned to the kitchen for her own drink. She expected Dahlia to come out of her room, long silk robe wrapped around her, carefully applied

13

crimson lipstick now smeared slightly past the edges of her smile. Dahlia never looked unattractive, even in disarray. If anything, the rumpled effect added to her allure and gave an appearance to Dahlia that not many people saw. Although more had in the few months since Dahlia had broken up with her steady boyfriend, Dante. Not that Carolyn was counting. Or if she was counting, not that she'd ever let on.

As she poured herself a glass of her favourite white wine, Carolyn was mildly surprised that Dahlia hadn't emerged from her room. Then she heard the man speaking again, as if the lovers didn't know that she was home, or as if they didn't care. This, she quickly realised, was the more likely scenario. Drawn closer to the grate, Carolyn bent awkwardly, listening. Jason's deep voice grew increasingly seductive, not begging, not insisting, just stating in a low tone what he wanted Dahlia to do.

And he wanted her to do the dirtiest things.

That's why Dahlia hadn't come out of her room, why she hadn't blushed becomingly and apologised for the noise. It suddenly made perfect sense to Carolyn because Dahlia liked to do dirty things, then share them with her roommate later on, when she was all clean and shining. Carolyn now realised she could finally get a true idea of what happened on one of Dahlia's dates. Crouched near the grate, she sipped her chilled wine and strained to hear.

'Just like that,' the man said. 'Get it nice and wet for me.'

It was like listening to a porno movie, an X-rated dialogue put on for an intended audience of two, but an actual audience of three. On her knees, Carolyn pressed her ear closer to the grate, certain that she would have time to stand and brush the dust from her hair if either lover walked out of the room and down the hallway.

'Such a pretty girl,' the man said. 'Look at yourself in the mirror while you do that. See what a beautiful girl looks like when she's sucking cock. Suck hard, like you would a peppermint stick. Lick all around the tip.'

Carolyn took a deep breath. She was uncomfortable listening, not only because of the awkward position, but also because she was spying on her best friend. Still, she couldn't seem to make herself stop.

'You like that?' A pause, then, 'I can feel for myself just how much you like it.'

Carolyn bit her bottom lip, thinking. She knew that she should go back to her bedroom, shut the door and start to work. She had a stack of demo tapes to listen to, each one from a desperate band, dying to get airplay. As one of Los Angeles' premier DJs, Carolyn had final say over what she played. She liked to give new talent a chance, and was one of the few disc jockeys who dedicated air time to bands who weren't yet established, even though this meant listening to a lot of bad music in the first instance. With her headset on, she wouldn't be able to hear anything else in the apartment. Maybe Dahlia had been counting on that when she'd brought Jason home, certain that Carolyn was already safe in her bedroom with a head full of music.

For some reason, Carolyn couldn't force her feet to follow the mental command to return to her room. Instead, she remained frozen in place, only occasionally moving to take a sip of her wine.

When the man spoke again, his voice was muffled, and Carolyn wondered if the lovers were in a 69 now, with him pleasuring Dahlia in the same way that she was working him. Apparently, he still had the desire to keep talking. 'You taste so good,' he murmured. Dahlia's response was unintelligible, but Carolyn made out the cadence, a sigh of assent to his questions.

The wine relaxed her, and she pressed her ear firmly to the grate to hear every word. Dust didn't bother her any more. She was drawn, as if magnetically, to the metal of the grate, to the visions that waited for her in a room only one wall away. She could easily picture Dahlia holding herself above Jason, head to tail. Every so often, Dahlia would look up into the mirror and see her reflection – lips stained with what remained of her berry-coloured gloss, eyelids half shut in ecstasy.

The only thing missing from Carolyn's mental movie was an image of Jason, since she'd never met the man. It didn't really matter, though. Carolyn found that it was easy enough to insert a fantasy figure into her imagined scenario. Someone like Zachary Modine, the lead singer of Zoom Box. She was set to interview him the following day for her radio show and had been knocked out by the headshot his agent had sent her. Good-looking enough to be a model, rather than a musician, he worked well in her fantasy. Zach doing Dahlia. That was a pretty picture.

On her knees on the cool lino, Carolyn bent almost as if in prayer. She stayed in that position until the creak of the bedroom door forced her to jump up. Then she moved quietly through the kitchen to the living room to adopt a relaxed position next to Terrie on the couch, as if she'd been there all along.

To Dahlia, sex was a contact sport. One that she intended to win.

No, she hadn't planned on sleeping with Jason on their first date, but look at the way he treated her. She hadn't freaked him out by playing footsie at dinner, not even when her toes had sought out the crotch of his slacks, stroking his erection up and down during the second course of their meal.

This was one of Dahlia's favourite forms of flirting. Teasing a man mercilessly when there was little he could do to respond. She adored being in total control of the situation, yet at the same time out of reach. At least, for the moment. Some dates, when put to similar challenges, had failed, wanting to leave the restaurant at once, taking her overture as a demand for instant sex. Not what she had in mind at all.

Jason had understood. Yes, his hazel eyes had opened wider in a combination of obvious shock and delight, but he had actually impressed her. Reaching forward, he'd offered her a bite from his plate, sliding the cold metal fork between her lips, feeding her. Playing with her. Exactly as he should have responded. Her under-the-table foray was meant only as an appetiser – a peek at what was potentially yet to come, *if* the man behaved himself.

His willingness to go along with the game – even though she hadn't explained the rules – had made her up the ante, trying harder to see if he would continue to match her desires. And he had. The fact that he'd actually added his own rules simply won him more points. Of course, what Jason didn't realise was that Dahlia's rules tended to change by the minute. She grew bored easily when things became routine, and wanted excitement. Adventure. She liked to create make-believe scenarios, always asking herself the one important question: who did she want to be tonight?

This evening, she'd started out by casting herself as a glamour queen from the age of the silver screen. She'd dressed the part in her forties-style outfit, a voluptuous vixen play-acting her film-noir fantasies. Jason, even if he hadn't fully understood what she was envisioning, had managed to star in his role to perfection. Tying her to the fence with her own bra had been the ultimate move. Less predictable than a pair of regulation steel handcuffs although, in Dahlia's opinion, those did have a time and place of their own. And the choice had been more sensuous than if he'd used his black leather belt around her slim wrists.

Not since Dante had she felt so connected with someone.

Literally connected, she thought, as he brought her back to the present by rocking his cock inside her warm, wet mouth, letting her feel the head pressing against the back of her throat. His eager intensity further fuelled her pleasure. She loved it when a man became hard because of something she did – whether simply from the way she looked at him, a coy glance from under her long lashes, or from the moves she made. To reward Jason

17

now, she worked him slowly, taking her time, slipping her tongue up the length of his rod, then moving so that she only held the tip in her mouth. She tightened her lips around it, sucking hard, as if it were the rounded ball of an all-day sucker.

Or an all-night sucker, in this case.

It had been several weeks since she'd last had sex, and being next to Jason's lean, naked body made her feel alive again. Since breaking up with Dante, her world had been off-kilter. Sure, there were plenty of guys who wanted to do her, but she needed to experience an electricity with any prospective bedmate before doing the nasty between the sheets . . . or against a fence. She had that electricity with Jason.

Oh, did she ever.

Taking a breath, she chided herself for lying. Most definitely, she had planned on sleeping with him. At least, subconsciously. Why else would she have worn her most expensive red satin bra and panty set if she hadn't thought he would get to peek at them? She wouldn't mourn their loss, even though the set had been one of her favourites. Losing them had actually been more pleasurable than wearing them.

Closing her eyes, she visualised the way the lacy bra had looked, still tied to the chain-link fence where Jason had fucked her after dinner. Spanked her and then fucked her. What a thrilling surprise. When they'd first met at Ed's Diner, the hipster cafe next to the salon where she worked, she'd thought that he might like to do the sort of things she did. The way he'd stared at her had given her an array of naughty ideas. But one could never be sure. There were plenty of kinky people in Hollywood, yet there were also loads of actors. Men who looked as if they could walk the walk, but ended up melting under pressure.

Not Jason. He was a keeper. The man had incredible stamina and required almost no 'down time' between rounds. Because now he was taking her again for the second ride since they'd arrived back at her apartment.

Even more thrilling than his staying power was the fact that she didn't have to tell him what she wanted. His tongue thrust into her pussy just the way she liked it, his teeth gently nipping at her clit. Although at the beginning of a session she always liked a soft touch, as the passion rose another level, she could take it more firmly. He understood this instinctively, responding a beat before she even knew what she desired herself. That took skill, and she sighed and ground herself against his mouth as he drew the point of his tongue in sensual, spiralling designs.

'Oh, yes,' she moaned, unable to stop herself. 'That is so good.'

He responded with a new trick, tightening his lips around her clit and giving her a solid suck that made her shiver all over. It was as if every nerve ending in her body was connected to the magical gem between her legs. Warm pulses of pleasure burst through her so intensely that she could picture them as radiating bands of colour. Red. Gold. Violet. An aura of erotic sensation shimmering around her. To match the way he was pleasing her with his mouth, Jason ran his fingers along her ribs, stroking her in synchronicity to the rhythm that he was using on her clit.

Then he returned to drawing teasing, tickling patterns with his tongue that didn't touch her clit at all. He volleyed back and forth, taking her to the edge, and then sliding her slowly down. Not letting her reach it. Even when she thought she was seconds away from coming, he was able to keep her teetering on the brink. The fact that he was in control made Dahlia suddenly second-guess her own abilities. Maybe she wouldn't win this round, after all . . . unless coming first meant winning, because she was definitely going to climax.

Now. And loudly.

Who would have guessed they would have reached this point so quickly?

Thoughts of Carolyn flickered briefly through her mind. But her roommate wouldn't be disturbed. She was hard at work in her room, listening to one god-awful garage band after another. That's how she always spent her free time, searching for the future Stones or Chili Peppers or Wallflowers. Every other night away from the radio station, Carolyn would be closeted in her room, expensive headset in place, feet kicked up on her thrift-store wooden desk, encased in a private capsule of music. That was her idea of a good time.

Besides, the two girls had roomed together since college, and Carolyn had never complained about noise before. And there *had* been noise from Dahlia's room in the past. She was, without a doubt, what the boys in high school had called a 'screamer', a moniker that she appreciated. It was important to have the confidence that went along with showing a man how good he made you feel. Girls who were eerily silent when they came just didn't understand the point.

'You like that, baby?' Jason asked softly, moving his mouth away from her body just long enough to ask the question. 'If you like it, then show me. Let me hear it. I loved those noises you made out on the hill.'

Knowing that Carolyn was most likely secluded in her own bedroom, connected with a series of wires from her fancy headset to her expensive, high-tech stereo, Dahlia did exactly as Jason asked. She gave in loudly, arching to press her body firmly to her new lover's lips.

Screaming as the pleasure slammed through her and carried her away.

'What the fuck?'

Carolyn had been DJing since college, and early on had trained herself not to swear. There were words (seven, specifically) that were banned from on-air usage, and she never wanted one to slip out by mistake. To say that a band was 'fucking awesome' or that an album was 'total shit' would be a career-damaging move. But sometimes, away from the studio, she couldn't help herself, and simply had to turn the mental censor off. Times like now, in the privacy of the kitchen, when all

20

she could think was, *What the fuck is Dahlia doing?* Because Dahlia had clearly gotten into something brand spanking new, and as Carolyn sipped her wine, she tried hard to figure out exactly what it was.

Moments before, the bedroom door had opened with a creak and then closed again quickly, as if someone had paused, listening, wanting to know where she was in the apartment. As soon as the door shut, Carolyn had returned from the living room to her newly designated spot on the black and white squares, trying to get a handle on why her roommate was behaving in this new, and loud, manner.

It wasn't that difficult to figure out. She knew Dahlia's tricks ... or at least some of them. After being friends for eight years she was aware that her roommate liked to cast herself in the role of some other person, either real or make-believe.

'You get to try someone else on for an evening,' Dahlia had once told her. They'd been at Sammy's Mango Hut, their favourite neighbourhood bar, on one of those rare dateless nights.

'Like playing dress up?'

'This is the funky grown-up version,' Dahlia had explained, vibrant curls bouncing as she moved. 'Choose your role for the evening, and try to stay in character.' She'd locked eyes with Carolyn, before adding, 'Every once in a while, I don't want to be me any more. I want to be someone else.'

In a way, Carolyn played the exact same game. At the radio station, she became a different person entirely: Stormy Winters, her on-air self. But it made less sense that Dahlia would want to play make-believe. With her stunning good looks and her ability to capture every man's attention in any situation, most women would die to be her.

'I get bored easily,' Dahlia had said, and Carolyn realised that her roommate didn't mean to sound stuck up, that she was actually being honest. 'When I make a game out of it then I can have a good time,' Dahlia said.

Suddenly, Carolyn had to stop thinking and just listen, mesmerised, as her roommate reached that sexual point of no return. From the kitchen, she heard Dahlia scream Jason's name, as if her volume dial had been cranked up to the max. Was Dahlia lost in some role-playing mode, forgetting that Carolyn might hear? Or was she being her normal self, out to get pleasure without caring what other people might think?

Carolyn didn't know. All she was sure of was that until she was certain that the lovers were finished, she couldn't make herself walk away.

Chapter Two

*I*n the morning, Carolyn was hit by a wave of guilt so strong that her normally pale skin flamed up as if she'd been messing with Dahlia's cosmetics. She decided to come clean about eavesdropping as soon as she saw her roommate. Confess and suggest that Dahlia flip the little lever on the grate to close it, effectively sealing off the sounds from the kitchen. That was her plan, and she felt secure in the decision. But an hour later, when she looked up from her desk and caught Dahlia in her emerald robe, standing in the doorway radiating pleasure, Carolyn deftly changed her mind. She wasn't going to tell. Easy as that.

'Last night was fantastic,' Dahlia said, smiling sleepily.

Carolyn slid into her role of the confidante, a part she'd played since college. Over the years, Dahlia had shared loads of her experiences: fucking one of her co-workers on an amusement park aerial ride; seducing the teacher's assistant for her English composition class. Will Davis had been a shy but attractive grad student, and they had actually done it on his desk during office hours. Even with her poor attendance record, Dahlia had received an A for her 'extra-curricular' activities. More recently, she'd divulged every detail about the time her ex-boyfriend Dante had done her at a Hollywood movie theatre, his long leather jacket hiding the place where their bare skin joined, the film's soundtrack masking the noise.

But it was different this morning because Carolyn knew all about Dahlia's evening. Much later, alone in bed, she'd had no trouble picturing each frame of their living movie, one hand snaking beneath the sheet and into the bottoms of her old flannel pyjamas. Was this what had her feeling the most guilty?

'Did you have fun with Harry?' Carolyn asked, stalling for time. Of all Dahlia's salon cronies, Harry was Carolyn's favourite. He wore women's clothes, slinky skirts paired with tight lycra turtlenecks, and his long black hair captured high in a ponytail. His job as the star make-up artist at Chez Chaz, the high-end salon where both he and Dahlia worked, meant that he could actually turn himself into a fairly convincing woman. At least, until he spoke. His deep voice, with his sexy Irish accent, gave him away every time.

The only problem with Harry was that, just like Dahlia, he was always after Carolyn to go out on dates. 'Gorgeous,' he'd trill, 'take it from me. The first plunge is the hardest and then it's all icing on a cake. Chocolate. Vanilla. Butterscotch swirl – whatever you're in the mood for.' Harry could make anything sound sexual. The way he said 'swirl' was positively X-rated. That was part of his appeal.

Carolyn would grin at him but ignore the suggestion, changing the subject back to Harry's own love life. She wasn't ready to rejoin the dating scene. Honestly, she might never be. But she still cared about what was going on with Harry, and paid attention as Dahlia told her the scoop.

'Harry's just having trouble with his latest beau,' Dahlia explained. 'He only wanted to talk.' In Carolyn's opinion, one of Dahlia's best attributes was that she could listen when that was all someone needed, stifling the urge to spout words of wisdom. At the salon, people confided in her constantly, using her as cheap therapy.

'Really, he should dump Jake and move on,' Dahlia explained. 'But Harry has to come to that decision all by himself.' Now she looked at her roommate expectantly, as if to ask, 'Can I tell you about my evening now? Can I, please?'

Carolyn said, 'So back to Jason,' and Dahlia beamed at her.

'He was even wonderful at dinner,' she said softly, making Carolyn wonder whether the man was nearby, perhaps getting dressed in Dahlia's room, pulling on his wrinkled slacks, looking around for a missing sock, wondering what the heck had happened to the buttons from his shirt. Maybe he was sitting on the edge of the bed and guessing how long he was required by etiquette to hang around.

Let's see, we made love twice last night and she woke me up with one fuck of a good blow job, so I have to stay here for breakfast and a walk in the park.

'We sat outside at The Bougainvillaea, out on the patio, you know?'

Carolyn nodded. She'd been to the twinkling hide-away for one of Virgin Records' star-studded launch parties. Hidden on Robertson, just off-centre of Beverly Hills, the restaurant offered a romantic setting to the celebrity crowd.

'He held my hand and looked into my eyes. He was so sweet.'

Now Carolyn camouflaged a disbelieving snort beneath a cough, as if clearing her throat. Dahlia liked the dirty boys, the ones with a little grease under their fingernails – designer grease. They should be rich enough to handle her desires, but twisted enough to satisfy her wild streak. If Dahlia told them to bring a pair of handcuffs to the theatre, they should have the balls to simply ask 'Fur-lined or steel?' and leave the rest up to her.

Besides, Carolyn had heard the things Jason had said. He wasn't sweet at all. She thought back to all the other times when Dahlia had talked about her dates and wondered whether she'd lied in the past. If not, why was she lying this time? Since Carolyn couldn't ask her those questions, she said, 'So you think he's the one?'

The dreamy quality faded slightly, as if a light inside Dahlia's brilliant smile had burned out. 'Who said there had to be just one?' she asked, giving Carolyn an evil grin.

The man must be gone, Carolyn thought. Would Dahlia say something like that if he could hear her?

Dahlia pulled a comb from the deep pocket of her robe and casually began to groom herself, dragging the tortoiseshell teeth through her loose, red curls. Sunlight caught in her hair and made the soft waves look gold-streaked, like a lion's mane. 'I wouldn't be happy with just one,' she added, turning to see her reflection in the window and nodding contentedly at what she saw.

Why did she change her story?

Dahlia couldn't explain it. Not even to herself. She liked sharing with Carolyn, liked drawing out the details, reliving the previous evening's events. From Carolyn's leading questions, Dahlia knew that her roommate relished the stories as much as she enjoyed telling them. And, in a way, she thought that discussing her experiences in such a straightforward manner might actually help Carolyn venture on some dates herself.

Of course, Dahlia understood why her roommate had stopped going out. Being stalked by some rabid fan would make anyone feel nervous and vulnerable. That's why Carolyn carried her mace, why she flinched whenever they received a hang-up on their answering machine. Carolyn had gotten it particularly bad when that guy in college had developed a fantasy relationship with her radio personality. He'd actually believed that she was his girlfriend. Steven had been a total psycho. But awful things happened to lots of people, and most

26

recovered. Carolyn hadn't. She'd shut down that part of herself, pouring all of her energy into her work, refusing to consider dating again. Fearful of men, of strangers, of closeness.

Now, it had been years, actual years, since Carolyn had let herself enjoy the company of a man. Poor thing. The company of men was one of the true pleasures in life. At least, in Dahlia's opinion.

But, still, sometimes Dahlia changed the facts when she shared her stories with her roommate, making things more – or less – exciting than they actually had been. She'd always been a creative liar, constantly stretching the truth to suit her purposes. Told little white lies, or big black lies, without an ounce of guilt. Usually, she had her reasons. She never told a guy that she was seeing more than one person, and wouldn't consider confessing that she'd tried a particularly wicked activity before.

Who benefited from those sorts of truths?

Then there were times, like this morning, when she didn't know why she lied. Leaving out the fact that Jason had fucked her against a fence hadn't been planned. She'd thought about telling the whole thing, about making Carolyn's dark blue eyes widen in surprise. Thought about confessing how cool it had all been. Watching the city, the lights twinkling like fireflies below as she'd felt Jason's body pressed hard against hers. The words were on the tip of her tongue when she'd sat on Carolyn's bed, but the story just didn't come out.

Maybe it was that she liked to keep part of her world secret, to relive in private all of the different things that she experienced. That made sense, except she never kept anything from Harry. Not one single thing. So what did that mean?

As she got ready for work, following her normally intricate make-up ritual, she met her gaze in the bathroom mirror and tried to decipher the look in her own eyes. Tried and failed.

27

What Dahlia was more than anything else was an enigma.

Sometimes even to herself.

She was also an enigma to her ex-boyfriend, Dante, who was waiting for her outside of Ed's Diner, the cafe situated next door to Chez Chaz. Waiting because Dahlia had called him from her cell phone on her way to the salon and asked him what he was doing this morning. He didn't know exactly what she had in mind – he never did – but when Dahlia rang, Dante came. Often both literally and figuratively.

As Dahlia approached, he ran a hand through his longish dark hair, pushing it away from his forehead. He wasn't nervous, just excited. It had been several weeks since they'd gotten together and he felt the need for her building within him, a wrenching desire that started somewhere in the base of his stomach and worked down lower, making his cock harden just from watching her walk. And what a walk. Her trademark strut made her hips swivel in the most dreamy way beneath her short skirt. Dante knew he wasn't the only one affected by the way she moved. Several male customers at the diner turned to admire Dahlia's approach as well.

'Baby doll,' Dante said, as she reached his side.

'Lover boy,' she replied, as always. 'Whatever are you doing here?' she asked in her slightly Southern Belle fashion, as if she didn't even remember that she'd called him twenty minutes before. She couldn't hide her smile at the fact that he was waiting for her.

'Hoping that I'm going to be doing you,' Dante said.

Dahlia felt something flutter in her chest at the way Dante was eyeing her. She had to be at the salon in less than a half an hour, yet there was always time in Dahlia's schedule for a little afternoon (or morning) delight. What was the point of life if not to take advantage of the fun parts?

'Where?' she asked now, although she knew. They

had often played like this in the past, and scattered around the city were several of their favourite places to fuck. Places like the mirrored unisex bathroom at the elegant Shim-Sham Club. Or the large, tiled swimming pool in Dante's back yard. Or even the salon's private elevator that whisked celebrities from the parking garage to Chaz's private penthouse without forcing them to ever merge with the public.

'Is the red carpet unfurled?' Dante asked, the code for finding out whether a celebrity was due to visit the salon for an early cut and dry.

Dahlia shook her head then turned around, knowing that Dante would follow her. Didn't men always follow wherever she led? They walked quickly around the corner to the parking level entrance. Dahlia had a key to the private elevator, and she and Dante entered it without a word.

Although she'd been charged up from her experience with Jason, she had felt only momentarily satisfied. Sex always made her want more sex. And Dante was the one man she knew who would always give it to her exactly the way she wanted it. So this morning she had dressed for the experience, wearing only garters, stockings and a lavender G-string beneath her silvery mini-skirt. No pantyhose to get in the way. It was important to be prepared. Wasn't that the Boy Scouts' motto? Maybe she should do more Boy Scouts . . .

As the doors shut, Dante took her in his arms and kissed her. He knew exactly how to do it, starting slowly, just tickling her lips with the tip of his tongue, then parting them and meeting her tongue with his own. Good kissing to Dahlia was like a dance, and for this particular samba, Dante was her favourite partner.

What was there about kissing him that made her body feel as if it were melting? She didn't know, but her legs trembled, and she was grateful when he lifted her up off the floor, holding her so that she didn't have to think any more and could let him control the situation. The kiss lengthened, and Dante moved his mouth slowly away from her lips and along her throat, lingering there, teasing the delicate hollow of her long neck. He nuzzled against her and she felt herself grow even more aroused. Often when they made love in a public place, it was rushed. But Dante seemed to want to take his time this morning. To make it last.

He released her only long enough to undo his black gabardine slacks, and then lifted her in his arms again, slipping her lacy nothing of an undergarment aside with his fingers. She shivered at the sensation of his fingers on her sex, just the brush of his fingertips against her as he positioned her body just right. With two fingers he held her lips open. Then, still without a word, he entered her, giving her a taste of how turned-on he was as he slipped her up and back on his rock-hard cock.

In Dahlia's mind, Dante was always hard.

The elevator took them on a silent ride to the top floor. Effortless. Totally quiet, just like his fucking technique. His hands on her hips, he worked her powerfully up and down as they rode to the top floor and back, five times. Fast. This was the kind of tryst that Dahlia lived for; the type of story other people only read about in the letter columns in men's magazines: 'I honestly can't believe I did this, but my ex-boyfriend and I fucked before work at our office elevator . . .'

He always seemed to know the mood she was in. It was why they were so good together. At least in bed. Some couples got into ruts, routines – touch breasts then stroke ass then kiss lips – every time doing the same thing in order to reach the final results. Dante wasn't like that. It was his personal belief that good sex never need be the same. In fact, he had a goal to always make something different. If they did it twice in the same position, he would talk to her, paint an imaginary picture that took them both somewhere else.

Right now, as he fucked her, he broke the silence, sharing a brand-new fantasy with her. The story involved her, him and a famous movie star they both admired. Dahlia loved the way he spun his tales. He was a writer, and as such seemed more capable than other men of creating make-believe worlds. Better still, he never pressured her to make the fantasies come true, and could leave the erotic story in the bedroom. Another plus. Some ideas were best left at the fantasy level.

'When the door opens, all the people will be waiting to greet us,' he said softly. 'We'll stroll naked out on to the red carpet, and when we get to the very centre, we'll stop.'

She imagined him, her and the movie star on the scarlet carpet while the paparazzi flashed their cameras at them – ménage à trois fucking to a medley of strobe lights. It was a unique image, and the thought of it made her hotter and wetter as he continued to thrust his slicked-up cock inside of her.

'You'd like that, wouldn't you?' he murmured. 'All those people watching.'

'Yes,' she sighed. Oh, she'd definitely like it. And then she imagined seeing the photos afterwards, perhaps displayed in the 'Living' section of the *LA Times*. What a fucking thrill.

'Tell me,' Dante demanded, wanting her to take part in creating this fantasy. 'How do you see it?'

'They'll all be dressed in black tie,' she said, easily visualising the image as she spoke. The fact that everyone else would be clothed while they would be naked gave her an extra charge. 'And they'll watch us as if we were the paid entertainment for the evening.'

Her descriptions made Dante sigh and drive harder inside her. There were no more words after that. Just fucking, long and deep. She could see their reflections in the mirror on the polished silver back of the elevator doors, focused on what it looked like as he worked her up and down. Dante was, she'd always thought, too handsome to be just a writer. He had inherited his dark hair and eyes from his Italian father, and his high cheekbones from Native American blood on his mother's side. The mixture reminded her of a silent movie star –

someone like Rudolph Valentino. His smouldering gaze was able to tell her secrets without parting his lips.

Then she had to close her eyes, to concentrate, as he found a special rhythm and moved her to it. With Dante, sex was like slow dancing to your favourite song, one that you hoped was never going to end.

Carolyn spent the morning in her plush office at the radio station, daydreaming as she waited for Zachary Modine to arrive. Despite her guilt at eavesdropping on her roommate the previous evening, she couldn't help but lose herself in the erotic memory. What a thrilling life Dahlia led. Being able to let go in that way, to vocalise her pleasure. Carolyn was more contained. *All* contained. Her face was like the surface of a deep lake. Nothing deep inside ever bubbled up to the top. Yet for some reason, remembering her roommate's actions made her feel excited and sort of pre-date jittery.

Was it because she was about to come face to face with a local icon – the incredibly attractive Zach Modine, he of the blue eyes and subtle half-smile? It was a dangerous combination that was famous for making even the most jaded Hollywood girls melt when he took the stage. His photo stared up at her from her desk, and she absentmindedly stroked the shiny black and white surface with the tips of her fingers, tracing the strong line of his jaw, the indent of his cheek.

Man, she was acting like a love-struck teenager.

There was a second picture beneath the first, and she slid it out to take a look. This one showed the band together on their instruments – Zach, Roger, Melody and Freddy at a gig. The energy between them was visible, tangible. She believed that they were going to make it, and she always had a good feel for things like this. Their single, 'Stay Cherry', was already climbing up the charts, and she had a sense that even if it took months, they would ultimately explode to the very top.

But what she really wanted was for Zach to explode inside her.

Had she actually thought that? This wasn't like her at all. She rubbed fiercely at her temples with her fingertips, trying to get her professional self back under control, but failing. All she wanted to do was lock the door to her office, slip her cobalt-dyed jeans down her thighs, and stroke herself. She would pretend it was Zach touching her, pretend he was doing the things to her that Jason had done to Dahlia the night before. All of those dirty things that she'd listened to for hours. That she'd fantasised about afterwards.

What was wrong with her?

Instead of acting on her urges, she stood up and paced the length of her office, thinking that maybe a change of position would help clear her mind. On the lilac walls around her hung a motley collection of framed vintage record covers. The Velvet Underground. Bob Dylan. The Stones. In Carolyn's opinion, something had gotten lost in the trade to CDs. Album covers were a type of folk art. The records themselves held a mystical aura. Nobody ever delicately cradled a CD or a cassette, admiring the feel of it. Even the smell was enticing to her. When she went into Groovy Grooves, her favourite used-record store on Melrose, she would just stand there for a moment, breathing in. It was as if the music itself had a scent.

Sitting again, she kicked her feet up on her desk, comfortable in her surroundings, although still nervous at the thought of conducting this interview.

'Pull yourself together,' she said out loud. 'Come on, kid.'

In general, she was completely at ease with her life as a DJ. It was, she knew, a dichotomy in her personality. How could she be so insecure away from the station but so in control behind a microphone? Scared of her shadow when out in the real world, larger than life when at the studio, able to actually make other people nervous. Didn't make any sense.

As it didn't make sense that she was nervous about this particular interview. Over the years, she had comfortably chatted with many of the world's most famous music celebrities. Much more famous than Mr Zachary Modine. At the radio station, she could count on being calm and collected, feeling lit up from within.

Music did that for her – it always had. She understood its power, and she respected it, never questioning the ability of a melody to change a scenario. You could turn happy to sad and vice versa simply by pressing a button and cueing up one special song. But away from the station, she was plain Carolyn Winters – slightly shell-shocked, inescapably shy. With her long dark hair and slim body, she considered herself just nondescript enough to fade into the background. Her eyes-down attitude further helped her to blend into crowds.

In actuality, her features were razor-sharp, delicate in a beautifully fragile way. And what she didn't realise, despite how often Dahlia tried to tell her, was that when she smiled, everything came alive. Her blue eyes took on a cool, clear glow. Her lips became full and inviting. She never smiled at her reflection; not any more, not since Steven. She did her best now to camouflage herself with the rest of the world.

Usually, the two personalities contained within Carolyn never met. Her DJ self stayed in the workplace while her shy self remained at home. But today, at the thought of her impending interview, she found that she was feeling much more like the insecure, mace-carrying Carolyn than the girl who spun discs for a living.

And what was she going to do about it?

Nothing. Because the intercom buzzed, her secretary announcing that her afternoon interview was on his way. And, my, what a fine boy he was. Quickly, Carolyn slid his headshot into a manila folder and slipped the folder into a drawer. No need to let the man know that she'd been fantasising about him. Moving on autopilot, she traded her masculine black frames for a pair of Stormy's trademark red-tinted lenses, covered her shoulder-length dark hair with a gingham bandanna, and slithered her way into the shiny black jacket that hung on the back of her chair. Paired with the dyed blue-on-blue jeans, she looked every bit the rock goddess that she portrayed on air.

As an afterthought she did something almost inconceivable: bit her bottom lip to give it colour, and pinched her cheeks to make roses bloom on her pale skin. These were two tricks she'd stolen from watching Dahlia. Lastly, she stretched, performing a quick yoga move that left her body feeling elongated and panther-like.

Then there he was: Zachary Modine, striding forcefully into her office clad in worn leather pants, a vibrant blue long-sleeved T-shirt, his gold-red hair pulled back into a ponytail. He was carrying a well-worn guitar case in one hand and a braided black leather leash in the other.

'Stormy,' he said as he approached her, not asking, but stating, as if, in a way, he was naming her. 'Stormy' was the pseudonym that Carolyn had created for herself back in college. She loved the way the words sounded together when she said them: 'This is Stormy Winters, coming to you live from downtown Los Angeles.' It was the perfect name for her to hide behind, indicating a mental state that was somehow both icy and turbulent.

'Zachary,' the musician said as he bestowed upon her his famous half-smile, 'or Zach, if you want.' He put forward a hand to shake hers.

She tried to get hold of herself then, tried to regain her composure. What was it about this man? Yes, he was good-looking, but so what? Every third man in LA seemed to be movie-star handsome. Besides, unlike Dahlia, Carolyn was rarely blindsided by looks. With music, the package wasn't nearly as important as what was inside. Think of all the ugly singers who had reached a cult level of rock 'n' roll status. So it had to be something else – a glimmer of sexual intrigue, a hot pulse beating between them. It was a feeling that she hadn't experienced for years, and she didn't know exactly how to react. Luckily, Stormy took instant charge of the situation.

'This way,' she said, leading him from her office towards the studio, her heart still pounding at triple speed. She'd listened to his band several times before setting up the interview. Maybe that was it. His music was amazing, so good in fact that she felt a bit like a groupie, which was exactly how Zach said he felt as they settled into the studio. He grinned at her as he kicked his battered black Doc Martens up on the chair next to hers.

'You're my favourite,' he said, sounding slightly awed now. 'Better than Suzanne deLong on K-SIX. Better than Jordan Right over at K-LUV. Simply the best DJ in LA. Couldn't believe it when my agent said you wanted me on the air.'

Wanted him off air, too. Wanted him right there, in the chair. Oh, she could see it. Ripping off his T-shirt, stroking his fine body through his leather pants. There was always something decadent about the feel of leather against naked skin. Maybe he would leave the pants on, at first, just take off his top, let her feel his bare chest against –

Was this the Stormy persona having these thoughts? Or was it because she'd heard Dahlia in action the night before, which had been entirely different from hearing Dahlia tell the stories of her dates afterwards? Listening to a 'date' in progress had made Carolyn suddenly aware of how many years had passed since she'd last been in a man's arms. So long. Too long.

'You are legendary,' he added, as if he hadn't flattered her enough.

She'd been buttered up before, but Carolyn was affected by the words in spite of herself. In response, she explained the routine, helped him with the headset, and let the engineer cue up the clock and give them the go-ahead. While she waited for air time, she looked down at her notes, trying to force the blush from her face.

As always, she was well prepared for the interview. Dahlia teased her about listening to music 24/7, but Carolyn did more than that. She *learned* music. She drank it in. It was something that felt necessary to her. Like food or water. Like cosmetics to Dahlia. Prior to interviewing a musician, she not only listened to his or her songs, she liked to revisit the band's own inspirations. If a group claimed to be influenced by Hendrix or Van Halen, Bo Diddley or the Beatles, she would search the songs of the predecessor to find the connection. To understand it for herself.

In this manner, she was able to get a full feel for a group, know all of the titbits about them, learn their musical tics, before introducing them to her listeners. Her show was special in that way. She gave a little more of herself, but always got it back in return. The music, and everything connected to it, made her feel truly alive.

Up until now, it was the only time in her life when she did.

Chapter Three

*A*s usual at Chez Chaz, things were beyond busy. Dahlia had a fading celebrity in the private room upstairs who was unhappy with her new haircut. She claimed it was too bouffant, but Dahlia knew the real problem was that the cut hadn't made her look twenty again. Chaz was good, but he wasn't a magician. Or a plastic surgeon. So Harry was on his way upstairs with his cosmetic kit and make-up brushes to try to fix the unfixable.

When Dahlia scanned the bank of phones, she saw that all eight lines of the salon switchboard were lit up. But she breezed through the chaos with finesse, at ease when the world bubbled angrily around her. She knew how to do her job, working easily to soothe troubled waters. Today, she played her role even better than usual because she felt in tune again, as if her morning with Dante, following her night with Jason, had oiled her up and made her interlocking parts work smoothly.

She was seeing Jason again this evening, and knowing this helped her to focus: appeasing the angry, calming the crazed, making the salon run in its calculatedly pleasurable manner, which was what Chez Chaz was known for. Located in the heart of Beverly Hills, it was the number one spot to go if you wanted to look beautiful. And even if occasionally customers had to wait, as they did now, huffily stalking about the lobby, nobody would ever pitch a true fit. Being banned from this place of magic was tantamount to arriving ugly at the next awards show.

Harry flitted back downstairs in a sleek black dress and elegant black ostrich feather boa. He paused, like a humming bird in flight, with a quick and pointedly sexual question about how Dahlia's evening had gone. Just like Harry to want to know all the erotic-charged details.

'Later,' Dahlia said, giving him a wicked smile and a wink, which was all he needed to know that she had scored. She hadn't had a chance yet to tell him about doing Dante in the elevator. She'd share that in the afternoon when they next had a free moment to sip coffee and dish dirt together. Dahlia and Harry had no secrets from each other. It was what made their relationship so close, and so unusual. How many gay men wanted to hear about the love life of their straight female friends?

Harry responded with his classic, 'You go, girl,' and strode off on his six-inch zebra-striped heels, on his way to turn ugly into lovely. (A trick that had earned him the nickname Harry the Fairy Godfather.)

'Dahlia, line one,' Amy said. 'Personal call.'

Dahlia nodded and pointed to Chaz's office, indicating that she'd take the call in privacy. She didn't know who was on the other end of the line, but she guessed correctly, as usual, that it would be a man. As she pressed the blinking button, she learned that she was right. It was her date from the night before, calling from his car. Jason was a location scout and his auto was his mobile office. She visualised him in his red convertible, the black top down, breeze mussing his curly, light brown hair.

'Jason,' she cooed, settling herself in Chaz's plush fuchsia chair made of butter-soft velvet. 'What are you up to?'

'Eight inches,' he responded, and Dahlia let herself giggle, a pleasing, tinkling sound that wasn't anything like her real, husky laugh.

'And what are you doing with it?' Dahlia wanted to know.

'What would you like me to be doing with it?'

Dahlia squirmed in the chair slightly, getting comfortable. She adored phone sex, but knew that it was a rare treat to find a man who was a willing partner; someone who could actually give good lines. Licking her bottom lip, she thought for a moment, then said, 'I could tell you, but you might have an accident.'

'I can drive and talk,' he said. 'I'm good at doing two things at once.'

'Only two?'

'Tell me what you want, Dahlia,' he said, his voice holding a darker tone that made Dahlia instantly wetter. As much as she liked being in control, she loved it when a man took charge. But that didn't mean she wouldn't challenge him and test him to see if he could remain on top.

'I want you to touch yourself while we're talking,' Dahlia told him.

Jason assured her that he could do that. He had her on the speaker phone, and he only needed one hand on the wheel as he manoeuvred through the freeway traffic, congested any time of day in Los Angeles. 'But only if you touch yourself as well,' he said.

'Already am.' She wasn't lying. She had her short skirt up and was lightly running her fingertips up and down the seam of her G-string panties.

'Are you wet?'

'So wet,' she said. 'You wouldn't believe it.'

'Tell me.'

'I'm sliding my lacy panties aside,' she told him, doing the action as she spoke. 'And I'm putting just the tip of my middle finger inside me.'

She could hear the phones ringing out in the salon, and the sounds of the receptionists as they frantically tried to regain control of the afternoon's appointments. If she were at the counter, she would definitely be able to help them. But she was much more interested in helping Jason get off and in helping herself to climax for the third time today.

'Now what?' he asked.

'I'm slipping my whole finger into my pussy,' she said, drawing that final word out, the way she knew that guys liked to hear it. 'And what are you doing?'

'My hand's around my cock,' he said, 'and I'm working it up and down.'

'Can people see?'

'If they looked over. Especially the ones in Range Rovers.' Jason's little Italian convertible put him down below most of the SUV traffic. 'But you know LA drivers. Lost in their own little worlds. Can't even be bothered to look out the window.'

'I like that image, anyway,' she said. 'The thought of you being caught.'

'I know you do. That's because it's naughty, and you like to be a naughty girl.'

Oh, good. He was speeding things up. These were exactly the type of words that Dahlia needed in order to reach her climax. As Jason spoke, she played with her clit, running the ball of her thumb over it, harder than she liked a man to touch her. For some reason, the sensation was different when she was the one touching herself.

'I'm going to take care of you tonight,' he promised. 'But I want you to do something for me right now.'

'Anything,' Dahlia sighed, wondering what filthy request the man would make. She hoped it was good. Maybe he'd tell her to lick her fingers, or to pinch her clit, or to lightly spank her pussy with her fingertips.

'Stop touching yourself.'

Because of the serious way he said it, she froze at the command, but she didn't take her fingers away from where they were, deep inside her. 'What do you mean?'

'I don't want you to come again until you can come on my tongue.'

She sighed into the phone, liking the way that sounded, but unsure whether she could do as he said. She was so close – just a few more strokes and she'd get off. If she didn't come now, she'd be all worked up for the rest of the day.

'Stop it, Dahlia, or I'll have to be very strict with you tonight. And let me assure you, I'll know if you disobey me.' A pause for effect, and then he repeated the statement. 'I'll know.'

Dahlia removed her fingers and, sighing, she straightened her panties and her skirt, sat up in the chair and tried to concentrate on anything other than the urgent pull that came at her from between her legs. She had to get back to the phones anyway. Who did she think she was, wasting the day like this?

'Go back to work,' he said, as if reading her thoughts, 'like a good girl. But be ready for me tonight.'

She promised him that she would, then stared at her reflection in the glass top of Chaz's desk. She looked untamed, and she concentrated hard on getting her mind back into her managerial mode. It took her a moment, in Chaz's private bathroom, where she washed her hands and splashed cool water on her face. Then, after a few deep, cleansing breaths, she unlocked the door and re-entered the world of turmoil waiting right outside.

'Dahlia, line three,' Amy said, not glancing up from the desk. 'Emergency make-over.'

Dahlia nodded, then looked at the clock. Before answering the phone, she turned the radio to Carolyn's station. She always listened to her roommate, even on hectic days like this. She liked to hear what was going on in the world.

At least, the world according to Stormy.

'And about that leash?' Stormy murmured, her voice a sweet, sultry combination, like whisky and honey. When the mike was on, the final transformation was complete.

42

Carolyn, and all the nervous energy that went with her, seemed to have vanished into the ether.

Zach eyed her quizzically, but leaned into the mike as if he were an old pro. 'You interested in that, are you?'

'Well, Zachary,' she said, her voice rich with a sexual promise that Stormy alone created with no help from Carolyn, 'you show up to play for me with your acoustic guitar in one hand and a long leather leash in the other. I gotta admit, it does give a girl ideas.'

He laughed, and his grey-blue eyes sparkled with mischief. Without speaking, he seemed to be telling her that he could play this game, too. Perhaps even better than she could. For an instant, she again saw what it would be like to be with him. How he might be up for the type of scenarios that Dahlia often described. What *would* someone do in bed with a leather leash? She waited, breathless, as she knew all of her female listeners – and possibly a few men – would be waiting to hear his answer.

'Just the leash?' he asked, those blue eyes flashing. 'Or are you into collars as well?'

'Depends on the situation,' she replied casually, making him laugh again. 'You never know when a good collar will come in handy. Black-tie event, diamond-studded collar optional.'

The words just came to her. This was the type of banter that her fans adored, and it flowed naturally on air. 'Don't you have a song about that?' she asked next, knowing full well that Zoom Box had a great little number called 'Chains' that included a plethora of sexual innuendoes. About being tied down – emotionally and physically – restrained in the most pleasurably perverted of ways.

Zachary seemed pleased that she knew about songs other than his band's solitary hit, and he gave a little back story about the one she was referring to. While he did, Carolyn thought about how easy it was to talk to him – even on air. It was when she was away from the studio that she flailed. Dahlia, who listened to her show

43

whenever she could, didn't understand. 'How can you be so sexy at work and forget how to be a vixen when you're not?'

Carolyn couldn't explain. It was as if Stormy owned the part of her that was a sexual creature. Without an audience to listen, she just wasn't the same.

Now Zachary gave the real reason for why he had the leash with him. He owned a dog, a black Lab puppy, and was picking him up at the groomers after the show. He hadn't even realised he'd brought the leash with him until she'd pointed it out. The story made Carolyn like him even more. Men who hung out with dogs were a special type. She didn't get into that, though. Instead, she started talking seriously about the music, letting him tell the history of the band, how the four members had found each other. How they'd created their unique sound.

She made a special effort to ask Zach questions about his female drummer because she knew that the demise of their relationship had almost taken the band down with it. Knew, also, that 'Back-stabbing Baby,' her absolute favourite of their songs, had been written about Melody. Some bands made it through relationship trauma, but for others it was disastrous. Zach talked openly about the break-up, and then, at Stormy's lead-in, he began to play.

> Back-stabbing baby makes my heart turn over
> Every time we get in bed.
> Back-stabbing baby, who'd you rather be with?
> Who are you doing in your head?

The real line was 'Who are you fucking?' but Zach knew enough to censor himself before the radio station did. The music sounded different without the rest of the instruments. Colder and more haunting, and Carolyn liked it. Yes, he was the integral part of his four-person band. But there was something interesting about separating members in a group. Isolating them. Seeing what they were capable of on their own. Alone, Zachary was more than capable. His voice was low and soothing. His fingers tricked along the strings of his guitar, making Carolyn imagine those fingers playing something else.

What was up with her? Where were these feelings coming from? She didn't know, but as she moved slightly to the beat of Zach's music, glancing at him through her red-tinted lenses, she wished for something she hadn't had in a long, long time.

'No, no, no!'

Melody Jones sat hunched like an angry cat on the bed in her studio apartment, listening to her ex-boyfriend flirt with some stupid fucking DJ. Her hands were clenched into fists around her drumsticks, her black-varnished nails digging into the flesh of her palms. She tossed her head angrily, swinging her shoulder-length mane of straight blonde hair so fiercely that it stung her cheeks.

What did Zachary think he was doing?

So they'd had a fight, and she'd been wrong. She could admit that. OK, maybe she hadn't actually admitted it yet, but she definitely could. If that's what it would take to get him back, she'd admit that on her hands and knees, naked in front of him. She'd do anything he wanted. Fulfil any twisted desire he had.

But why the hell was he telling some stranger – and all those listeners – about their private lives? About how difficult it had been for the band but that they would survive. Fucking hell, yes, Zoom Box would survive. And so would she and Zach. She knew it, could feel it inside her. What they had together was rock solid. At least, it had been before she'd had a little bit of a flirtation with a singer from another band, and that flirtation had led to a fiery fling. And, bad fucking luck for her, Zach had found out in spite of her best efforts to keep the relationship undercover.

Wasn't that what the world of rock 'n' roll was all about?

It was worse than all that, though. Not only had Zach found out, but an asshole music columnist for an LA alternative weekly had found out, and had written a gossipy piece about the whole thing. People loved to worm their way into places they didn't belong. Even though she and Zachary had tried to make it work several times since the big fight, seeing the words in print had made Zach finalise their break-up, officially calling it quits for good.

'No more,' he'd said. 'I can't keep it up. You make life too hard.'

She had a tough attitude, no doubt about it. But that's what had drawn him to her in the first place, wasn't it? Her edge. That, and the way she looked in tight, leather pants, as if they'd been painted on to her sublime body.

Come on, Zach, she thought now. Recover already.

The singer she'd fucked, Zorg Ozone, a man with a stupid name but an amazing ten-inch cock, hadn't meant anything to her. He'd simply caught her eye and her interest, and she hadn't been able to get him out of her mind. They'd done it repeatedly in the dressing room at the Painted Lady before his gigs, had fucked against Melody's Harley-Davidson up in the hills, had even screwed at her own apartment when Zach was away. For several weeks, they'd been connected nearly all the time. But it was over now. She'd moved on. Why couldn't Zach?

Furiously, she pounded out an aggressive rhythm with her sticks on the edge of the bed – a bed Zach had refused to return to. He'd left their apartment and moved into Freddy's. He'd even replaced her affection with some puppy, which she could deal with. What she couldn't deal with was another woman. Was he trying to replace her with Stormy Winters?

She was better than a DJ, wasn't she? She could play music, actually *play* it, not just play other people's music on the radio. Frustrated, she flung her sticks across the room and jammed her fists into her eyes.

She'd win him back. All she had to do was get herself under control.

Then she could focus on her mission.

Jason was on a mission as well. Since having phone sex on the 10 freeway, he couldn't get Dahlia out of his mind. He'd try to pay attention to his latest assignment, but end up blanking out, driving without seeing anything other than some erotic image of her in his mind: Dahlia tied to the fence by the Hollywood sign; Dahlia looking up in the mirror at him as he took her from behind; Dahlia stroking her pussy in the middle of the busy salon.

Now that he was in his mid-thirties, women rarely affected him in this way. Usually, he was the one to get under their skin, to field their phone calls and ultimately break their hearts. But not Dahlia. He was consumed by thoughts of how he might take the satisfied, knowing smirk off her face. To erase it, if not permanently, then momentarily. That would be enough.

Finally, he gave up on the day's task, heading to his favourite adult store instead. He paced the aisles of Sasha's Sexy Somethings, a kinky shop on the cusp of West Hollywood, filled with naughty things for the bedroom and beyond, looking for something unique. Something that would surprise her . . . but not scare her away.

Shouldn't be too difficult, right? Jason was a catch, and he knew it. He had this wild streak that he generally kept hidden beneath his good-boy exterior, but that was showing itself now as he lifted a battery-operated dildo from one of the shelves. A wild streak that potentially even surpassed Dahlia's own.

It was what made him stand out from the rest of the suit-clad drones at the Culver City studios. They might be equally as good-looking, might be able to bed the starlets, but they couldn't keep them. Jason had something else going for him. Some hot filament within his soul that showed in his eyes if you knew what to look for. He sensed that Dahlia had the same power, and that if he harnessed it they would reach limits together that neither one had thought could realistically be achieved.

That was what Hollywood was all about, right? Fulfilling your dreams.

'Stormy,' Zach said, catching Carolyn off guard. He was standing at the door of her office, waiting, a black Lab puppy bouncing at his heels. He'd picked up the pup after the interview then returned to the studio and hung around until she'd finished her show.

She walked forward, unconsciously doing her arm-rubbing thing, the move that made it look as if she were cold, but only truly served as something to keep her hands busy. Noticing quickly, she lowered her hands to her sides, but that was somehow worse. Finally, she dropped to one knee to pet his dog, something that put her much more at ease. Animals were far easier to deal with than people.

'Thought that went really well,' he said, and it seemed that he was waiting for her to open the door to her office and invite him in. She reminded herself that she was still Stormy. Had on her red shades, her rock 'n' roll jacket. She looked the part, so she could damn well act the part, couldn't she? She'd been doing this for too many years to let some up-and-coming rock star shake her balance, just because he was Jim Morrison beautiful and had a glimmer in his eye that made her remember what it had felt like to be sexy.

With a nod, she opened the door and then watched as he kicked back in the comfortable old leather chair next to her desk. While the dog roamed the corners of the room, sniffing excitedly, Zach took in the albums on the wall, nodding in approval, before saying, 'You ever go to shows?'

Of course she went to shows. It was a main perk of her job. She got free tickets to just about everything. She often slid into a concert after it had started, stayed for the body of the show, and then departed before the crowds dispersed. That was the way to hear the music live but not have to deal with the fuss of her mild celebrity status. But what she said was, 'Depends on my schedule.'

'Come to ours?'

Now she shrugged. What was he really asking her?

'I'd like it if you would,' he said. 'I –' There was a hesitation, as if he were nervous. Could that be possible? 'I mean, I'd really like to see you again.'

She thought of Dahlia, and how her roommate would act in this situation. Subtly teasing. The flirt. Make him think that maybe he had a chance with her and maybe he didn't. Carolyn could hardly remember how it all worked. But she liked him. He was different than the other rock studs.

She nodded, and heard herself say that she'd try to make it. That was the best she could do. But it was also the best she'd done in years. Bravo, Carolyn, she thought to herself. Or was it, Bravo, Stormy?

After Zachary left, Carolyn had half the day off before filling in for a DJ buddy who was on vacation. The station was a second home for Carolyn. She liked the smell of the studio, the high-tech feeling of being in an enclosed glass box, surrounded by blinking coloured lights. Sometimes, like tonight, she didn't want to leave. But at 2.30 in the morning, she finally drove home. She didn't even have the energy to turn on the radio, something she normally did as a professional courtesy to the DJ who came on after her. Instead, she mentally replayed Zach's deep voice in her head.

When she got to the apartment she was still thinking about Zach Modine. With his long hair, sleek physique and colourful tattoos, he fit and surpassed the Hollywood standard of attractive musician. She wished she had more guts when interacting with the opposite sex. It had been too long since she'd tossed her hair and pouted her lips. At least, away from the studio. There, she could be the sexpot of her dreams. Marilyn Monroe with a radio show. She could fuck her audience all night long with music, knowing exactly how to manipulate the lyrics, lining up one sexy song after another. But when she got right down to the actual act, to being flirtatious with a man one on one, that was another story, and one that she didn't want to waste any more time thinking about tonight.

Finally home, she unlocked the front door and tossed her slinky, fingertip-length leather jacket towards the sofa, missing by several feet. It was nearly three now, and she planned on stumbling down the hallway to her bed. She didn't have to be up until noon the next day. But as she passed the kitchen, she heard the noises, even louder than they'd been the day before. Noises that instantly erased her memories of Zachary Modine.

The lovers were in the middle of an encore, and for this show, Dahlia was talking, too. Could Carolyn ignore the entertaining erotic fun or would she be forced to crouch in front of the grate and lose herself in the visions of Dahlia fucking Jason? After a moment's hesitation, it turned out to be an easy call. Just as Carolyn thought she was going to do the right thing and consider it a night, Dahlia murmured, 'I've never done that before.'

But Dahlia had tried everything. What could possibly be new to her?

'You want to, baby. Right?'

When she said, 'Yes,' it was almost like a purr. Long and drawn out, a cross between a sigh and a moan.

Carolyn mentally inventoried the escapades her best friend had shared with her in the past: her foray with Dante into light bondage; the silliness of food play with the head chef at the Dream On cafe; a string of dates with boys who liked costumes. She'd even had an ultra-short fling with an older guy who needed her to call him 'Daddy' in order to get off. What could remain on her list of pleasures yet to try?

'You ready?' he asked, and Carolyn was ready, too, bent down low, ear to the grate, breathless. 'I'm going to turn it on now,' he said, and Carolyn had an instant image to go with the picture. Jason, the naughty boy, had brought a sex toy with him. And Dahlia was lying to her new bedmate. She'd done it with a vibrator before. In college she had dated a deviant football player who'd liked to tie her down to his four-poster bed and break out two triple-C-powered vibrators. 'One for each of his favourite holes,' Dahlia had said as she reported the evening's events in extreme detail.

The humming sound let Carolyn know that she was right, but that didn't stop her listening. As enthralled as she had been the previous night, she got herself into a comfortable position, ready to hear the entire show. She could tell from the dialogue that Dahlia was teasing Jason, playing shy and sweet, telling him that she'd never had a vibrator on her clit before. 'It feels so good,' Dahlia crooned, 'so sexy.' Carolyn could picture her, slender legs spread, hips forward, giving herself over to the magical pleasure of it.

Jason said, 'God, Dahlia, I love the way you move,' and now Carolyn figured that she was shimmying her body in rhythm with the toy. When Jason's, then Dahlia's moans grew louder, Carolyn had to strain to hear her roommate giving him directions. 'Lower, baby. Just like that.'

Carolyn closed her eyes, painting a dirty scenario on the canvas of her mind. This time she saw Dahlia on her hands and knees, Jason entering her from behind. Dahlia could look in the mirror easily this way; could see as Jason worked the toy between the lips of her pussy and gripped her waist with his free hand, pounding into her, driving in deep. From the sound of his ragged breathing, Carolyn bet that he felt the vibrations pulsing through her body to his, making it difficult for him to stave off his orgasm. But he didn't want to come too quickly, didn't want to disappoint her. Nobody ever wanted to disappoint Dahlia.

In Carolyn's mental X-rated movie, Jason let go of Dahlia's waist and grabbed a handful of her thick mane, pulling on it, tilting her head back so that she looked over her shoulder at him. That did it for him, because

Carolyn heard a guttural moan and, rising above it, Dahlia's rich laughter, as she came with him.

Carolyn made out a click and a thud as the toy was finally discarded, and then she was left in the silent loneliness of the empty kitchen, seeing in her mind Dahlia snuggling up against Jason's chest, letting him stroke her fiery hair away from her face.

'Kitten,' he said softly. 'Did you like that?'

'What do you think?' she asked, obviously playing with him.

'I've never seen anyone get so wet.'

'I still am,' she said, and Carolyn sighed as she crossed her legs in a lotus position on the linoleum floor, waiting to see if Jason could rise to the challenge.

As Yogi Berra said, it was déjà vu all over again. Except Carolyn didn't think he was talking about masturbating to fantasies of your sexually adventurous roommate and her latest boyfriend.

Regardless, as soon as Carolyn was absolutely sure that Jason and Dahlia were finished, she retreated to her bedroom. To Terrie's dismay, she left him to sleep in the hall, as she wanted some privacy. Climbing beneath her black duvet, she got one hand inside her panties, fingers playing their favourite melody over her clit and between the slick, wet lips of her pussy. She didn't touch herself like this often, but when she did, she knew exactly how to do it. Just as she had the night before, she fantasised about herself with Dahlia's new Don Juan. There wasn't anything really wrong with that, was there? Fantasies couldn't hurt anyone.

Closing her eyes, she imagined Jason on the bed with her, sliding a thick, flesh-toned toy between her legs, adjusting the power so that it hummed back and forth from soft vibrations to Harley-engine rumbling. But no, that wasn't good enough. She didn't want Jason. Didn't even know the man. If she was going to be honest with herself, then she should choose the one she really wanted to be with: Zach Modine. Accepting this desire, she took the fantasy from the top, picturing Zach in bed with her. In her fantasies, they didn't have to talk. Not like Dahlia and Jason. They were together and that was enough.

Or almost enough.

Without opening her eyes, Carolyn reached into the drawer of her nightstand to find her own rarely used vibrator. As she turned it on, she dipped back into the fantasy again, picturing Zach working the motorised plaything back and forth between the lips of her pussy before thrusting it inside her.

The feeling of the toy against her clit had Carolyn so wet, so excited, that it was easy for her to slip in the vibrator. The sensation was overwhelming, a kind of pleasure that had her cheeks flushed, her heart racing and made her fantasies expand. She wanted something in her mouth now. Another dildo? Zachary's cock? Or maybe Dahlia's pussy pressed against her lips? This was only in her dreams. No one knew. Nobody got hurt. So, yes, she brought Dahlia into her mental movie, had her sprawled out on the bed, like a fantasy feast.

Her roommate was beautiful, her hair fanned out around her head in a red-tinted halo. Dahlia's skin was a deep caramel colour from lying out at the beach on her days off, tanned everywhere except the area around her breasts and her pussy. Carolyn knew this because her roommate didn't understand the concept of modesty, and would walk naked around the house when she went from the shower to her bedroom.

Those pale parts of Dahlia's body made the places seem extra special, and in her mind, Carolyn pressed her mouth against Dahlia's cunt, licking at her, parting her pussy lips with her tongue, until it was too much. Too good. But just as Carolyn was about to come, the batteries on her vibrator sputtered sadly to a stop and then died.

She couldn't believe it. Desperate, she used her fingers to take herself to the finishing line, plunging them forward, pressing them hard against herself. She made

53

the circles she needed, pressing her fingers against the inner walls, trying her best to regain the sense of free-falling pleasure that she'd had only a moment before.

And as she finally reached it, two thoughts reverberated in her mind:

I need a new vibrator.

No, I need a man.

Chapter Four

'*I* need a man,' Harry said urgently the following Saturday night. 'I mean, I neeeed one.'

'You *have* a man,' Dahlia reminded him, glancing up from the edge of Carolyn's bed, where she sat filing her red-varnished nails into perfect spade shapes. Just looking at them made Carolyn think about Dahlia dragging the sharpened tips down some lucky man's naked broad back. What was wrong with her? She had sex on the brain, that was for sure. All week long, she'd been in a heightened state of arousal and she didn't know how to deal with it.

'A new one,' Harry explained. 'I'm through with Jake.'

Dahlia gave Carolyn a knowing 'I-predicted-this' look, but didn't comment.

'Maybe you'll find one tonight,' Carolyn offered. Harry was at their apartment to get dressed for one of his frisky Hollywood parties. A come-as-you're-*not* affair, 'boys only' embossed in large silver letters on the invitations. Harry looked great in some of Dahlia's outfits.

Carolyn's room had been chosen for the site of the fashion show since Dahlia's bedroom was now Harry's dressing room. 'One must never watch a star dress,' Harry had informed them in his sexy Irish brogue. 'That would destroy the magic of the illusion.' Carolyn loved listening to Harry talk. Even though he'd lived in Los Angeles for years, his accent remained unaffected.

'Remember that scene in *All About Eve*,' he said now, 'where Bette Davis is sitting backstage with her wig off and her face covered in cold cream?' He looked pointedly at Carolyn, who was wearing a neon-green seaweed beauty mask that Dahlia had brought home from the salon. 'That's a sight nobody should ever have seen.' Harry was all about illusions, in both his job and his personal life.

'What a dump,' Dahlia drawled, attempting to impersonate Bette, but failing.

'Wrong movie,' Harry sighed, as if wondering what idiot could get one Bette Davis film confused with another. He turned his attention to Carolyn. 'Come on, gorgeous,' he said, 'what do you think?' Harry's long black hair fell past his bare shoulders, covering the top of the strapless party dress. This particular number was made from a crinkly-looking silver material. It went well with the costume jewellery necklace Harry had picked up from a street vendor down on Melrose, and was a cheap version of the blue heart-shaped gem from *Titanic*.

'Leo,' he sighed, whenever anyone asked him why he liked *Titanic*. 'Lovely little Leo.' DiCaprio made the whole stilted story worth it for Harry. He'd watch the thing on mute just to see Leo's pretty face.

'The blue was nice with your eyes,' Carolyn said honestly. Not that it really mattered which outfit Harry finally chose. They all knew that he would be the stunner at the party regardless of what he wore.

'The blue was a little snug,' Harry admitted. He raised his eyebrows and said, 'What's a boy to do when he's trying to slide into a size six dress?'

'I've got body-shaper stockings,' Dahlia offered. 'They might help a bit.'

Harry nodded, accepting the suggestion without being insulted. While Dahlia told him where to find her new pair, Harry twirled so that his skirt raised up, providing his audience with a glimpse of frilly purple panties.

'I see London, I see France,' trilled Dahlia as Harry headed down the hall towards Dahlia's room for another change. As soon as the girls were alone, Dahlia focused her attention on Carolyn.

'Let's do *you*, next,' she suddenly suggested. 'Make you up and send you out.' Dahlia was a lot like Harry in this respect. Both were constantly trying to get Carolyn to date again, although each had a different method. Harry would cajole, assuring Carolyn that once she tested the water she'd see it was warm and delightful. Dahlia was more direct. 'You need to get laid,' she'd say. 'One rowdy fuck will change your entire world view.' Before Carolyn was forced to come up with some sort of random excuse to avoid playing dress-up, a blast of seventies rock crashed their party.

'She's a brick . . . house! She's mighty-mighty. Letting it all hang out!'

They were both shocked, and when the voice stopped singing, there was a moment of total silence followed immediately by Harry's pitiful moan from the other room. 'What the fuck was that?'

'Isn't it "shaped mighty-mighty"?' Dahlia asked Carolyn seriously, since she was the expert. Carolyn shrugged. 'You should know –' Dahlia started, but was immediately interrupted by the singing.

'Yes, she's a brick . . . house . . .'

The doorbell rang, and Dahlia and Carolyn looked at each other again. As the buzzer sounded for a second time, the phone rang in Dahlia's room and she sprinted down the hall to get it. Harry screamed as Dahlia opened the door, but she calmed him quickly. 'I've seen it all before,' she said, catching the phone on the third ring as the doorbell sounded insistently again.

'Will you answer it, Carolyn?' Dahlia yelled from her bedroom.

'Harry, can you?' Carolyn called back.

'Like *this*?' he asked, apparently tired of his talk about

illusions, stepping into her room dressed only in Dahlia's panty-shapers and then striking a pose against the wall. Sighing, Carolyn walked down the hall and looked through the peephole, Terrie at her heels. Outside stood a tall, long-haired man holding a huge amplifier. Carolyn swallowed hard. It was Zachary Modine, but what was he doing here? How had he managed to get her address, and why was he holding that amp?

With shaking hands, she reached for the bolt, prepared, as always for her next move, forever aware of the nearest exits. Yes, there was something inherently sad about having these thoughts, but she couldn't help herself. Still, she knew Zachary, knew that he wasn't a threat, so she opened the door. She and Terrie poked their heads into the hall at the same time, coming face to face – or face to knees, in Terrie's case – with Zachary.

He looked at Carolyn first, then stared down at Terrie, who for once wasn't off on a barking spree at the sight of someone he didn't know. 'Didn't think that anyone was home,' he said as he set the amp on the floor. Carolyn suddenly realised that he hadn't come looking for her; he didn't even seem to know who she was. She'd interviewed him only the week before, though, so why didn't he recognise her?

'Now, I can tell you were making yourself all beautiful for me,' he continued, and Carolyn remembered the green mask on her face, remembered the fact that away from the studio, her special aura faded. At home, she didn't have on those red-tinted lenses, her cool bandanna, the rock 'n' roll outfit. She was wearing her usual attire of ripped jeans and a white T-shirt, and her hair was scraped back from her face in its standard, no-nonsense ponytail.

'I'm your new neighbour,' he said next, sticking his hand forward. He seemed to appreciate the neon hue of the mask, grinning broadly as he looked her over.

'It washes off,' Carolyn said, looking pointedly at the tribal tattoos climbing his bare arms, shown to perfection in a rip-sleeved shirt. Those don't wash off, she was thinking, but she didn't say it out loud. Adhering to the tattoo fad hadn't marred his good looks, high cheekbones, a strong chin and those blue eyes . . .

Terrie got his big paw up, interrupting Carolyn's thoughts, and this made Zach laugh. 'We're moving in tonight.' He tilted his head upwards, indicating the apartment directly above. A woman, who Carolyn quickly recognised from the press photo as the drummer for the band, was on her way up the stairs with a large box in her arms. Melody Jones was the woman that Zach had dated in the past, and Carolyn took her time checking her out.

'Mel's helping, but she's not going to live here. It'll just be me and Freddy.'

The drummer looked back once at Zach, but didn't speak. She was stunning in a blonde goddess way. Exactly the type of person Carolyn would pick for Zachary. She wondered about the real reason why they had broken up. She'd read the stories – that Melody had been making it with Zorg something, the lead singer from Feast of Flesh. Did she have something for men with names that started with Z? Still, Carolyn knew that you never could trust gossip in the trades.

As Melody disappeared upstairs, Dahlia, drawn to the voice of a man she didn't know, appeared behind Carolyn, then stood in the doorway at her side. Carolyn moved back, letting her roommate step out on to the tiled landing as if claiming her rightful space. She appeared oblivious to the connection between Carolyn and their new upstairs neighbour, which suited Carolyn just fine. Dahlia, her robe partially open to show off the shimmer of her red silk chemise, smiled at the musician. 'Was that you singing?'

'We're in a band,' Zach explained. He slid one hand into his back pocket and pulled out a flyer. 'It's why I rang. I wanted to see if you guys could make our next gig. A way to get to know your new neighbours, and a way to help you to overlook us rehearsing in the garage late at night.' Carolyn looked over Dahlia's shoulder at the lizard-green flyer. It announced a Zoom Box gig, on stage at Two Moons in Hollywood.

'I'll put you on the list if you'd like to come. You can't get a better deal than free.'

'Me, too?' Harry asked, now joining the conversation. Like Dahlia, he was pulled to the sound of a male voice and, looking at Zach, he obviously had ideas of his own. 'No free pass for little old me?' he asked. Faux crystal earrings brushed his shoulders, and he had wrapped a lemon-yellow feather boa around his neck. 'Never go out without a boa,' Harry liked to say. Someday, Carolyn thought, the fashion police would take out a hit on Harry, but Zach didn't flinch at the get-up.

'Of course,' Zach said magnanimously.

Melody made her way back downstairs. She didn't pause by the group and simply headed outside to get more boxes. Carolyn took in her half-sneer, like a blonde Joan Jett from her days with the Runaways. Melody was stunning – no question about that – but she looked mean. She also looked sexy, wearing snakeskin pants and a long-sleeved lipstick-red T-shirt with the words 'Rock Star' on the front in tiny silver sequins. Dahlia didn't even seem to notice the girl; her gaze was focused on Zach.

'I'm generally busy on Saturdays,' Dahlia cooed. He'd have to work harder than that to get into her little black book. Zach gave her an understanding smile, and it seemed that he'd already summed her up after this briefest of meetings.

'Just show up if it turns out you're available,' he said kindly. Then, as Dahlia and Harry returned to the apartment to finish dressing, Zach picked up the amp and started to lug it up the stairs. He looked over his shoulder to call back, 'Hope to see you later –' pausing for effect before adding, 'Stormy.'

So he *did* know who she was. Carolyn's smile cracked the crust of the mask.

Chapter Five

*H*e didn't like to think of himself as a killer. Instead, he preferred the term 'artiste'. Weren't those who reached the highest levels of their professions given this title? Yes, they were. And he was good at what he did. No questions about it. An expert. The police didn't have a clue, hadn't even gotten close.

In a way, it didn't seem fair. Why should he be so competent at this particular skill, one that he wasn't able to get any real credit for? He tried to assure himself that later, when he was finished, he would be written about in the history books, like Jack the Ripper or Son of Sam. He'd get credit either posthumously or after they caught him, which they never, ever would. Not if he kept to his carefully orchestrated plans. Who would guess his secret? He was too thoughtful, too prepared, to ever fuck up.

That was something to keep up his spirits. And as he polished his favourite knife, he closed his eyes and meditated on his next move.

Chapter Six

'Walk Terrie before you go to the studio?' Dahlia asked two nights later.

'No problem,' Carolyn replied as casually as possible, but after a beat, she said, 'Are you going out with Jason tonight?' As she vocalised the question, she realised that the thought of the two of them doing it aroused her intensely.

'No,' Dahlia said, 'Dante.'

'Oh, Dante,' Carolyn responded enthusiastically. *Too* enthusiastically. Dahlia looked at her, and Carolyn, recovering quickly, said, 'I haven't seen him for weeks.'

Although Dante and Dahlia had officially broken up six months before, they continued to fall into bed together on a fairly regular basis. It was as if their definition of 'breaking up' meant that they no longer went out to dinner or did 'couples' things together. All they really did now was fuck. Dahlia claimed Dante was so good in bed that it was difficult for her to turn him away. After nearly a year together, they knew the choreography of their lovemaking down to each individual moan.

Carolyn was not the slightest bit disappointed that Dante would be replacing Jason in the line-up. Dante possessed a wild streak that Dahlia loved to share. 'He tied me up last night,' she'd say, giving Carolyn a wicked grin. 'He used my own nylons and bound me to the bed.'

Tonight, it took longer than usual for Dahlia to dress. She discarded one outfit in favour of another, then momentarily gave up and walked down the hall in hose, no underwear, and a shiny blue blouse. From the rear, Carolyn caught sight of a bright tattooed heart on the right cheek of Dahlia's haughty ass. It was a decal tattoo. Dahlia changed her mind too often to have a permanent one. Still, its appearance made Carolyn think that Dante was going to get a look at Dahlia's derrière tonight. Why else would she decorate her behind if not for him?

'Where are you guys going?' Carolyn asked, probing casually for information.

When Dahlia turned to face her, Carolyn was startled enough to suck in her breath. The tattoo was nothing. Dahlia's nude hose had a space in the front, as if she'd taken a pair of scissors to them and cut out the crotch. But these stockings were obviously made this way, the hole sewn cleanly around the edges. The mink-coloured fur that covered her pussy let the viewer know that Dahlia was not born a redhead, something Dante was undoubtedly already well aware of.

'I ordered the pantyhose through the mail,' she said, aware of Carolyn's fascination. 'From one of those *naughty* catalogues.'

'Sexy,' Carolyn said, trying not to sound shocked. Dahlia lived to shock people. Carolyn lived to try not to let on when she succeeded. Their relationship had been built on this bond for eight years.

'We shouldn't be back too late,' Dahlia called out from the bathroom as Terrie loped to Carolyn with his favourite ball in his mouth. She threw it down the hall and watched as he raced gracefully after it. 'We're having sushi in Hollywood,' she continued. 'Then maybe a movie.' She paused. 'At the Chinese.'

'Oh, the Chinese,' Carolyn said happily, once again winning an odd look. She made a mental note to be more careful with her responses. Still, she knew Dahlia's history at the famous movie theatre. Some people visited Mann's Chinese Theatre for the history, or to place their hands in the concrete prints left by movie stars from a long-gone era. Dante and Dahlia had a different reason entirely for patronising the landmark. They liked to do it in the back row of the cavernous movie hall, with her sliding into his lap after he'd undone his slacks, climbing on top of his cock and then riding him. She remembered the look on Dahlia's face when she'd described that expedition. 'The thrill,' Dahlia had said, 'at almost being caught, but not.'

Knowing the state of those pantyhose made Carolyn think they would be taking a trip down memory lane this evening. She'd much rather that they come home so she could listen, but there was simply no tactful way to suggest this.

Terrie brought the wet tennis ball back and dropped it at her feet. He looked up at her, waiting, and she lifted it, pretending to toss the ball towards the living room, then throwing it in the other direction. Terrie knew her strategy. He hesitated for only a second, then headed for the lime-green ball, catching it easily on the second bounce.

'Good dog,' she said, when he returned to her side, ready to play again.

Dahlia emerged from the bathroom, her shiny hair falling in dark cherry curls to her shoulders. She looked from Carolyn to Terrie and then back to Carolyn. Head cocked, she gave them both the same smile. For a moment, Carolyn felt as much her pet as Terrie, and when Dahlia put out her hand, Carolyn wondered for an instant if it was her head that she was going to stroke.

After Dahlia had gone out, Carolyn walked into her roommate's bedroom and looked around. Maybe she *would* go to Zach's gig. She could borrow something from her closet: a pretty dress, fishnet stockings, high-heels. After years of urging her to get back into the dating game, Dahlia would undoubtedly be thrilled to help her dress up for the occasion.

With this concept in mind, Carolyn slowly entered the closet, a large walk-in lined on both sides with two rows of bars. Carefully, she touched Dahlia's red satin gown, recalling the way the dress looked on her, how it nipped in at her waist and flowed gently over her hips. Dahlia saved the dress for special occasions, so Carolyn wouldn't try on this one. Instead, she reached for the one behind it. Pale blue, soft as cashmere, it was a short T-shirt style that Dahlia wore with a white crocheted cardigan and cork-soled sandals straight out of the seventies.

Quickly, before she could talk sense into herself, Carolyn stripped off all of her own clothes, including her plain white cotton underwear. Still moving fast, she reached for a pair of Dahlia's silky hot-pink panties and one of her special push-up bras. Then she tried on the blue dress, let her hair down from its severe ponytail, and approached the full-length mirror. She was more excited than when she'd listened to Dahlia and Jason. But before looking in the mirror, she remembered to take off her black glasses, setting them on the night table.

Carolyn's reflection was fuzzy to her eyes. Shoulder-length hair, so dark that it was almost black, framed her face. Dahlia's blue, figure-hugging dress didn't fit Carolyn the same way as it fit her roommate. She was lacking some of Dahlia's famous curves. Still, with her eyes squinting, she could tell that it showed off her long legs, her slim waist, her small breasts. She ran her fingers over the soft material, turned around and caught how she looked with her straight hair flying around her head in a circle. It reminded her of models on shampoo commercials, tossing their hair then pouting seductively at the camera.

But then some masochistic side of herself won out and she slid her heavy glasses back on and took a step closer to the mirror. Light blue eyes stared back at her. A pretty oval shape, they looked older than she actually was. Older inside. Every time she looked in a mirror, she saw two reflections. The person she'd been before Steven, six years ago, and the person she was now.

With great care, Carolyn took off Dahlia's lovely dress and hung it back in her closet. Then she slid back into her own clothes. It was time to head to the station.

Melody Jones sat in the converted garage of her apartment complex, banging ferociously on a set of bongo drums with both hands. She wasn't playing to any particular rhythm, just pounding on them to soothe her mind. The drums had been a gift from Zach the previous Christmas, and she loved the way the tightly stretched skins felt beneath the palms of her hands. She loved the way Zach's skin felt, as well, if she wanted to think about it.

But that wasn't what she was fixating on right now.

So the DJ lived downstairs from Zach. How fucking convenient. Or, rather, how convenient for fucking. Knowing that Zach and 'Stormy' practically lived together was a little hard to take.

She looked at her battered man's wristwatch, saw that Stormy's show was on in half an hour, and headed upstairs to listen. Melody was in her research mode right now. In order to get Zachary back, everything had to go just right. If her plan didn't happen tonight, that was fine. It would work out another time. But for it to work, the timing had to be perfect.

That was OK.

Weren't good drummers known for their excellent timing?

Dahlia and Dante hardly needed to speak any more. They were so in tune that, at least for most of the time, their eye contact alone was enough. More than enough. It sizzled. Before even leaving the driveway, they had an in-depth conversation in the car without parting their lips. Dante's dark brown eyes stared into Dahlia's green ones, imparting secret fantasies. There was no tension between them aside from sexual tension, and this they both enjoyed. Finally, Dahlia broke the silence, laughing. Who else could say 'I want to fuck the daylights out of you' without speaking a word?

'We going to sit here all night?' she asked in a low voice. 'Or do you have other plans?' She knew, though, knew all about his other plans, what they might include, where they might take the two of them.

Dante responded by backing his silver convertible out of the driveway and on to Rosewood, a quiet tree-lined street that took them to La Brea, where he made a left at the lights. They drove in sex-charged silence past the vintage clothing stores, now closed for the night, then past the array of design studios and the old-time movie house.

Dahlia leaned back against the plush leather headrest and looked out of Dante's moon roof. Strobe lights played across the sky, shooting beams into the heavens as they tried to capture the attention of the masses, announcing the opening of some new hotspot. Another dance club, restaurant or music venue. As if Los Angeles needed any more. Dahlia had been to her share of openings and could visualise the people hustling against each other shoulder to shoulder in some gallery or club, trying to act cool. The really cool people didn't have to try.

That made her think about her different men of the moment. Jason and Dante, with a few other possibilities on the horizon. Who was the coolest? Jason had definite potential, but Dante still turned her on like no other man could. Well, she could excite him as well, she thought, moving her hips slightly in the bucket seat.

Stopped at the busy intersection of La Brea and Melrose, Dante turned his head to observe Dahlia as she shimmied around as if trying to get comfortable. He had plenty of dirty ideas. No need for help from her. Still, he enjoyed the show, and when the light turned green again, he spoke.

'Remember the game?'

'*The* game?' she repeated. Which one did he mean? There were many games. Food games. Dressing-up games. Bondage games. Doing-it-in-public games. Name an activity and Dahlia and Dante had tried it at least once.

'You know, Dahlia,' he urged, not willing to spell it out. She had to participate in this, had to bring some of the fun with her. And, of course, she knew. Yes, there were a wide variety of games that they played, but only one which he would have thought of based on the changing traffic light.

'Red light, green light?' she asked, with a lilt in her voice that made her sound innocent and daring at the same time.

'Are you up for it?' Dante asked.

'That's more of a question that I should ask you,' she said, reaching casually with one hand to cup his hard-on. He *was* up for it. But after enjoying the tickle of her fingers through his pants, he took her hand away and set it gently on her own thigh, wanting to make the evening last.

'Starting at the next intersection,' he said, preparing her. They were approaching Hollywood Boulevard and it looked as if the light was going to stay green – a good sign for Dante. It did, which meant that Dahlia had to remove one item of clothing. That's how the game worked. At red lights, the driver took off an article of clothing, while green lights meant the same for the passenger. Yellow equalled a draw, so nobody had to take off anything, unless the driver tried to race through it, which was a foul and meant the driver would have to remove two pieces of clothing at the next red light.

The game was one definite way to make any trip enjoyable. They had played it often when they were together, and now they started for the first time since their break-up, with Dahlia slipping one dainty high-heeled mule off her foot and tossing the shoe into the back seat. Luck was on Dante's side for three more lights, and by the time they reached Franklin Boulevard, she had lost her other shoe, her white fishnet stockings (which she'd ultimately chosen to wear over the ones with the hole cut in the crotch), as well as her delicate cashmere cardigan.

Then they hit two reds, so that Dante was driving barefoot, his expensive leather loafers thrown in the back seat along with Dahlia's growing pile. Other things in the car were growing, as well, as they slipped through two more greens, forcing Dahlia out of her shiny cobalt-blue shirt and short black silk skirt, now down to her lacy silver bra and panties. Dante's erection was reaching mammoth proportions, which his date could see clearly outlined through his boxers once his pants joined her clothes in the rear.

She wondered if they were still going to dinner. Not dressed – or undressed – like this. But Dante definitely seemed to have an idea of where he was taking them, because he manoeuvred the car through traffic without any instructions from his companion. Although she did like to be in charge, as she had been with Jason on their first date, she knew that giving over the power was a rush, too. Especially when she was with someone as knowledgeable as Dante. Because here she was, sitting in her silky underwear, growing wetter at each intersection, especially the intersection between her thighs.

Would they make it to their destination before they were naked? That was truly the exciting part, the part that made her look out for cops, the part that made Dante adhere carefully to the speed limit. This whole experience would be a heck of a lot less fun if they were pulled over by some hot-headed officer who wanted to know exactly what they thought they were doing, streaking through the city.

The cops must have been busy busting people more dangerous than nudists, however, and they continued to motor along, moving through the streets near Griffith Park without interruption or flashing lights. And soon, as they reached the stoplight at the bottom of the hills,

Dahlia found that she was forced to focus on an important question. Not whether or not it was smart to fall back into bed again with her ex. Not whether she loved him or whether he loved her. Her final, who-wants-to-be-a-millionaire question was much more difficult.

Which of her two remaining items would she remove next? Bra or panties?

'Stormy?' the caller said, sounding somewhat suspicious, as if not believing she'd gotten through to the right person.

'That's me.'

'This is Melody Jones, the drummer of Zoom Box.'

How interesting. She rarely knew the people who called up for a song. Except for Harry and Dahlia, who often liked to mess with her throughout her show, asking for odd numbers like 'Lil' Red Riding Hood' by Sam The Sham and the Pharaohs or 'Coconut' off the 'Nilsson Schmilsson' album.

'I wanted to call to tell you that I thought the interview was great,' Melody continued. 'So nice of you to give us a plug.'

'You guys deserve it,' Carolyn said honestly. She had a really good feeling about the band, one that extended beyond her feelings for Zachary. But she didn't say this to the drummer. Instead, she pictured the way Melody had looked in her body-hugging snakeskin pants as she'd helped Zach move into the apartment.

'I'm actually calling to make a request.'

'What would you like to hear?' Carolyn, as the sexy Stormy, murmured.

'"Hurts So Good."'

'Mellencamp,' Stormy said automatically. She visualised the eighties video that went with the classic song. The song and images were entwined in her mind: bikers and leather babes in S&M gear dancing poorly on top of a bar. It was a video that had been made long before videos became the multi-million-dollar mini-movies they were today, but Carolyn had always been charmed by it, none the less. The way John Cougar Mellencamp had tried to force a smile on his face as he'd led the pack of bikers on a winding road. It was difficult to smile into the wind while riding a motorcycle.

'Dedicate it to Zach, if you wouldn't mind,' Melody said, breaking through Carolyn's thoughts, 'because he always does it for me.'

'Does what?' Stormy asked, falling right into the trap, as the drummer had so obviously hoped she would.

'Makes it hurt so good,' Melody said, dragging the words out, implying with the lyrics alone that she and Zach were still together. And then she was off, and Stormy was holding a dead line.

As she cued up the song, still one of her all-time favourites, she wondered why the woman had called her. Music was filled with messages. This particular song was ripe with imagery, and you didn't have to think too hard to figure it out. Yet she was left sitting on the edge of her stool, thinking hard.

Ultimately, she guessed that when Melody had heard the interview, she'd sensed the same connection that Carolyn herself had felt. Whether or not Zach had felt it, this meant that it had been real. Women always sensed these things better than men, didn't they?

'Sometimes love don't feel like it should,' Mellencamp sang from the speakers.

That was the truth, wasn't it?

The lovers were both completely naked by the time they reached Dante's house. He lived on a cul-de-sac high up in the hills with only two other neighbours: a sometime movie star on one side, and a director of cult status on the other. Dante had bought the house five years before with the money from his first movie. His first and best. Ever since then, he'd been able to get work fairly easily but he'd never been able to write anything as hard-hitting. He wasn't sure why that was, and sometimes it bothered him. Turned him into an insomniac and kept him sitting out on his porch, overlooking the city, chain-smoking as he tried to convince himself that he wasn't a total sell-out. Convince himself that someday he'd be famous for a reason.

Most of the time he was able to push the thoughts out of his mind, satisfied with his level of financial success and able to accept the fact that in this part of the world money was king. Because in Hollywood, that's all that really mattered. You didn't have to make anything good, anything that was art. You just had to make money. To drive your fancy car and wear your expensive clothes. And fuck beautiful women who looked like Dahlia.

It was what he was planning on doing right now, and he raced her into the house, both of them streaking through the sparsely decorated living room to the pool out back. They knew exactly where they were going, and Dahlia was the one to hit the light switch so that the large, kidney-shaped pool was lit up from within.

She dived in without looking back, her body becoming silvery beneath the water, moving cleanly through it, swimming almost the full length underneath the surface before coming up for air. Dante watched the spectacle for a moment, enjoying the feeling that Dahlia was putting on a show for his pleasure. Then he followed after, swimming to where she stood, in the cool water between the deep end and the shallows. He didn't have to ask what she had on her mind. He simply lifted her in his arms and entered her.

'Oh, like that,' Dahlia murmured. 'Just like that.' Being in the water transformed her, made her feel like a different person than the one who had so carefully prepared for this date. Forgotten was her perfectly coiffed hair. Now, her long, wet curls fell over her shoulders and down her back.

As Dante fucked her, he moved them slowly down the gentle slope into deeper water. Dahlia found the weightlessness thrilling, intensely erotic, the ripples lapping against her skin as they rocked back and forth. Her breasts were caressed by the water and made buoyant by it.

'Now you,' Dante instructed, and Dahlia locked her feet around his thighs and pumped herself up and down, working herself on his body. The glistening moonlight created a perfect sheen on the water and on their slick, wet bodies. They might have been in any tropical paradise, where the turquoise ocean licked at pure white sand.

And then, Dahlia changed the rules again. Pulling off Dante, she swam further into the deep end, her strokes smooth and athletic. When she reached the diving board, she stopped and grabbed hold of the rough lip of it with her fingers. Her back was towards Dante, her body exposed out of the water almost to her waist, and he could see the sinuous cords of muscles beneath her skin as she held herself straight. He understood what she wanted instantly. Instead of them making it where he could stand and support her, she wanted him to take her in the deep end.

He reached her easily and held on to the board with one hand, using the other to slide his cock between her thighs. Then he gripped on to the diving board and started to move against her. Dahlia clung to the board, keeping her body as still as possible, while Dante did the work. He fucked her hard, but the water created resistance, slowing him down.

It was like fucking on Quaaludes. Everything seemed slightly unreal. The way Dahlia moaned, her voice muted, as if she were trying not to make any noise. The way he couldn't just slam into her, fuck her hard and take them both quickly to the limit. He had to go slow, to play it just right, moving within her, finally staying sealed inside her and letting her muscles work him. A tight embrace, a quick release, a powerful grip that made him feel as if she were the one fucking him.

How strange was that?

At the end, Dahlia let go of the diving board entirely. Dante, still joined to her, was forced to do the same or pull out. They slid under the water in slow motion, still connected as they came together. The water surrounded them, embraced their bodies, stretched out their pleasure.

Afterwards, they parted slowly, and then broke the aqua blue surface together, turning towards each other and smiling as they swam to the tiled edge of the pool.

Chapter Seven

Melody was pleased with herself. She knew that Stormy wanted to get into Zach's pants. It was obvious. Well, lots of girls had wanted to visit that location before. If Stormy was going to try to seduce Zach with her big-time radio show and her sultry voice, then Melody was going to have to play hardball. Let the bitch know to back off.

Having made her request, she threw herself down on her leather sofa and picked up a pony-necked beer. Her good feeling started to melt away as soon as she looked around. The apartment should have seemed bigger without Zach in it, without all his shit crowding her space. But it didn't. It seemed smaller. Lonelier. When he'd simply been living in Freddy's tiny one-bedroom pad, the move hadn't felt so permanent. But now that he and Freddy had found a bigger place together, had actually signed a lease, things seemed different.

Keep it together, babe, she told herself. He'll be back.

She'd been playing her hand expertly so far, had even helped him move into his new space. Boxing up his stuff as if they were just buddies, even decorating the apartment with him, offering ideas and buying a housewarming gift. Shit like that. He kept telling her that she didn't have to bother, but she just gave him her sweetest smile ever and said it was her pleasure.

A lie.

Her pleasure wouldn't happen until he moved back in with her, or until they both moved into a bigger space together. Something that could definitely happen if the music kept going well. At least they had that. When the four of them got together and played they were still magic. She just had to make sure he stayed away from all the cute groupies until he got over his anger and came back to her.

What an idiot she'd been fucking Zorg. She drained the beer angrily as she recalled the quickies she'd shared with the Feast of Flesh singer in the dressing room at the Painted Lady. While Zach had been out in Redondo Beach surfing with Roger and Freddy, Melody had been playing with fire again. Not the first time, but the first time Zach had found out.

She'd be a good girl from now on. If she got him back, she'd be an angel.

She just had to get him back.

People often told Carolyn that time healed all wounds, but she didn't agree. She thought that time simply faded wounds, like a scar turning from livid red to a muted silver. It was still there, just harder to see.

Every once in a while, she'd force herself to relive that night, if only to remind herself that she'd survived. That she was fine now. Well, 'fine' was a relative term. How fine could she be if she hadn't been on a date since it had happened, hadn't considered being alone with a man she didn't know well? A man like Harry or Dante, someone she could trust if only because he wasn't interested in her. Harry because he was gay. And Dante because, well, because he was so obviously in love with Dahlia.

Was reliving it a good idea? She didn't know. But after putting on Parliament's 'The Goose', a nine-minute-and-ten-second song, she closed her eyes and made herself mentally walk through it. Seeing each frame as if watching a movie.

A scary movie.

Steven said, 'I want to talk to you,' and Carolyn went. She knew him. He worked at the radio station in the record library. So she walked away from the lit path without thinking. Who knew where trouble lurked? Now, after it had happened, a part of her stayed focused. A part of her watched, the way people watch a horror movie, wanting to call out to the actor not to go there, not to open that door, but knowing all the time that the actor can't hear you, that you can't save him. It's all part of the masterplan.

Steven said her name as she joined him in the space between the two buildings. He said, 'Carolyn,' in a normal-sounding voice. Nothing odd yet. Nothing frightening. No audience members in the theatre screaming for her to take a different way back to the dorm. Why should they? It wasn't that odd for him to be there. The alley was a short cut to the other side of the student centre.

But something was wrong. Even though it took a moment for her to tell what. He had his backpack on, and his threadbare black sweater, and there was a bright, shining object glittering in his hands.

Carolyn's producer brought her back to the present, announcing that she had another request on line two. As she hit the blinking red button, she had a sudden premonition of exactly whose voice she was to hear. And she was right.

'You take requests from anybody?' Zachary asked.

'Anyone with an ounce of taste,' she replied. She was glad that a long song was already playing, and that she could take her time with him.

'I just heard an old Mellencamp classic,' he continued, letting her know that he was listening to her show, and that he was ready to respond.

'That's one of my favourites,' she said, hesitating. What she wanted to do was ask whether he and Melody were still together. Whether he had made her hurt or whether it had been the other way around. Too many questions and not enough time – or guts – to ask them. Not even as Stormy.

'Got my own request,' he told her and then he hesitated before saying, 'Carolyn.'

Oh, she liked the way he said her name. And for once, she liked the feeling of being Carolyn instead of Stormy. Carolyn was real, and it was Carolyn he wanted to talk to. She sensed that, thinking that Zachary was someone who understood all about real life versus stage life. He must have known, since he was someone who climbed up on the stage at a venue and transformed himself into someone else.

She waited, breathless, for him to make his request. What was it about this man? What hold did he have over her?

'Play "Baby Did A Bad Bad Thing", if you would.'

'Chris Isaak,' she said immediately, even though she knew it wasn't a test. Wasn't one of those 'I can name that song in three notes' types of games. He would know that she would know the song, as he would also know that she would sit afterwards, listening to the lyrics, trying like a maniac to decipher them.

Was he just using her to send messages to Melody or was he telling Melody to back the fuck off? Maybe she should get out from between the two of them. Or maybe, and this thought put a smile on her face, she should join in, choosing her own songs to add into the line-up. There was a great one off Madonna's *Erotica* album, 'Thief Of Hearts', that told another girl to stay away from her man, although Zach was in no way her man. At least, not yet. Could she get into the fun, play songs and dedicate them to either one? It wasn't the same as dating, or being truly involved, it was just doing what she did for a living.

Carolyn thought of her all-time favourite Bowie song, 'DJ'.

She was a DJ, and it was suddenly apparent to her that she had believers believing in her, too.

Terrie whimpered Carolyn awake in the middle of night. He made a half-hearted bark at the door before settling himself again on the foot of her bed, easily re-entering the world of doggy dreams. He must have sensed that the newcomers to the apartment were Dahlia and Dante, and that there was no reason to bark at his mistress and her old boyfriend.

Carolyn was not so fast to hit the pillow. Quietly, she walked to the bedroom door and pressed her ear against it, listening. Would Dahlia and Dante go into the kitchen or stay on the sofa in the living room? She pictured the layout of the rooms, trying to plan her next move.

The refrigerator door opened with a metallic click, and she heard the pop of a wine cork. There was soft laughter, a low voice talking, then more laughter, the sound becoming high and girlish. Dahlia must be drunk. Her roommate's normal laugh was a sexy sound that had always reminded Carolyn of jazz. A saxophone riff. She wished she could hear better but Dahlia's room was next to the kitchen, blocking her. It was easier for her to listen if she pressed her ear to the door.

She was in that position when they turned on the TV in the living room. It came on tremendously loud, and after a few seconds of an infomercial, in which Carolyn envisioned the two lovers fumbling drunkenly with the remote control, the sound was muted. After several more seconds, the volume came on again at a much lower level, but she could make out funky theme music, then the hiss of the fast-forward mechanics. From the noises that rose above the soundtrack, Carolyn got a clear image of what was going on: they were watching a porno movie. She knew what people did when they watched pornos, and she was surprised that Dahlia and Dante were going to do that in the living room.

On her couch.

More than surprised, however, she was disappointed. If they stayed in the living room, she wouldn't be able to hear very well. All she wanted to do was to listen in. She closed her eyes, thinking again, trying to figure out a way. She would have to remove the window screen, climb out of the bedroom window, walk around the side of the house, press up against the living-room windows and hope that the windows were open but the shades were drawn. A bit of effort, but she actually considered it. Then she looked at Terrie and realised he would undoubtedly wake up and bark like crazy, either at the unusual sight of his favourite master climbing like a fugitive out of the window or at the concept of some stranger prowling around the house.

Finally, Carolyn resigned herself to hearing Dahlia's edited version of the night's events in the morning. And, after ushering a disgruntled Terrie out into the hall, she made do with a replay of her new favourite fantasy: the one starring both Dahlia and Zachary. Pushing back the duvet so that she could slip one trembling hand beneath the thin cotton of her pyjama bottoms, she was startled when she realised that she still had Dahlia's silky pink panties on. But somehow that helped with the fantasy and took her further and deeper than she had lost herself before.

In the living room, Dante peeled open his faded black jeans and helped position Dahlia's flexible body so that she could slide back easily on his stiff cock for the second time of the night. His large hands looked huge and powerful on her slender waist, holding her steady, controlling the scene. A nearly silent movie flickered on the large TV screen in front of them, but they didn't even see it, being too focused on their own action on the centre of the plush suede sofa.

'Slowly, baby, slowly,' Dante said, giving her just the head of his cock, the bulbous helmet-head that filled her slick opening and rocked deliciously against her. She wanted more, though. The first taste of him made her want the whole thing. But when she told him this, when she said, 'I'm hungry, Dante. Fill me up,' he wouldn't. Instead, he said, 'Greedy girl, you wait your turn. You take it just like I tell you.'

As always, she loved the way he talked to her. She *was* greedy, wanting more than he was willing to give. Yearning, she tried to disobey, to slide her body all the way back down, to sit on him and let his cock impale her. But he guessed what she was planning and was ready for her.

'None of that, Dahlia.' His tone was strict as he gripped into her hips to keep her body poised above his. Then he gave her only the first bit of his cock. Just enough to make her arch her back and beg.

'Dante, please. I can't wait –' Her voice was low, hoarse. She didn't want to attract the attention of her sleeping roommate, but she wished she could scream for him to do what she wanted him to. Fuck her. Hard. Now. It was different to being with Jason. Dante had fucked her so many times in the past that his fingers played over her as if on automatic pilot. They knew where to go and what to do. Jason was good for the excitement of the new, and the man was definitely clever in bed, but Dante had months of practice behind him, and knowing what was coming made Dahlia desperate to reach it.

Yet, now that they'd already blown off steam during their first round in Dante's pool, her ex was able to take his time. And this meant that he was on some sort of a teasing kick. A *cruel* teasing trick, in Dahlia's estimation.

'It will be so much better if you wait,' he said, kindly sliding his fingers forward to stroke the outer lips of her pussy. This move spread her even wider, and she thought she might actually die if he didn't touch her clit.

'You won't die.' He laughed, when she told him in desperation how she was feeling. 'You'll just come. There's a major difference.' She could tell from the sound of his voice that he was smiling, and she resigned herself to going at his pace, regardless of how slow it was. But then a different idea bloomed in her mind. Two could play at his game. She could be as sexy as the porn star in the movie they were ignoring. Devilishly, she squeezed the head of his cock with her tight inner muscles, trying with all her will to get a reaction out of him.

That worked.

Dante groaned and arched his hips, helping her by giving her a little more of his cock. She squeezed him again, and he called her a dirty girl, but he slid his bone all the way inside her, just like she'd wanted. Now Dante was the one who was suddenly impatient. He lifted Dahlia into a standing position, then bent her over the armrest of the sofa. She gripped on to the soft material as he started to work her with more serious intent. His cock was large, and it felt delicious as it reached all those secret places.

For the first time since they'd started, Dahlia looked up at the TV screen, at the lovers fucking to the outrageously silly beat of the background music. There was a close-up of the place where their bodies were joined. As Dante worked his cock within her, Dahlia watched as the actor's own mammoth member slid into the actress's pussy, her petal lips parting over his large, demanding rod. Dahlia couldn't get enough of this picture, her eyes widening as she watched the action.

She hadn't paid much attention to the notes on the box when they'd rented the movie, and she was pleasantly surprised when another woman joined the fray. There was a medley of skin colours as bodies slid against each other. What looked to be baby oil, a clear and slickly glistening liquid, was poured along the front of a nubile blonde, and then rubbed into her body by her darker, cinnamon-skinned lover. The man in the movie took a step back as the two girls slid against each other, breasts pressed to breasts, pussy to pussy.

'Oh, God,' Dahlia moaned. With all her experience, this was one of the few things she'd never done before –

she'd never been with another girl. The look of it, at least between these two luscious co-stars, was far sexier than she could have imagined. That these two beauties were doing the action as a show for the man added to the eroticism. Dahlia understood the thrill of having an audience.

On the screen, one of the girls bent down to part the lips of her co-star. The camera took in a tight shot as the blonde began to lick the other woman's clit. It was pierced, which added to Dahlia's excitement as she watched the porn star pull and tug on the silver ball that adorned her co-star's pussy. A woman knew just how to touch a woman, Dahlia realised. It was so pretty watching the blonde's delicate fingers probing and sliding in the juices of her mate. Breathless, Dahlia listened as the second woman began to moan, low and urgent, searching for release.

'Come on, baby. Do me. Do me harder.'

That was on film, but it could just as easily have been Dahlia begging Dante. When the two women got themselves into a 69, their hair cascading over each other's breasts, their hands strumming up and down each other's fantastically beautiful bodies, Dahlia let out a harsh, hungry-sounding sigh. She couldn't help herself.

'You like that, don't you, baby?' Dante whispered, reminding Dahlia suddenly of his presence. How could she have forgotten? He was still fucking her. But she'd been captivated by the screen, so in tune with the action on the film that she'd actually lost track of where she was and what she was doing. Or who was doing her. In response to his question, Dahlia made some sort of assent, the sound coming deep in her throat.

'The thought of you and me and another woman –' he probed.

'Yes,' Dahlia said, even though she really had never wanted to try it before, not wanting to share a man's attention with someone else. But now she realised that a threesome wasn't necessarily about sharing a man. It could also be about a man and a woman sharing *her*.

What a totally decadent thought: two lovers fighting for her attention. The man equipped with a tool to give her pleasure, the woman using her tongue and fingers expertly, seeking out the places that would most please her. She could do it. Play-act at being a lesbian for a night. Nothing wrong with that, was there? Nothing at all.

This sensual vision was all that she needed to come, and as Dante drove hard and fast inside her, she pressed her fingers against her clit and felt the wetness surround them.

Drowning in sexual honey.

An unmistakable aroma of French Roast coffee woke Carolyn next morning, the scent making its way down the hall and into her bedroom. Generally, Carolyn was the one who made coffee, always awake long before Dahlia, even on days when she didn't have to be in the studio until late. This morning, she walked into the kitchen in her striped pyjamas and accepted the proffered black mug from Dante. The two were both early risers, while Dahlia needed three separate alarms to jump-start herself. That's why she insisted on spending work nights at her apartment; she didn't want to have to worry about oversleeping at a man's place. Her clocks were positioned around her room so that she couldn't simply hit a buzzer and fall back to sleep. She had to actually get out of bed and turn off each one.

Bright sunlight shined through the kitchen windows, picking up shimmering dust motes in the air and making them gleam. This reminded Carolyn that the cleaners were coming later; she had to write them a cheque and leave it on the refrigerator if she went out. Her brain was busy with this type of inconsequential detail but Dante pulled her into the present by saying, 'I made it strong, the way you like it.'

She smiled at him, leaning against the sparkling fifties-style Formica counter and putting both hands around the mug to feel the warmth. Dante was one of the few men she felt truly at ease with. When he turned to get a blue gingham towel by the sink, she continued to appraise him. He was striking, like all of Dahlia's men, with heavy dark hair that constantly fell over his forehead. When he tilted his head back to toss his hair out of his brown eyes, he looked like a surfer – 32 going on sixteen.

Finished rinsing up, he offered Carolyn a coaster. It was slightly odd to be treated as a guest in her own apartment, but she didn't mind. She could imagine having someone serve her coffee every morning, someone tall and dark like Dante. Someone who knew at least the sketchy outline of her history and would never ask her any stupid or embarrassing questions. Although this morning he did ask her something that made her stare at him.

'Did we bother you?' he wondered, looking away as if suddenly captivated by the rhinestone-studded Elvis clock on the far wall. Elvis's legs swung back and forth to tick off the seconds, hips a-swivel in a way that would have made Ed Sullivan jitterbug in his grave.

Carolyn shook her head, took a sip, and murmured that the coffee was great.

'So we *didn't* bother you?' His voice made it sound almost as if he wished they had; as if he'd like to know that she'd spent her evening listening to their sexual gymnastics. Carolyn wondered what he'd think if he knew that she had actually considered watching from outside.

'I went to bed right after I got home from my show,' she told him honestly. 'Did you guys have sushi?'

Dante made a face. 'I don't do raw fish any more.'

'Why not?'

'I read this article about a man who got one of those sushi worms inside him.' He grimaced. 'When the thing died, he put on this pair of rubber gloves and pulled –'

'Don't tell me,' Carolyn begged. 'I like sushi.'

'It was twenty-seven feet long.'

'Urban legend,' she said, but he shook his head,

85

apparently ready to give her more details, which she didn't want. 'How was the movie?' she asked before they reached a point where she could never eat sushi again.

Dante flushed. His skin was so tan that it wasn't easy to tell, but she knew him well enough. Instantly, she understood that he thought she was talking about the X-rated one they'd viewed in the living room.

'Didn't you go see some action flick? *Bruce Willis Conquers Van Damme*?'

He caught himself. 'It was sold out. We rented something instead.'

Terrie, set for a morning sprint, trotted into the room, looking expectantly from Dante to Carolyn. 'Hold on,' Carolyn said to the dog, 'I've got to finish my cup.' She talked to Terrie a lot, sometimes forgetting to stop when other people were present. Terrie didn't understand the concept of patience, and he probably didn't have a great grasp of English either, but Carolyn always felt better when she kept him posted. Now, he nudged against her as if he hoped he could physically force her to the door.

A blare of synthetic horns sounded from Dahlia's bedroom, the alarms going off in rapid succession. Terrie was accustomed to this noise and didn't even look up, continuing to push and now adding excited little yips as if that might help Carolyn understand what he wanted.

'I'll go,' Dante said, reaching for Terrie's black leather leash hanging from a hook on the back door. 'I was headed out to Fairfax for bagels anyway.'

Carolyn simply nodded and watched the two leave. Dahlia emerged moments later, obviously awake the whole time but not ready to deal with company – even her own.

'Did we bother you last night?' she asked casually, just like Dante.

Carolyn shook her head. What was up with these two?

'We rented this wild tape,' she said, and Carolyn sensed that Dahlia was dying to tell her, and had simply

86

been waiting for Dante to leave so that she could share her erotic exploits. 'I thought we might do it in the theatre,' she said, 'but Dante suggested we rent a porno. It's been a long time since I'd seen one.'

'Have you watched many?'

She ignored the question. When something didn't suit Dahlia, she simply moved on. 'The titles kept cracking me up. *Edward Penishands. Private Ryan Meets Private Benjamin. A Few More Good Men.* Finally, we brought one home, and it was just awesome. I was worried we'd wake you, but we couldn't help ourselves.'

Carolyn was starting to think that maybe they had wanted her to wake up, that maybe the fun was the thought of someone listening in. Or could they possibly have wanted her to join in? That concept made her echo Dante's blush, and she tried to cover with a quick question.

'Which film did you end up with?'

'*Sinderella*.' Dahlia started to laugh, taking a moment to compose herself before adding, 'With an "s", like "sin".' Another pause and smile. 'If you thought the stepsisters were evil in the storybook, you'd be surprised by how wicked they were in this one.'

While Dante was still out after the bagels, Dahlia got ready for work. As always, she paid as much attention to her appearance for days at the salon as she did on date nights. It was her job to represent Chez Chaz. If she didn't look good, Chaz didn't look good. Chaz had it easy in this department because Dahlia *always* looked good.

'Tell Dante I'll vibe him,' Dahlia said, referring to Dante's silent vibrating pager. This concept appealed to her intensely. She could let a man know she was calling by making the pocket in his pants start to twitch. Every time he felt that rumbling motor, he'd think of her. It was as if the designer had Dahlia in mind when creating this device.

When Dante returned and learned that Dahlia was

gone for the day, he didn't appear to be in any hurry to leave. He played with Terrie for a while, then wandered down the hall to find Carolyn. She was at work at her computer, headset in place, but when she felt Dante's eyes on her, she looked up. He was holding the front page of the *LA Times* in one hand, a red mug of steaming coffee in the other. She could see the banner headline screaming about some political scandal. Below was a picture of the missing girl from the flyers and news bulletins. The headline made it clear that the young girl was dead.

'Where did they find her?' Carolyn asked, pressing the 'pause' button on her micro-disc player.

'Up in the hills. Someone simply stumbled on the body by accident. Lucky break for the police.' He paused. 'I want to keep the piece. It fits in well with my latest project. You're supposed to write about what you know, but I honestly don't know anything about this.'

'What are you working on?'

'Nothing,' Dante said. 'I've got writer's block.' He sat on Carolyn's bed and stared at his reflection in the windows, reminding her of Dahlia, the way she preened. When he looked back at her, it was obvious that he wanted Carolyn's attention, and she took off the headset.

'What are you *supposed* to be working on?'

'Made-for-TV movie.' He shrugged as if he knew that it wasn't the great American novel, but what could you do? Dante had high expectations and a low work ethic, a combination that didn't always meld together to create the best results. 'A movie-of-the-week deal. It should cover my cell phone bill for the next year.'

'What's the plot?'

'Average murder. Some fancy but slutty girl is found dead and the police aren't sure if she was killed by her jealous older sister, her cuckolded fiancé, or, perhaps, her sexually deviant stepfather.'

'So who did it?' Carolyn was awful with mysteries, and could only read a chapter or two before flipping to the back of the book to find out the answer. It made her too jittery not to know. She'd never understood people who wanted to be scared for pleasure.

Dante winked. 'You'll have to wait until prime time to learn that.' He looked out the window again. Californian sunshine created a halo of pinkish gold light on the panes.

'When's the deadline?'

'Soon,' he said, running his hands through his hair. No matter how many times he brushed his glossy dark mane out of his eyes, that wayward lock fell right back into place. Carolyn thought that he must have his hair cut that way on purpose, to give himself something to do with his hands – a way to contain his obvious endless amounts of nervous energy. 'Can I listen to your music with you?'

Company while she worked was rare for Carolyn, yet nice. But before she let Dante plug in, she warned him first, 'I have to stop a lot.' She was reviewing several band interviews, choosing excerpts to play before showcasing their music.

'No problem.'

Carolyn connected her extra headphones and set Dante up next to her on the desk. They listened to two band interviews back to back, Dante never complaining when Carolyn had to stop and rewind, or when she swore at herself for putting her hands on the keyboard wrong and getting lines that looked like an alien language. It was his fault, really. Having Dante so close to her made it difficult to concentrate. Carolyn took in his smell: remnants of a musky cologne mixed with a scent of fresh air. She was aware of the way his body moved every time he shifted in his seat, and she wondered, suddenly, why he and Dahlia broke up.

She knew Dahlia's stated reasons, but she'd never fully believed them. It was difficult when you only heard one side of an argument. Dahlia's claim that she simply needed more space was too clichéd for Carolyn to accept. Space from what? Dante was so non-threatening that she couldn't imagine him putting any pressure on her. No way was he after her for marriage or a serious commitment. But then, they hadn't really broken up, had they? All they'd done was taken a few months off from each other and now they were dating again. Although Dante might not be aware, Carolyn realised, that Dahlia was also serial dating other men on the side. What would he do if he knew?

Dante suddenly said, 'Earth to Carolyn. Are you with us, Carolyn?' sensing that she'd gotten behind on the transcription. He broke her from her reverie, and she quickly pressed rewind to back up the disc, then got her hands on the keyboard to type in the real question.

'Hey, Carrie, it's us!' Billy called when he entered the apartment. He always hollered to let Carolyn know that he and Max had arrived. Carolyn had given the magic cleaning duo their own key when it became obvious that she was never going to hear the doorbell over her headset.

Billy and Max were both post-grad students waiting for their big breaks. In the meantime, they cleaned other people's houses to pay the bills. When Carolyn had initially received their flyer in the mail, she'd been hesitant. Big bold letters had proclaimed that the Confidential Cleaners would take care of all those dirty little chores most people hated to do. 'We won't tell if you won't,' was their motto. They would vacuum. Dust. They even did windows.

As usual, Carolyn had disliked the thought of strangers coming into her house. Somehow it didn't feel right. Still, she liked cleaning even less. And Dahlia liked cleaning not at all, which had occasionally caused friction between the roommates. Now, Billy and Max were a regular part of her routine, flying through the place once a week and leaving everything clean and shining in their wake.

Max was all business. Slim, with the angular features and golden-blond hair of someone with Nordic blood, he rarely spoke to Carolyn at all. Seemingly lost in his own world, he walked into the apartment with his green plastic bucket and blue rubber gloves, grabbed the various supplies from under the kitchen sink, and made his way directly to the shower.

Billy was his opposite. Dark-haired and dark-eyed, he was always fun to talk to. When Carolyn was at home, he cleaned her bedroom first, chatting her up while he worked. She'd sit on her sofa and listen to him talk about his weekend activities. Billy was an outdoorsman, always filled with interesting tales of fishing trips, hiking at Joshua Tree, or bungee jumping.

Carolyn scheduled the cleaners for times when Dahlia was at work because her roommate hated the smell of cleaning products. That always struck Carolyn as odd. How could someone who was accustomed to the scent of perm solution be so sensitive?

This afternoon, Carolyn watched as Billy slipped Terrie a doggy treat, then she followed the cleaner into the kitchen, sitting on the counter with her feet off the floor while he mopped the black and white chequered floor. Dante had just left, and she knew she should go back to work, but for some reason she was in a mood to procrastinate.

'Did you want us to do the windows today, Carrie?' That made her smile. Billy was one of the few people to give her a nickname. 'It's been several months.'

'And the rugs?' she asked hopefully. This was the one thing they wouldn't do – shampoo the super-shag, seventies-style carpets spread through the apartment.

'You know the rules,' Billy said. 'We'll do windows. Most people won't even do that. But we won't attempt those monster rugs. You need one of those special steam-cleaning machines for those.'

Carolyn shrugged, as if she couldn't be blamed for trying, and then listened as Billy told her in great detail about his weekend spent windsurfing. While he talked, she pictured the scenes, watching as he carefully polished the grate that led to Dahlia's closet. As he rubbed the soft grey flannel cloth over the old metal, a hinge suddenly squeaked and the bronze-coloured plate fell open into his hands.

'Shit,' he said, looking up at her sheepishly. 'I think I broke your –' He didn't know what to call it. 'Your *thing*.' Curious, he peered through the opening, lowering his body and then disappearing, head and shoulders, into the wall. 'Holy shit,' he said, his voice slightly muffled. 'Look at all the shoes!'

Carolyn couldn't believe it. The whatever-it-was-called opened. And if Billy could wriggle through, then she most definitely could slide inside, getting right into Dahlia's closet without her roommate ever knowing. Excitement bubbled within her. If listening to Dahlia and her dates had been enough to fuel several days' worth of fantasies, she could hardly imagine what watching would be like.

When Billy backed out, brushing dust bunnies from his hair, he gave Carolyn an interested look. 'What are you thinking, Carrie?' he asked. 'Come on. Spill it.'

She was thinking that she was off tonight. She would be home when Dahlia came home. Would she have the nerve to slide inside Dahlia's closet?

'Nothing special,' she lied, looking into Billy's choc-olate-brown eyes. 'Just daydreams.'

Part II

'Everybody knows that you've been faithful,
give or take a night or two.'

Leonard Cohen, 'Everybody Knows'

Chapter Eight

*D*uring Dahlia's morning coffee break, someone slipped stealthily behind her in the tiny employees' lounge and covered her eyes. She knew exactly who it was from the moment his warm hands touched her skin, but she didn't let on. Dahlia was good at games like this, and playing dumb was all part of the fun.

'Oh, honey,' she purred, shimmying her curvy hips in a sensuous way against those of her hidden suitor, 'I like the way you move.'

'You ain't seen nothing yet,' the man said, his voice a rough whisper, but then he started to laugh, unable to keep up the charade for more than a millisecond. Harry couldn't fake at being heterosexual if his life depended on it. Once, for Halloween, he'd actually gone in costume as a straight guy, but his swish walk had given him away from the very first step. Now Dahlia said, 'Harry, you nut, either follow through or get the hell away from me. You know how much I hate a tease.'

'But you're all sexed up,' Harry said, hoisting himself up to sit on the chrome-topped counter and smile at her. In his ultra-femme fashion, he crossed his legs and began to fluff the feather-trimmed edge of his short, black skirt. Attached to his belt were a pair of silver handcuffs, an accessory that Harry was rarely without. Today, he looked like a cross between a woman and a raven, every bit of his outfit trimmed in shiny, dark feathers. It was a good look for him, and while Dahlia appraised the outfit, Harry appraised Dahlia. 'You're positively exuding that scent again.'

'Scent of a woman?' she asked sweetly. 'Like in the Pacino film?'

'I don't think that's exactly what the movie was about.'

'Speaking of movies . . .' Dahlia said, starting to fill him in on all of the details from her wild romp the night before. She knew that Harry would get a big kick out of the story, especially when she described the deliriously decadent behaviour of Sinderella's fairy godmother in this particularly kinky version. But then Chaz came steaming into the room, looking for Harry to solve another hideous and desperate make-up emergency, and Dahlia was left alone again.

Alone for a heartbeat.

Standing at the counter, she'd only had time to take one sip of her coffee, to reach for a copy of the *Weekly* and start perusing the personal ads, before footsteps behind her alerted her to the fact that another man had entered the room. Then a second set of hands covered her eyes, hands that this time most obviously did not belong to a feather-dipped drag queen.

'Mmmm,' Dahlia murmured. 'Now let me see. I'm guessing that I'm supposed to name the mysterious person behind the hands.'

There was silence, but the man's body now pressed into her from behind, giving her an added clue with the feeling of the suitor's package against her ass. Dahlia took her time to really enjoy the moment. Savouring the suspense. Still, as she had before, she knew exactly who was playing with her, and she also knew that it wouldn't be smart to start tossing out names of random men. Most men didn't appreciate it if they thought they weren't the only one putting a particular hole.

'Jason,' she murmured. 'You know, I could get in trouble.'

'You *are* in trouble,' he whispered back, his voice holding a dangerous yet undeniably sexy edge.

'You're breaking one of the main rules of the salon.'

'Fucking the manager? Can I see the rule book which lists that as a no-no?'

She laughed as she said, 'No, you're just really not supposed to be back here.'

'Back where?' he asked, pressing harder still, so that she could feel that he was erect and that he was wanting it. 'Back *here*?'

Oh, the naughty, naughty boy. What a find he was turning out to be.

'Rules,' he continued now, 'are made to be broken. Isn't that right? Isn't that what all the bad girls do? Break the rules.'

She turned around, wriggling in his embrace so that he felt her pert breasts against his chest and her lithe body up against his own.

'What were you planning?' she asked. He had obviously snuck himself past Amy, the most rabid of their receptionists, a woman who never let anyone take one step past the lobby without an appointment. The Chez Chaz salon was a little like the court of the Wizard of Oz in that sense. No lay people were supposed to see what went on behind the curtain. For Jason to go to this much trouble made Dahlia figure that he must have more ideas than simply playing peek-a-boo.

'I was planning on giving you this,' he said, grabbing her tightly and pulling her even harder against his body. Oh, she wanted that. Definitely. But then Jason continued. 'That's what you *were* going to get, but I couldn't help but overhear you and that flaming friend of yours discussing your activities from last night.' He said 'activities' as if the word were in quotes, almost daring Dahlia to confess to him that she'd spent the evening with another man. She remained silent. Why shouldn't she have been with Dante? She and Jason hadn't made any

promises to each other. They'd only been out – or in –
two times. Much too soon for any commitments.

Instead of saying any of this, she looked up into his
strikingly handsome face, and from his half-smile she
could tell that he was still playing. That he was as
excited by the whole situation as she was. Jason had a
look that was overall less boyish than Dante, even
though the men were about the same age. She found
their differences enticing. Why date cookie-cutter men
when you could sample a wide selection?

'And what are you planning on giving me *now*?' she
asked him.

He eyed her for a moment, but didn't speak, letting
her read the future in the simple expression on his face.
And oh, my, her panties were wet already, just from this
sexually charged exchange. If he did what she thought
he might then he would discover just how turned on she
was. 'Well, little girl,' he finally said, walking away and
locking the door to the small, pink-walled coffee room,
'I'm thinking something else entirely now. I'm thinking
that you had better get that fine ass of yours over my
lap for a bare-bottom spanking. That is, if you know
what's good for you.'

'A spanking is going to be good for me?' She could
hardly get the question out. Simply saying the word
'spanking' made her legs feel watery and she held on to
the counter with one hand to keep herself steady.

'It'll be better for you to get over here yourself,' he
explained, 'than to force me to come over and get you.'
He shook his head, and made a 'tsk, tsk' noise. 'Such a
bad girl, going out with another man. What am I gonna
do with you?'

As he spoke, he pulled out one of the high-backed
armless pink leather chairs and sat down. He looked
entirely at ease, as if it wasn't at all unusual for him to
burst into a place where his date worked and punish her
in the middle of the day. Then he stared at her with an
expression on his face that let her know he could wait as
long as it took.

Dahlia, even though she meant to play it tough, changed her mind and quick-stepped over to his side, her patent leather stack-heeled shoes click-clacking on the polished tile floor. Sometimes, when it was really good, she was unable to deny herself the pleasure. This was one of those times. She knew exactly how it was going to feel, how powerfully she was going to come afterwards.

Jason took hold of one of her wrists and pulled, draping her over his waiting lap. Then he dragged the back of her micro-mini plaid skirt up her thighs, flipped the pleated nothing of a skirt over, then slid her silky white panties down her thighs. Moving slowly. Taking his time.

What a deviant player he was, doing this to her at work. He must have guessed that if it hadn't been OK, she would have said no. And since she was saying nothing, he was meant to go forward. To spank her. Hard. Which is exactly what he did. Dahlia was all a-quiver as Jason's hand connected with her naked bottom, and she had to work not to let herself squeal each time his hand met her skin. When he slid one hand beneath her body, letting his finger just rest between her sex lips, she thought she might actually faint. Each time he smacked her, she ground her hips against him, and his fingertip made contact with her pulsing clit. That mixture of almost unfathomable pleasure juxtaposed with the smarting pain from the spanking had Dahlia ready to climax in almost no time at all. And when Dahlia came, she generally came loudly.

Thankfully someone, in all likelihood Harry, had turned the radio up in the salon, masking the noises emanating from the coffee room. Dahlia suddenly heard her roommate's voice over the airwaves, announcing a request for a particularly faithful listener. As Jason continued spanking her, Dahlia made out the opening words to Fiona Apple's song, 'Criminal', one of her all-time favourites.

'I've been a bad, bad girl,' Fiona crooned.

'Yes, you have,' Jason said, agreeing, and it was obvious from the sound of his voice that he had something to do with the fact that this song was playing now. Maybe he'd had Harry call ahead. No one Dahlia had been with before had ever thought to choose music for a sexual encounter, and she was thrilled at the thought. It added something to what they were doing, made their little scene seem even larger.

Just as she was wondering which song was up next, the music changed to Madonna's spicy soft-core hit from the *Dick Tracy* soundtrack. 'Don't want no hanky-panky. Just want a little spanky.' Dahlia would have broken out laughing if Jason hadn't taken this opportunity to up the intensity of their session, really letting her have it, so that she kicked up her heels and gripped on to the metal legs of the chair to try to hold herself steady.

'Such a pretty ass,' Jason muttered. 'I mean, it's fucking gorgeous. From the first time I caught sight of your haughty rear at Ed's Diner, I couldn't wait to get you over my lap.'

Dahlia remembered that day well. She'd been wearing a pair of vinyl short-shorts that were red and white striped, like peppermint. Her roommate had been in shock when she'd seem them. 'Who are you today?' Carolyn had asked. 'An X-rated candy striper?' What did Carolyn know? The shorts had most definitely attracted Jason's interest, as well as the interest of several other local players. But she couldn't waste time thinking of any of them right now, as Jason continued to spank her.

It was as if he was punctuating his sentences with the sound of his hand meeting her naked skin. 'If you can believe it, it's even prettier now that it's all blushing for me. But you know it's going to feel so good when I fuck it. Your hot skin against mine.'

He let her up then, and without a word bent her over the glitter-topped Formica table, taking her from behind. He was right. The man definitely knew what he was talking about; knew the road to Dahlia's . . . not heart

. . . her clit. The spanking had simply brought her to a simmering point, and now that his cock had been introduced to the recipe, Dahlia was only one beat away from coming.

And all it took was Jason calling her a naughty girl, a sinful fuck, as he rode her. What a good choice this man had turned out to be. With his flair for the dramatic, like showing up at work and doing this, to his comic side, by getting Harry to call up her roommate and create his own personal sexual soundtrack, she couldn't have been more pleased.

Or maybe she could be just a little more pleased, because coming took her even higher. She tried to stay quiet, holding on to the edge of the table with her hands and shuddering all over as the warmth of the climax flamed through her.

Zach had sensed an intense connection with Carolyn from the moment he'd first entered her office at the station. To be perfectly honest, he'd developed a bit of a crush on her. Seeing her in person had simply solidified those feelings for him. The fact that he now lived upstairs from her only added to his interest. Maybe it was destiny that had told him to answer that particular ad.

But still, there was something odd about the girl.

When he called her at the station, she seemed like a different person. Sexy and sultry, she sounded more than happy to talk to him, to play what he liked, to banter and be somewhat of a tease. Then, when he'd see her at home, she'd nod 'hello' and disappear quickly into her apartment or her shiny black pick-up truck, off somewhere away from him.

This hadn't ever happened before. Ego aside, he really had never been interested in someone who didn't want to go with him. He found that for the first time since finalising his split with Melody, he was really fixated on a girl, rather than the other way around. Was he into the thrill of the chase? No, it was deeper. He liked her. He liked her taste in music, liked listening to her radio show, and he liked calling her up and making requests. Letting her know the type of music that he was into.

Choosing one song after another to really reveal himself was the most drawn-out method of foreplay he'd ever experienced. Today, he called her with Peter Gabriel's 'Your Eyes'. A classic. There were so many different lines to analyse, but his favourite was about the resolution of all the fruitless searches.

She might actually be his resolution, and this realisation hit hard. It made him the most insecure he'd ever felt.

Stormy, fielding phone calls, didn't know exactly how it had happened. She and Zach were playing this strange game of musical dating. Every day, he'd call her up with a song to play and then she'd respond with one of her own. Their exchange gave her a feeling of power, because she knew music. It was the one thing that had always been there for her.

The insertion of Melody into the picture was something that neither talked about. Because for every one song Zach would request, Melody would ask for two. She was obviously listening, paying attention to the little lyrical discussion. Stormy would dutifully play Melody's requests: The Stones' 'Under My Thumb', then wonder who was under whose. Then The Divynls' 'I Touch Myself', which didn't have to be dissected at all.

Zach never talked about Melody when he called, and Carolyn, although she was desperate to ask whenever she saw him at home, didn't have the same need when she was in the Stormy role. For some reason, as Stormy she felt superior to Melody. She wasn't acting like the crazy ex-girlfriend. She was simply doing her job, playing the music and interacting with the callers.

Carolyn avoided Zach at the apartment because that was easier. Safer. If he wanted to play with her over the phone, then fine. They could start like that. Besides, there were other things on her mind at the moment.

Other things like Dahlia's closet.

Keeping her relationship with Zachary confined to her times as Stormy let her continue with her eavesdropping when at home. Losing herself in the visions of Dahlia and her dates when they played at the apartment, which was just how Carolyn wanted it. At least, for now.

'If I ever hear Enya again I am going to kill someone,' Dahlia announced when she arrived home from work that evening. She was still aglow (on all four cheeks) from her midday tryst with Jason, but she didn't think she was going to share this with her roommate. Sometimes she felt the desire to confess all that happened, and other times she didn't. She never questioned her feelings, simply went with them.

'That bad?' Carolyn asked. What she really wanted to ask was why Harry had made a double request earlier that day, and what those songs had meant to him or to Dahlia. She knew something was up but she wasn't able to probe. Funny how she had no problem eavesdropping, learning in secret all about Dahlia's world, but she couldn't ask the things she wanted to when the women were face to face.

Carolyn had played exactly what Harry'd requested, taunting her listeners with a bit of bedroom talk, all the while wondering what was going on in Dahlia's life. She'd guessed it must be something erotic, and she had loved the concept as much as Dahlia had, momentarily lost in a fantasy about what different soundtracks would be appropriate for which sexual activities. Sort of like which wine to choose with a meal. There was George Michael's 'Outside', just perfect for playing in public with his lyrics about being done with the sofa and through with the kitchen table. The Chili Peppers had many, but the one that she loved best was 'Sir Psycho Sexy' because it was filled with an array of fantasy situations, including one with a lady cop and her big black stick. And then there was Prince. Name the song. She especially liked 'Cream', 'Head', and 'Kiss.'

Now that she was home, she wanted to hear about what Dahlia had done while listening to the songs. She also wanted to talk to her about Zach and Melody, but that would mean admitting that there was something going on. Admitting that she wanted something to go on. And she couldn't face it yet. Too many years had passed since she'd last had these sensations inside. She needed to get comfortable with them herself before including her roommate in the situation.

'Give me anything other than the language of fucking trees,' Dahlia continued on her anti-Enya rant. Enya was Chaz's favourite singer, and when the radio was off, that was the CD he chose. Dahlia paused in Carolyn's doorway and stared in at her. As always, Carolyn had a week's worth of demos stacked up and was sorting through them, choosing which ones she'd discard and which deserved a second hearing. Next to these were three rock interviews she wanted to edit.

'What's your schedule?' Dahlia asked.

'I can walk Terrie,' Carolyn told her, anticipating the question.

'But could you walk me?'

That made less sense. Carolyn stopped organising and looked over at her roommate, eyebrows raised to ask a silent question.

'I'm dateless,' Dahlia said, frowning, and twirling in a circle absentmindedly. 'Dante's at a screening and Jason has to work late.' Her short skirt floated up, reminding Carolyn of Harry the night that he'd dressed for his kinky cross-dressing party. Carolyn could see Dahlia's toned thighs, the laced edge of her day-of-the-week panties, a new rage in Hollywood. On Dahlia, the fad worked. It was almost too cute that she was wearing Monday panties on a Tuesday, as if she'd forgotten which day of the week it was.

'Maybe what you need is a third boyfriend,' Carolyn suggested, and even though she was teasing as she said it, she realised the idea appealed to her. Someone new in Dahlia's line-up to listen to, and potentially to watch.

Someone who might surprise both of them with something Dahlia had never done. Was that even possible?

'Third,' Dahlia repeated, giving Carolyn her calculatedly evil grin. 'So you're keeping track. Well, good. Someone ought to follow up on me. I know that I never have time to.'

Damn. Carolyn realised that she needed to pay more attention to what she was saying. She really didn't want Dahlia to know how much energy she had invested in fantasising about her. Luckily, Dahlia was busy with her own thoughts, as always on to something else.

'I *had* a date,' Dahlia explained. 'I just turned him down. He struck me as a little too confident. Needed to take him down a notch.' She continued to pull at the hem of her skirt. Watching her fidget, Carolyn was reminded of a little kid with nothing to do. Dahlia wanted someone to entertain her. If male company wasn't available, than female would have to suffice.

'Why don't *you* walk Terrie?' Carolyn asked, knowing ahead of time that this idea wouldn't win her any points. Walking Terrie was neither glamorous nor fun. It wasn't the way Dahlia wanted to spend an evening after she'd slaved over a hot counter all day long.

Dahlia sighed dramatically, moving back over to Carolyn's bed and throwing herself on it. Carolyn considered giving in to her – going with Dahlia to her favourite bar, watching her flirt. It could be entertaining. Dahlia always played games when she went to bars, sliding into her make-believe world, pretending she was someone else. 'I'm Julia tonight,' she'd announce as they walked into Sammy's. 'Don't forget. I'm Julia.'

'Come on,' Dahlia urged, 'you can play any of the CDs you want on the jukebox.' She always used that bribe to get Carolyn to go with her. Now with Dahlia staring at her expectantly, Carolyn weighed her options. Work all night, lost in the droning sound of some hotshot rock star who probably couldn't even get it up. Or slink into a smoky bar and listen to Dahlia's soft whisper. As usual, on the rare occasions when Dahlia thrust Carolyn into this type of decision, she opted for the latter. And, as usual, Dahlia was all smiles at getting her own way.

She bounded over to Carolyn in an energetic leap that was reminiscent of Terrie in his happiest moments, and gave Carolyn a quick squeeze. Then she was off down the hall to her room, and Carolyn could hear the noises that indicated her roommate was getting ready. Dahlia must have known all along that Carolyn would say yes, because she was back in almost no time, her work outfit replaced by something very tight and black shot through with silver strands, her hair pinned up into a style that looks like it takes a long time to create but actually is an illusion.

She had on sheer hose and tall, chunky heels – a funky fad from Europe that was apparently ahead of its time for Hollywood because Carolyn hadn't seen anyone else wearing them yet. Dahlia often previewed the next rage, knowing instinctively what other people would be wearing in several months, and discarding the style long before the rest of the world caught on. Sensing Carolyn's eyes on her, Dahlia took position against the door frame, one foot kicked up under her, like a shot from the cover for an old-time pulp novel.

'Ready?' she asked, smouldering grey lids lowered, mouth pursed as she blew a kiss in Carolyn's direction.

'Just about.' Carolyn bent to tie the laces on her heavy black boots, then rummaged through her closet for her favourite thrift-store cardigan. It was a pretty jade green, and as Carolyn slid into it, she imagined what it would look like on Dahlia, bringing out the colour in her eyes. Squinting, Carolyn took a peek at herself in the mirror, just to make sure everything was tucked in, and suddenly Dahlia was at her side, staring for once at Carolyn's reflection rather than at her own. She lifted Carolyn's masculine black glasses and then looked at her again.

'Do you *have* to wear these?'

'I can't see without them.'

Of course, Dahlia knew this, but she handed the lenses back with reluctance, then started to fluff Carolyn's hair. It was easy to see what Dahlia would be like at the salon, moving from one celebrity client to another, sleeking back a wayward curl, brushing away a few remaining snips of hair. Carolyn shook her off, pulling her dark hair back into a ponytail and capturing it with a dime-store band.

'Let me do your make-up?' Dahlia asked.

Carolyn was suddenly sure that when Dahlia was little she had one of those dress-up Barbies, the plastic heads that you could make up, hair you could tease into fashion after fashion. 'Let's just go,' Carolyn said, moving through the apartment. She was no good at being anyone's doll.

Chapter Nine

*O*K, Melody was plenty fucking smart enough to realise that she was losing it. As she circled Zach's new apartment on her Harley for the third time, staring up at the second floor to see if the windows were lit, she understood that she was now a borderline stalker. Couldn't get him out of her mind. Needed to keep tabs on him. To know exactly where he was and what – or who – he was doing.

The craziest part about going nuts was that when she saw him at rehearsals or when they had a gig, she could actually keep it together. Act as if she had accepted their break-up and was ready to settle for friendship and partner in the band.

Not true. She would never settle.

Another time around, zipping along beneath the purple-blossomed jacaranda trees, manoeuvring easily through the light traffic on her turquoise Sportster. No lights were on in the place. He must have gone out to a bar, or over to Roger's to rehearse. They were all supposed to meet up there later. Roger had the best place for music, way the fuck out in Venice where people didn't mind loud noises. If the occasional gunshot didn't disturb anyone then they could be secure in the fact that nobody would call the police because of some loud bass line.

She hoped he was at Roger's, and not out with some slut. Not that it really mattered. She knew that no other woman was right for him. Once he was back with her, all the rest of them would fade away. Even that DJ he seemed so enamoured with. Stormy Weathers. What kind of a fucking name was that?

It was getting late, almost time to go rehearse. But first, Melody was off to meet Zorg. Shit, Zach couldn't expect her to totally give up sex, could he? Just because he was taking the long way around to get back with her, he had to realise that she was a sexual creature. That she needed her fix. He'd been with her long enough to know that she couldn't go too many days without a good fucking.

Come on, she'd already quit using drugs. What more could he want?

One final time around the block just to make sure he truly wasn't home, and then Melody headed over to the Sleeping Buddha, where Feast of Flesh was playing a 9 p.m. show.

She'd meet Zorg backstage for a quick one between sets. Then she'd head over to Roger's, and act the subdued good girl who would do just about anything to win back Zachary's love.

It was only several blocks to Sammy's, but Dahlia didn't like to walk in her heels. Didn't like to walk much at all. She was a firm believer in the immortal song lyric, 'Nobody walks in LA.' Carolyn didn't mind, because the drive gave her time to think. Yes, she *was* counting the men in Dahlia's life. It was true.

So how many lovers *had* Dahlia been with? Carolyn believed that she knew most of her roommate's sexual history. Friends shared things with friends, and Carolyn had a good memory when it came to facts and figures. She knew that Dahlia had lost her virginity senior year in high school to – and this was almost too classic for words – the captain of the football team. She'd had that type of high-school experience, a member of the popular set, the cheerleading team, the party crowd. She'd done it under the bleachers after a game, and then again in the back of his daddy's pick-up truck. That had been the start of her sexual career.

In college, both girls had dated extensively at first. It was what you did when you left home. But Dahlia had surpassed most people even then. She'd dated, Carolyn suddenly realised, like a man. Without expectations of a relationship, without needing to be coddled or called the morning after. Maybe it was because most men fell for her. Fell hard. Wanted more than she was willing to give. Since she was the pursued and never the pursuer, she never had to worry about whether or not a man would call for a second date.

They always called.

Now, at 26, how many men had Dahlia been intimate with? Carolyn tried to mentally track the number. Josh in high school. Bryan, Reed, Declan, Paul, and then a hiatus while she'd gone steady with a grad student named Will – a man that Carolyn had never met because he was Dahlia's T.A., and they'd had to keep their romance on the hush-hush. Dating students would have gotten him fired. Dahlia had loved the secret quality of their relationship, but when the semester was over and they could have gone public with their romance, she'd left him.

Back in the circuit, she'd picked up with Blaine, then Todd, Hunter, Eden ... and finally Dante and Jason. Carolyn lost count, but guessed there were at least twenty. Not too bad, considering Dahlia could have been with many more. She could have said yes the way some people say good morning.

Carolyn's own record was totally different. A virgin when she'd arrived at UCLA, she had waited until she found someone she truly liked before she gave it up. And then he'd dumped her right away, forcing her to reconsider her position on sex. Dahlia, who had been her roommate from freshman year, looked to Carolyn as if she were having a lot more fun. So she tried that.

Tried dating around, and in the beginning she'd liked it, too.

Adventure was a high, and going out with so many different men was thrilling. Empowering. But then she'd had the run-in with Steven and she'd closed down, seen everything in an altered light.

Was that light finally changing now?

Zorg had his big rough hands locked around Melody's naked waist, holding her up against the concrete wall of the dressing room as he rocked his cock inside her. Outside, they could hear the sounds of Feast of Flesh getting ready to perform – a high-pitched feedback screech that made up the preliminary notes to their biggest hit, 'Ozone Man'. But they still had a few moments before Zorg was required on stage. Just enough time to take care of the need that burned inside them.

'Fuck me, baby,' Melody whispered. 'Fuck me like you love me.'

Zorg didn't respond. He rarely ever spoke. Now he had an intense, urgent look on his face and his eyes were shut, giving Melody the opportunity to observe him. He was attractive to her in an animalistic way, with his shaved head, hard jaw, strong lines in his face. When he was on stage he was possessed, the way he screamed into the microphone, flailed across the stage. Although he and Zach were both musicians, they were polar opposites.

With Zach, she was never exactly sure what was going on in his head. He'd grow quiet sometimes, and she'd have to ask a million questions before he'd tell her what was troubling him. Usually, it was something about her – the way she'd flirted with someone at a party, the way she'd ripped her shirt off at the end of a gig, showing her breasts to the howling crowd.

She didn't have the same problem with Zorg. It was easy to guess what he was thinking about because it was

111

always the same thing: sex. He was a bit like a Neanderthal in that way.

As they fucked, Melody turned her attention away from her lover and to the way her own expressions changed in the cracked mirror hanging on the wall behind him. She looked like a porn star, cherry-glossed lips parted, a flush to her cheeks that came from an impending orgasm. She was close now.

Getting closer.

There was something special about riding Zorg's cock. Not only was it big – and it was huge – but it was also thick. The times when she prepped him with a quick hand job, she couldn't fully wrap one hand around it. And she'd tried often, liking to jerk him off at the start of their sessions just so she could play with his stick. He got even bigger as they fucked, so that when he thrust into her, she felt absolutely impaled. Fucking him was the only time that she could forget about wanting Zachary.

Almost forget, anyway.

The way Zorg felt opened her up to other possibilities. That was a big difference from Zach. Not that Zachary was some sensitive mama's boy, but Zorg was rough and ready. And that raw, hard-boned quality connected with something inside Melody.

Why, then, was she so fucking adamant about getting Zachary back? She couldn't explain it, simply couldn't stop herself from wanting him. As she couldn't stop coming when Zorg drove into her. Fucking her so hard, she could almost taste it at the back of her throat.

'Hello, Dolly,' Chester sang out loudly when the girls arrived at the bar. No, he didn't have much of a voice, but Carolyn mentally gave him an 'f' for effort. Chester was young, too young to be of serious interest to Dahlia, but she obviously enjoyed the attention he bestowed upon her. Like a puppy, with his shaggy long hair and gold-streaked goatee, he practically bounced behind the bar when Dahlia chose her place before him, offering him her brilliant half-smile as she perched on a stool.

Several of the businessmen close by stopped talking about the markets and turned to stare at her. Dahlia acted as if she didn't notice, but she did. There was no way that three pairs of wandering eyes would get past her radar. They were so fixed on her that Carolyn wondered if Dahlia could actually physically feel them looking.

As usual, Carolyn headed immediately to the well-stocked jukebox. Focused on the glass case, she flipped the CD covers until the music she was looking for appeared. Tonight felt like a Jim Morrison evening. 'People are strange, when you're a stranger.' Wasn't that the truth? Then she'd move on to a faster paced number, a favourite tune from The Clash. What next? Maybe an unexpected song like 'Walk On The Wild Side' by Lou Reed.

When Harry was at the bar with them, he and Carolyn fought over the rights to choose songs. His picks ranged towards the sappy – The Cowboy Junkies, who Carolyn thought should just kill themselves and get it over with, or Irene Cara singing 'Flashdance'. Harry liked this song because of one particular line that he intentionally mis-heard as, 'Take your pants off, make it happen.' It was Harry's own personal motto. He'd put it on a bumper sticker if he allowed bumper stickers to come close to the rear end of his beloved Morris Minor. Harry wouldn't listen when Carolyn explained that the line was actually, 'Take your passion, make it happen.'

Carolyn liked this place. Sammy's Mango Hut had extremely tacky plastic pineapple lights hanging over the bar. The handsome waitstaff wore Hawaiian shirts and mu-mus in disgustingly vibrant day-glo colours. From her favourite table by the jukebox, she could watch everything that occurred in the bar, from the pool tables at the far corner – even *these* were covered with Hawaiian-style print fabric – to the bartender as he whipped up one tropical confection after another. Usually, once safely ensconced in her corner, Carolyn simply watched Dahlia go into action.

Tonight, however, her booth had been commandeered by a rowdy foursome who had already gone through a pitcher of Daiquiris and were waiting loudly and impatiently for a second round. As Carolyn looked for an equally out-of-the-way place, Dahlia waved her over. She had some sort of glittery polish on and when she moved her hand, her nails glinted in the light.

At the bar, she'd already been bought one drink by the suits. Chester, who only had eyes for Dahlia, finally noticed Carolyn and handed over a cold beer. No glass. At least he remembered what she drank, even if he didn't serve it with the same type of fanfare he employed when serving Dahlia. In fact, he barely seemed to notice that Carolyn was there. This was, Dahlia often told her, because of her attitude, not her looks. Carolyn put out a vibe that said, 'Leave me the fuck alone.' And men did. That was fine with her. It was exactly what she wanted. Dahlia, on the other hand, exuded, 'Come get me. If you can.'

While they listened to the second raucous number of Carolyn's jukebox selections, Dahlia introduced herself to the businessmen. Chester had ruined her game plan. She couldn't fake a name tonight, couldn't play at being a Marcie or a Julia or a Sian because Chester had called her 'Dolly' as she'd entered the bar. So instead, she faked an occupation.

'I'm a DJ,' she said, glancing over to see if Carolyn was listening. Of all the people she could play-act being, why would Dahlia want to be her? Carolyn wondered how far Dahlia would go with this little charade.

'Really?' one of the businessmen fawned. 'How incredibly interesting.'

'Oh, it is interesting,' Dahlia agreed, doing that flirty thing with the coils of her hair twisted around her fingers. Carolyn had read a magazine article that explained there were certain ways a woman could tell a guy she was interested in sex. Playing with her hair was

114

high on the list; letting her foot slip slightly out of her shoe so that the shoe dangled slightly away from her heel was another. Dahlia had this move down as well. Carolyn watched as the smooth ball of her heel came into play. But was Dahlia teasing, or was she really interested in having sex with one of these men? Or two ... or three?

'Plus,' she added, 'I get to go to a lot of free concerts.'

'Who's your favourite band?' the first man asked. His friends seemed too enthralled with Dahlia to even speak. Every time she leaned forward, they could look down the front of her dress. She knew this and was arching her body to perfection, letting them see only as much as she wanted. Dahlia could give lessons on how to flirt.

'I'm into alternative rock,' Dahlia said, giving Carolyn another quick glance. Was she catching this? Was she proud of her? The funniest part was that Dahlia was doubly lying. No, she wasn't a total geek about music. But her favourite bands were the all-girl vocals. Bonnie Raitt. Tori Amos. Paula Cole. She didn't really know anything about the music Carolyn preferred.

'I like that stuff, too,' the man said. 'I did some DJing in college.' He named a famous Bay Area college station, K-IBU, known for playing breakthrough bands, and now Carolyn started to pay more attention, wondering how Dahlia was going to get out of this potential predicament. She wouldn't know the difference between Kid Rock and King Crimson, between Southern Culture on the Skids and Santana.

Carolyn could see Dahlia's reflection in the mirror behind the bar. She lifted her drink and swallowed it quickly, all the while keeping an expression on her face as if she were considering the answer. As soon as her glass hit the bar, Chester was back in front of her, offering a refill. Tonight, Dahlia was drinking good tequila, straight up. Chester, always trying, offered to do a body shot with her. He claimed that it was the one thing he wanted to do before his time on earth ran out. 'Please, Dahlia, let me die a happy man.'

Carolyn realised instantly what Dahlia had done. She'd diverted the attention of her newly smitten beau from the world of music to the thought of Dahlia engaging in a body shot with the attractive barkeep. Brilliant.

'You were just talking about your favourite bands the other day,' Carolyn said, teasing her by bringing the conversation around again. 'Remember? Compiling a list of the top five records you'd take with you to a desert island.'

Dahlia shook her head, as if that imaginary conversation had completely slipped her mind, but Carolyn wouldn't let up so quickly. It was fun to see Dahlia caught off-guard, as it so rarely happened.

'Come on, Dahlia,' Chester begged, turning the attention back to alcohol. He had his lime wedge, his little silver shaker of salt. All he needed was for Dahlia to agree to let him play with her and he'd pop the lime in his mouth and sprinkle the salt on the back of his hand. He was so excited that his body actually trembled.

'I don't remember my list,' Dahlia said softly, giving Carolyn a look. 'But I do know who I hate. And that's Enya.'

The businessmen nodded appreciatively. It was an easy comment. A cheat. Not really up to Dahlia's standards. It was like saying that she thought The Carpenters were melodramatic or that The Bee Gees were dated.

'But if you want to hear my favourites, just listen,' Dahlia continued. 'I think Carolyn picked out the ones that I like best.'

'Who'd you choose?' one of the men asked, for once directing a question towards Carolyn. She smiled at him and responded. She'd stocked the jukebox with an unusual mix: Parliament. The Talking Heads. Sublime. Tom Waits.

'Oh, yeah,' the man sighed next to her. 'Those are good.' Carolyn looked at him with added interest, but too quickly he showed his true colours, turning back to look at her roommate again. It was obvious that he only had eyes for Dahlia, who now shook her head at Chester and downed the second shot without his assistance. The smile she flashed Carolyn made it perfectly clear how she felt inside. She'd won again.

Without even trying.

Like Harry wasn't even trying. Not trying to flirt or to be noticed by any of the revellers nearby. He preferred it when his liaisons occurred naturally. To this end, Harry sat by himself at the edge of an oval-shaped swimming pool, his dainty feet kicking in the water, watching the ripples as they radiated outwards. He was gratified when the boy he'd been eyeing all evening finally strolled towards him. Ogling didn't count as trying in Harry's book. It only counted as letting someone know you were available.

And he *was* available. Always available. That's what these parties were about. Connecting with someone special – or at least someone right for the night – and he thought that the boy might be just what he had in mind.

Harry was one of the few men who didn't really have a type. 'An equal-opportunity slut,' Dahlia teased him. Sometimes he went with the big, teddy-bear-looking guys who wore leather and motorcycle boots. The men who hung out in Boys' Town at the hardcore clubs, indicating their preferences with coloured bandannas stuck in their back pockets. A throwback to the seventies, it was a gimmick that had become so out that it was actually in again. Other times, he'd find himself enmeshed in a flirtation with someone who looked a lot like he did: a small, sprightly flamer. But tonight, he'd had his eye on one of the waitstaff – a blond youth with short, cropped hair and eyes that sparkled like diamonds.

The kid had to be in his early twenties, or else he was doing a great job of maintaining – a highly prized skill in LA. Youth wasn't necessarily a good thing to Harry. He liked his lovers to have experience. But he was willing to make an exception in the name of beauty, because this youthful number definitely had that.

He got ready to make small talk as the boy approached and sat at his side, sliding up his shiny black pants and slipping his own feet into the cool water. Harry noticed instantly the delicate bone structure of the boy's ankles, the pearly polished nails – something that came and went in these circles. Ever since Mickey Rourke had appeared in public with Vamp nail polish on, it was sort of a hit or miss thing.

Harry opened his mouth, ready to charm the new love of his life, when the unthinkable happened. The kid beat him to the punch, taking Harry's face, cradling his chin, and kissing him first.

And what a kiss. An old-time, pre-censorship movie kiss that Harry felt all the way to the tips of his toes. He realised that he'd gotten goose bumps from the smooch, as if the boy had rubbed one of Harry's boas up and down his naked skin – a favourite bedtime activity of Harry's. Their lips were pressed together, tongues meeting, and for a moment the rest of the party faded away. All the giggling going on behind them in the cabanas by the pool. The trysts in the tent set up on the large, lush lawn. Everything disappeared.

Silently, the two parted, and the beautiful boy motioned for Harry to follow. Still not speaking. Sexier than hell, Harry thought. So many men had to fill up the space with useless conversation, nervously babbling and totally ruining a mood. This kid seemed to have already learned the lesson that sometimes it was better to say things without words.

Excited, Harry followed his new crush into the house, up the spiral marble staircase to the master suite, feeling his desire swell with each step. But as they disrobed, Harry's feelings suddenly changed as he saw the last thing he'd expected to find on a new playmate.

'If you give them the slightest chance, the men will do all the work,' Dahlia explained to Carolyn in the ladies' room. She was a little tipsy, but not too far gone. Not after only two shots. As she stared at her reflection, she didn't seem to notice that Carolyn's eyes were on her, focused hard. Dahlia paused in the middle of her dating lesson as she pursed her lips, preparing to redo the Merlot-coloured lipstick that she most favoured. She used one of Harry's tricks, dotting the deep colour in the centre of the lower lip and then blending it outward for an added intensity.

'Meaning?' Carolyn asked, confused.

'You tried to trip me up and have me name the bands.' Now Dahlia gave Carolyn a mild look that showed she didn't mind the tease. It was obvious that she thought Carolyn was simply playing a game with her, and Dahlia loved games. '*He* did it for me. You can always be assured that a man who's interested in you will never intentionally make you uncomfortable.'

'But Chester does.'

Dahlia shook her head. Her hair, loose now from its fancy style, floated around her face. 'He's a kid. He doesn't know any better.' She narrowed her eyes at Carolyn for a moment, before adding, 'And I'm not uncomfortable around him. I simply don't do what he wants me to. That makes him want to even more.'

Carolyn thought about that statement as Dahlia now touched up her mascara, then fluttered her lashes at her reflection. Carolyn's own face was make-up free, as usual, and she hardly noticed herself in the mirror, seeing through her image as she pondered Dahlia's advice.

'The man I turned down tonight, Marlon, will call me every day for a week. You wait and see.'

'Because you said no?'

Dahlia nodded. 'And because Marlon thinks he's special. He won't be able to get over the shun. Really, I could hardly believe that I said no. He's so good-looking it's like watching a statue of a Greek god come to life when he smiles. But there's something to playing hard to get that drives some men crazy. The hunter types. The ones who have to conquer the woman in order to feel in control.'

119

Carolyn didn't understand. Dahlia never played hard to get. Just look at how quickly Jason had managed to get into her bed, and look how she kept returning to the 'Dahlia and Dante' re-run of a relationship, reliving it again and again so that it would never end. Carolyn thought of bringing up these conversational gambits, but changed her mind as another woman entered the bathroom, joining the two roommates at the mirror. Instead, she left Dahlia to primp and headed out of the bar before her roommate resumed her spot next to the businessmen.

It was too much for her. She wanted to be home. Now. Occasionally being out with Dahlia made her long for her headset, her loud music, and a glass of good wine, all by herself in her bedroom. Could she honestly handle these types of games if she decided to jump back into the dating circuit? Was she ready for Zach?

No, she wasn't. Not at all.

Harry wasn't sure he was ready, either. Even though he'd had a hard-on all the way up the stairs, now he wasn't so sure. Because the waiter, stripped down to nothing, had turned out not to be a boy but a girl.

'Sorry,' Harry said softly, 'my mistake.' And what a mistake. Man, if his buddies found out about this one he'd be the laughing stock for weeks. He was ready to flee, to head back to the throngs of men down below and lose himself in the arms of a different, more suitable stranger.

'No mistakes,' the woman said. She was slim-bodied and hard-boned and had a type of figure that Harry generally adored: an androgynous look with only the slightest swell of breasts to give away her true nature.

'I'm just not wired that way,' Harry explained.

'You're wired for pleasure,' the woman said, taking a step forward. 'For things that feel good. Right?'

'Right,' Harry agreed tentatively.

'I'm not looking for a traditional fuck, if that's what you're worried about.'

Yes, it was. Exactly what he was worried about. There was no way he was putting his cock between her legs. But, as she kneeled before him on the floor and opened her lips, he had second thoughts about denying her wishes. If she was the type to get off at cross-dressing as a man, at playing as a boy, and if she could play the way her expression was promising him that she could, then why not give it a try?

Closing his eyes, Harry felt the blonde plaything take his cock between her lips. The woman knew what she was doing. She kept her lips slick, kept rolling her tongue along the underside of Harry's cock, searching out his favourite places as if she had memorised a map of his pleasure sites ahead of time.

With one hand, she lightly, so lightly, cupped his balls, and with the other, she made an L-shape with her hand, keeping his cock in the webbing between her thumb and fingers, resting her hand on his groin.

Oh, she was good.

The pressure was delicious, and Harry felt that he wouldn't be able to take much more. Suddenly there were no more thoughts about men and women. There was only the heat and the welcoming wetness of a hungry mouth, the urgent tug deep in his balls, and the need, that desperate yet lovely need, to come.

All consuming, it wiped away everything else.

Carolyn had left the building. Dahlia registered this fact, understanding that her roommate wouldn't have ditched her without the car, and must have walked home. Now she glanced over at her fan club – the three men who seemed to all want to go to bed with her. That wasn't going to happen, no matter how good-looking they were. She had her limits. But she liked the one who seemed to be the leader of the pack, and when he offered to buy her another round, she shook her head, reaching for her own leather wallet and slipping a crisp twenty-dollar bill on to the bar.

Chester didn't appreciate what was going on at all.

Usually Dahlia spent her time at the bar talking to him, ignoring the men around who wanted to flirt with her. Sometimes she would play little mind games with patrons, but she never seemed serious about any of them. Now, the youthful bartender found his voice.

'On me, Dahlia,' he said.

'You're buying this nice man a drink?' Dahlia asked, her comely arched eyebrows raised in mock surprise. 'What a treat for him.'

Chester flushed, clearly not knowing what to do. It was obvious that he wanted to take control of the situation, but he couldn't handle himself against a player of Dahlia's stature. Yet before she could say anything to make the situation worse, Chester seemed to find his confidence again, sliding the fancy tequila bottle out from behind the bar and pouring the man a refill.

'Body shot?' he asked, his face a wash of seriousness, his eyes bright.

The man shook his head, embarrassed at Chester's flirtatious tone, but Dahlia collapsed into giggles, thrilled at the response. Maybe she was going to have to reconsider her position on Chester after all. The boy had definite possibilities.

'What are you doing later?' she murmured when Chester set a fresh glass of tequila in front of her.

'After we close?'

She nodded.

'No plans, really,' he said. She could see it in his eyes that he understood what she was offering, but because she had turned him down so many times in the past, he couldn't actually believe it was real. As if waiting for the punch line, he tentatively asked, 'How about you? What are you doing later?'

Now she shrugged, acting instantly younger than her 26 years, playing at being a co-ed once again. The type of girl that Chester would normally go after. The type he might even feel comfortable seducing. Wouldn't it be fun to be that silly once again? That sorority-girl giggly? She tried the role on for size, twirling her curls around her fingers, licking her lower lip, acting just a little bit drunker than she actually was.

Chester was quicker to respond now, leaning forward over the bar and whispering, 'You gonna make my dreams come true tonight, Dolly? Is that what you're gonna do?'

A deep voice behind her answered the question. Jason, suddenly appearing at her side so that she could see him in the mirror over the bar, said, 'No, kiddo,' directing the words to Chester. 'She's got a full schedule tonight. She's going to make my dreams come true instead.'

Dahlia turned on her stool, swivelling around so that she was face to face with her newest playmate. How had he found her here? The question was answered before she could vocalise it.

Carolyn. He must have called and her roommate had told him where she was. But Dahlia found that she didn't mind at all. Jason had surprised her twice in one day, and still didn't seem to mind that she had her own life – her own wild side. That he was only a partner in it, someone along for the ride as long as she was willing to have him. Without a word to Chester, she slipped off the bar stool and followed Jason out to his car.

Tonight, he had on a dark T-shirt, a pair of faded jeans, engineer boots, and one of those wallets with a metal chain that ran from the front pocket to the back. He looked tough, which was somehow unexpected to Dahlia. She knew that he liked to play a little rough, but he was a professional, a location scout for movies; practically a Yuppie. She hadn't given him enough credit, she realised, because now he looked as if he could be any one of those young punks standing on the corner of Sunset Boulevard, daring people to start a fight with him.

That wasn't what she had in mind at all, as she stopped him and wrapped her wrists in the silvery links of his wallet chain.

'Like that?' he asked. 'I thought you might.' She

tugged, her wrists wrapped tight, and he smiled at her. 'You're playing,' he said, 'but I'm not.'

There it was again, that hot liquid look to his hazel eyes, as if he knew something about her – something she hadn't come to terms with yet herself. And she felt a wave of excitement wash through her, a bit of fear mingled with intense arousal. What a unique way this evening was ending up – from having no date to one she couldn't immediately read. How rare that was for Dahlia. Usually, the men wore their desire for her openly. Jason didn't fall into this category. It was as if he were testing her, trying to judge whether she could keep up with him.

Could she? You bet.

She suddenly deciphered the sensations going on inside her. She wanted to go on this ride. That was the feeling. Like being a little kid at an amusement park and seeing the height requirement. Was she tall enough yet? Yes, she was. She could go on any of the rides she wanted. And she let Jason grip on to the chain and pull her by her wrists into the back seat of his car. He hadn't brought his little European convertible. This time, he'd been thinking ahead, and had somehow acquired a classic American car – one equipped with those beautifully designed fifties-style fins on the back and a roomy bench seat covered in shiny red leather.

As Jason pulled her into the car, his hand tight on the metal chain, she mentally asked herself her favourite question: who was she tonight? Her identity kept slipping, kept changing. In the bar, with those men and then with Chester, she'd been on top. Out here, in the back seat of Jason's car, she was on the bottom. And she loved every fucking minute of it.

All Carolyn wanted was peace and not quiet. Noise. Music. Sounds that she understood filling her head. But when she arrived at the apartment, she saw Harry's car parked out front. He must be inside, she thought, hurrying towards the front door. Harry had a key to their place because he looked after Terrie on the few occasions when both girls were out of town at the same time.

As she opened the door, she saw she was right. There was Harry, waiting on her cream-coloured sofa, and he looked so shaken up that she forgot her own problems and quickly focused her attention on him.

'It was one of those happy parties that got a little too happy,' Harry explained as he pulled off his Madonna-style net gloves. 'Happy' was his pet word for homosexual. He thought 'gay' was overused, and he hated 'queer'. 'It makes it sound as if I'm strange, when it's the rest of the world that's queer. In my opinion, I'm normal.'

'Light in his loafers' had been Dahlia's suggestion, but that hadn't fared any better. 'As if I'd wear *loafers*,' Harry had sneered, pointing one elegant foot shod in a new Manolo Blahnik heel. '*Really*.'

Harry sighed dramatically while Carolyn hung his vintage vibrant blue ostrich feather boa on their coat rack. 'How happy?' Carolyn asked. Harry flushed, something entirely unusual for him. Carolyn came closer and sat on the edge of the coffee table looking at him. She did exactly what Dahlia would have done, putting one hand on his fishnet-clad knee and saying, 'Harry, spill it.'

'Breasts,' Harry said.

'Excuse me?' Carolyn asked, her eyes wide.

'I thought he was a guy, until he took off his vest and I saw his breasts. So stupid.' He shook his head dramatically. 'And I couldn't talk to anyone there. I just needed to talk, to confess, really, to someone who's not a drag queen. I mean, if they found out –' He grimaced. 'You simply don't know how catty those girls can be.'

'I have an idea,' Carolyn said. Harry had told horror stories of face-scratching fights, always sounding somewhat humorous in the aftermath, but apparently very serious when they were occurring. She imagined them to be something like the cat fights you sometimes saw in night-time soap operas.

'I guess you do,' Harry conceded, crossing his slim legs and fussing with the hem on his shiny black dress. Watching Harry was a little like watching Dahlia. They both seemed to know all the precious moves that made a woman feminine. Carolyn wished she remembered a few more of them. She'd read in one of Dahlia's magazines about 'sexual anorexia'. The article claimed that the longer a woman went without sex, the less she wanted it, the same way that anorexics felt about food. If this were true, Carolyn thought, then she would have completely starved her sexual side to death by now. It would be a skeleton.

Harry interrupted her before she could finish that thought, describing a bit of the scene he had fled. 'The men dress like women. The women dress like men. I just assumed since he was one of the bartenders – shit, I mean, *she* was – that it explained why she had on the man's suit. But she was a she. And she liked me.'

'But you kissed her and you didn't know?' Carolyn was having trouble fathoming this. Wouldn't she know the difference if she wound up kissing a girl instead of a guy? Probably not, she supposed, since it had been so long since she'd kissed anyone. 'So what did you do?'

'Well, we were there,' Harry said, 'and it's not like I'd never done it with a girl before. I mean, I'm a trisexual.' Before Carolyn could ask what that meant, Harry explained the pun. 'I try anything once. Twice to make sure I really don't like it. And, you know, occasionally a change is good.'

For a moment, Carolyn was surprised that Harry would tell her so much about his love life. Yes, he often regaled her and Dahlia with tales of his dating escapades, but this evening, Dahlia was still out at Sammy's Mango Hut, and probably hadn't realised that Carolyn had walked home. Yet Harry was Carolyn's friend, too. He didn't seem to mind that his co-worker was absent.

'Do you have any coffee?' he asked. 'I'd kill for a caffeine fix.'

'It's late,' Carolyn said, looking up at the clock.

126

'I'm an insomniac, anyway,' Harry said shrugging. 'Doesn't affect me one way or another.'

Carolyn could drink coffee any time, too. Working shifts a variety of times during the day or night had taught her how to catch sleep when she could. While she made espressos, Harry scanned the front page of the paper spread out on the coffee table. Carolyn could see him from the kitchen, and he appeared to be totally relaxed, fishnet stockings still on his slender legs, golden slave bracelet dangling from one slim ankle.

'Did you read the paper today?' he asked Carolyn, changing the subject.

'Most of it,' she lied as she brought the tiny cups into the room. She never read the front page. Bad news wore her out.

'Is there anything about Kathleen's murder?' Harry asked.

'Kathleen?'

'The poor little rich girl.' He paused, then added, 'The one from the posters.'

'Did you know her?'

'Her mother is one of my clients.' He named a socialite who appeared in the living section of the pages all the time, constantly giving money to some charity, or hosting a ball for a special cause.

'That's her mother?'

'The girl had her father's name, but the mother raised her. Well, the nannies raised her. But she lived with the mother.' Harry looked up at Carolyn with sad eyes. 'It's such a tragedy. Kitten was her only daughter, and she lived a completely secure life. Nobody knows how it happened, or why.'

'Some stalker,' Carolyn offered, that word catching in her throat. Harry looked at her again, this time sympathetically.

'That's what it must have been,' he said. 'Because how else would the killer know her schedule, pick the one time when she wasn't under her mother's careful watch?'

He skimmed the article. What he read made him swallow hard. 'Oh, God,' he murmured. 'Did you read what happened to her?'

Carolyn shook her head. She tried not to read stories like that.

'He cut her –' Harry stopped talking, folded up the paper, and stuck it back on the coffee table. 'Let's talk about the party,' he said, fluffing himself up with several colourful velvet pillows from the sofa and covering his knees with the pale blue afghan. Although his segue was poor, Carolyn smiled at him for trying.

'Do they know who did it?' she asked, bringing the conversation back again.

He shook his head. Long black tendrils curled over his forehead and he tossed them away. 'The police have leads,' he said, sounding just like Dante, 'but nobody's been arrested.' He sighed. 'And another woman is missing – a young mother from the same neighbourhood. The Beverly Hills cops are adding patrol units to that area. And you know the private security is going to go up as well. They'll catch him.'

Carolyn nodded, but she was happy that Harry – all five foot six of him – was with her this night.

Chapter Ten

*A*t first, Dahlia assumed that the back seat make-out session was simply foreplay. That Jason would decide to drive them to her apartment or his, where they could continue their romance in private. He surprised her. Instead of taking her home, he wrapped her wrists even more tightly with the chain and then fucked her against the back seat of his car. The leather had a smooth feel to it, and the smell was amazing. There was something about leather against skin that always turned her on.

Jason was winning extra points for this. He was definitely giving Dante a run for the winner of most decadent lover. Because just as Dahlia thought that she couldn't get any higher, he reached under the seat of the car and brought out a new chamois, a polishing cloth used to make a car's paintjob sparkle. He put it to use along her body, running it up and down her ribs, making her arch her back and consider begging. She had to have that between her legs. Had to know what it would feel like. But Jason took his time and wouldn't be rushed, no matter how she shifted her body, how much she urged him with her actions. Maybe he wanted to hear her ask for it, she realised, and she said softly, 'Please.'

'Please what, baby?'

'Touch me with that.'

'I am touching you, aren't I?'

What a tease. She wriggled her hips, helpfully, showing him exactly what she wanted. He understood. It was obvious. But he wanted her to spell it out.

'Use it on my pussy.'

'I like the way you say that,' he told her, rewarding her by doing exactly as she'd asked. 'Say it again.'

'Use it.' Now she was teasing *him*, but he stopped touching her for being a smart-ass, waiting for her to obey his command.

'On my –' she tried next, working hard to keep from laughing. The look that Jason was giving her was priceless. His face was hard, unreadable, and she was impressed that he didn't laugh with her.

'Pussy,' she finally said, and again he brought the impromptu, and improbable, toy back into play. The soft fuzzy cloth felt amazing, exactly how she'd imagined, and as Jason continued to polish her between her legs, Dahlia steeled herself for experiencing the most unusual orgasm she'd had in months.

'How does it feel?' he asked. Dahlia sensed that he liked it when she spoke to him. This was the man who wanted phone sex at work, who hadn't melted when she'd given him that hand job in the car. He was unique, and she decided to play that way he wanted to. No more stalling.

'Like silk,' she whispered. 'The way it feels against my lips down there is so good. Soft and tickling in the most decadent manner.'

'Maybe I should try it,' he said, releasing her wrists so that she could pluck up the toy and brush it along his hard cock. She could tell that he liked it – who wouldn't? – and she stroked him with the chamois until she could see the first drips of pre-come on the head of his cock. She took this as her sign to bend down and lick him, tricking her tongue in a circle around the head of his penis.

They had to manoeuvre themselves in the back seat, with Jason sitting up now and Dahlia crouched on her hands and knees. Jason took the toy from her and reached around her body to use it on her from behind.

That was sweet. So delicious. Having Jason's cock in her throat and the soft, tickling toy on her pussy. Every time he brought it down between her legs, she swallowed him deeper.

'That's right,' he said. 'Nice long licks.'

It was a natural response to her. The pleasure he brought her made her want to return it. But before either one of them could come, Jason stopped the action. He moved her so that she was facing away from him, and then he entered her from behind. The windows of the car were steamed up, reminding Dahlia of make-out sessions in high school.

But this was different. This was the grown-up world with a kinky partner. Because now Jason wrapped his wallet chain around one fist and he brought his hand under her body and between her legs. As he fucked her, he stroked her pussy with the cold metal links, working the hard steel in the most gentle manner over her clit. With his other hand he used the chamois, going back and forth between the two sensations. First one, then the other. Like hot and cold. Night and day. Dahlia couldn't decide which one she liked best. But then, she didn't have to choose, as Jason went back and forth, teasing and pleasing her until she couldn't wait any longer. She had to come, biting the back of her hand to stifle her cries as she did.

'"Human Nature"' by Madonna,' Melody slurred to Stormy several nights later. 'It's my favourite.'

The chorus lines were 'And I'm not sorry. It's human nature.' Melody had chosen it to show Zach that she didn't care if he knew that she'd done a bad, bad thing. Maybe it wasn't the brightest request, but when she'd called in she was a little too drunk to care. All right, so she knew it was too early for her to be this plastered, but she'd actually never stopped drinking after the night before.

She'd spent part of the night parked outside Zach's apartment waiting for his lights to come on, drinking directly from a bottle of vodka. She'd even walked around the building, trying to see if there was a way to get up to the second floor from the outside. There wasn't – not unless she suddenly developed super-human powers.

Late, she'd gone to see Zorg play again, and then had ended up back home with him. And they'd drunk away the rest of the night and all of today.

Zorg, looking blankly up at her from the couch, didn't say anything about her making a phone request. He simply lit another cigarette with the butt of the one in his hand and crushed out the old one against the wall. As Melody stared at him, she realised that Zorg never said anything. He could sing, or yell, whatever it was that he did when he was on stage, his lips right up against the mike, but away from a club, he didn't do much aside from grunt. Now, his hand on her hip, he rolled her over and entered her, still smoking. If he weren't such a good fuck, she would demand that he leave.

Zorg moved inside her, his body rutting up against hers, his mammoth cock driving in deep. Didn't work to erase her problems, though, even as he pressed his cock to the limits, stretching her. She thought only of Zachary. She knew that Zach was only messing with her by making phone requests. He wasn't the type to take it seriously, and, in fact, she guessed that he was actually flirting with the DJ. Was she driving them together by acting the psycho role out of *Play Misty For Me*?

That wasn't her intention at all.

Carolyn listened to the Madonna song, wondering about Melody. Was the girl really worried about her, thinking that she could actually steal Zach away? Should she take it at face value that the musicians were really broken up?

Whatever was going on, she used her Stormy side to mediate, playing Melody's request, and then losing herself in questions: was it Melody or Zach who wasn't sorry, and what would there be to be sorry for?

By the end of the night, she'd decided that she shouldn't care. Forget it. It was too hard. Instead, she'd focus on Dahlia and the soap opera of her roommate's love life. And as it turned out, she didn't have to wait long to eavesdrop again because that evening, both she and Jason got lucky again.

This evening, the lovers didn't even wait until after dinner. They went right at it almost from the moment that Jason arrived. His voice was deep with yearning as he told Dahlia to get on her bed on all fours. Facing away from him.

Carolyn, back from her walk with Terrie, put her ear to the familiar grate, imagining an instant mental picture of what was going on. She'd often watched Dahlia work out to exercise videos. Her roommate could get on all fours and do impressive leg kicks that would cripple the most limber of people. But Jason didn't want to watch her exercise. He wanted to do her doggy-style, and he talked her through it, every step of the way. The man *did* like to keep up a running monologue about what they were doing, which Carolyn was thrilled to have. Maybe it added to his excitement, describing the play-by-play even as he was going through the motions. Whatever it did for Dahlia or her date, it definitely added to Carolyn's own excitement.

'Do you like it when I pull your hair?' the man asked, his voice soft and soothing. Carolyn instantly owned that mental picture, Jason's strong hand wrapped in Dahlia's red-streaked mane, wrist-deep in her silky tresses.

'You're a little pony,' he said next, and Carolyn could see that image, too. Dahlia flipping back her head, arching her back, as if she were a show horse.

'Whinny for me,' Jason instructed, and now Carolyn had to bite the insides of her cheeks hard so that she

133

wouldn't laugh. She couldn't imagine it at all, not at first. Why would Jason want Dahlia to make a noise like a horse? It seemed impossible that this would be even slightly erotic. But then Carolyn heard her, sounding just like a pretty little filly, and suddenly it made sense. Dahlia was play-acting yet again. She liked men who would be rough with her, and they weren't always easy to find. Most men treated her with kid gloves, unable to play raunchy with a woman as beautiful, as perfect-looking as she was. Jason, however, seemed to have no such problems.

'That's my girl,' Jason said. 'Next time, I'm going to bring my bridle and reins –'

Dahlia whinnied again.

'– or my crop,' he continued, and Dahlia made a softer, different kind of sound. A moan? The pictures in Carolyn's head came unbidden, quick and fast. What a perfect porno star Dahlia made in the movies of Carolyn's mind.

Suddenly, she thought about the grate falling open in Billy's hands. Thought about his head and shoulders poking through into Dahlia's closet. Carolyn could tell by the clarity of their voices that Dahlia's closet door was at least partly open. If she were to peek inside, would they be able to see her?

When Carolyn was sure the couple was still going at it – she'd learned Jason's rhythm was start slowly, work up, then slow back down again before the climax – she carefully removed the grate and cautiously peered forward. Billy was right. Dahlia owned more shoes than she'd realised. Sandals. Boots. High-heels. Slippers. Moccasins. Mules . . . Terrie didn't like this latest development at all. His nails came clacking across the kitchen floor, making so much noise that Carolyn quickly replaced the grate and hurried to move him into her bedroom. She bribed him with his favourite chew toy, whispered for him to be a good boy, then closed the door.

Back in the kitchen, ready to finally put her voyeuristic

plan into action, she discovered that the show was already over. She sighed, disappointed. But there was always next time. With Dahlia, there would always be a next time.

Chapter Eleven

The man sat silently in a nearly empty room. The only items of furniture he had were a desk, hard wooden chair, computer, and an army mat. He crouched on the floor, looking at the photos on his walls. He liked to take pictures ahead of time, liked to plan out every move. He never left anything to chance.

This next one, such a beauty, was almost model-perfect. He reached out to touch her face, and then smiled. He didn't know why he was doing this, what urge led him from one femme fatale to another. But he didn't question it. As long as the cops were clueless, then he was safe.

Staying one step ahead was the important part, and he was smart enough to do that. Smart enough to have found a way into the world of the women he wanted without them ever guessing who he really was.

Hollywood was the ultimate place for blending. He'd simply joined the ranks of other actors, and so far no one had ever guessed what monster was hidden behind his mask.

Chapter Twelve

*I*t was time, Melody decided, to put on the finishing touches. Enough of the fucking over the airwaves. Enough of letting Zach and Stormy create their own personal soundtrack for the rest of the world to be forced to hear. That was too disgusting to think about. Each one choosing songs that they felt had messages, playing them back and forth. Shit, she practically threw up after hearing the song Zach had requested tonight – 'Choose Me' by Teddy Pendergrass. Had Zach lost his edge or what?

Well, Melody was going to take matters into her own hands. And coming to the decision gave her a thrill that was only surpassed by the way it felt to straddle Zorg's cock and ride him like a cowgirl.

When Carolyn came home from work early on Friday morning, she didn't notice the turquoise Harley Sportster parked outside the apartment. Night shows generally did her in, and she was actually too sleepy to notice much of anything. But as she turned the key in the lock to the foyer, she saw a blur of action up on the top steps.

Instinctively, she reached for her can of mace, her hand finding the trigger, holding on tight. Then she realised that the blur wasn't some random attacker, but someone leaving Zachary's apartment. She tried to look as if she were busy with her front door lock, paying attention to the figure of the woman as she made her way down the wooden stairs.

'Hey,' the woman said, and Carolyn turned, coming face to face with Melody Jones, whose partly open black trench coat revealed a red-hot lingerie set: bra, lacy panties, garter belt, and red fishnets that disappeared into knee-high crimson leather boots. The outfit was something that Dahlia would definitely have appreciated.

'Late night?' Melody cooed.

'Working,' Carolyn said, taking in Melody's tousled hair and her smudged lipstick.

'Just love your show,' Melody said as she caught the front door and exited. Carolyn watched through the glass as the woman straddled her Harley and took off, her black coat flapping behind her like a set of vampire wings.

So they *were* back together. Well, fuck it. Didn't matter to Carolyn. Not at all. Maybe if she told herself that often enough she would start to believe it.

Zachary, upstairs in his bedroom, rolled over at the sound of the Harley engine revving. Sounded like Melody's bike, but that didn't make any sense. He hadn't seen her since Zoom Box's previous gig. There must be thousands of Harleys in the city, he thought, then turned on his side and went back to sleep.

Melody was so pleased that she found herself humming as she drove through the city, making up some nonsense song in her head that went along with the sound of her Harley engine. Her plan had worked perfectly. She'd listened to Stormy's radio show, not even bothering to call in with a request this evening, and then headed over to Zachary's, knowing that he was undoubtedly already asleep. On nights when they didn't rehearse or have a gig, he always crashed out early.

Curled up in a corner on the landing, she'd waited until Carolyn had returned. And then, standing by Zach's door, she'd done her best to make it seem as if she were just leaving after a night of debauchery. Going as far as kissing the inside of her own wrist ahead of time so that her lipstick would be smeared.

Stormy had definitely looked surprised when Melody had come down the stairs. Surprised and sad. A few more little tricks like that, and she'd know that Zach was off-limits. As dawn striped the morning sky in pink and orange bands of light, Melody found that the rumbling of the engine between her thighs was working a dreamy magic on her. Like a 500-pound vibrator between her legs. She took her time winding through the city, not caring whether anyone could see her in her lingerie. Maybe she'd ride over to Zorg's and surprise him with a wake-up fuck.

Her engine was already plenty revved.

The run-in with Melody was a blow to Carolyn's ego. But more than that, it was a blow to her future. She'd actually considered dating again, trying to get past Steven. And look what had happened. Her expectations had been raised and now she didn't know what to do with herself. If she were Dahlia, she'd simply move on to prospect number two. But Carolyn wasn't like that. She wasn't ready. Maybe she would be someday, but not now. At the moment, she was sick and tired of reality. All she wanted was to lose herself in fantasies once again.

Specifically, the fantasy world of Dahlia's closet.

The next time she had a chance to watch, she wouldn't hesitate. She would do exactly what Billy had, and pull open the grate and slide through. With this promise to herself, she found that it was all she thought about. At work, as she chose records, she became so lost in daydreams that she actually played one song twice. It was during an eighties hour, and appropriately enough, the song she double-played was Rockwell's solitary hit,

'Somebody's Watching You'. Her station manager came in to talk to her about the double-play, a huge radio faux pas, and Carolyn struggled to formulate some bullshit of a response.

'A reason for the double-header?' the manager asked. Janice didn't look pleased, but Carolyn was too important to be yelled at.

'I'm giving away free concert tickets to the first caller who notices,' she said. Instantly, Janice's face lit up. The woman was always on the look-out for new ideas for promotions. 'It's a sequel Sunday,' Carolyn continued, simply pulling the idea out of her head. 'As soon as the audience catches on, I'll explain it further.'

When Janice left, nodding and murmuring the word 'brilliant' under her breath, Carolyn sighed with relief. Normally, her concentration at work was unshakable. She simply got into the professional zone and did the business. She always knew what she was doing. This mistake told her that she had to do something about the Dahlia situation, and quick.

So maybe if she finally *did* watch Dahlia, her mind would be put at ease. With the decision, her mind felt soothed. But that evening, Carolyn's plans for watching were put on hold. And all because Jason wanted to do it in the shower.

The prick.

Jason pulled back the clear curtain and stepped inside the white-tiled shower. Dahlia, who had been standing beneath the hot spray enjoying the water as it cascaded over her body, turned to face him with a smile. She knew exactly how good she looked. Her long hair, which appeared an even glossier shade of reddish-brown when it was wet, was slicked off her face. Tiny beads of water, like raindrops carved from crystal, ran down the curves of her body. The soft fur that covered her pussy had been waxed at the salon the day before into a heart-shape, and it looked so gosh-darn cute she knew that any man would be charmed.

In a welcoming stance, she waited to see what Jason would do next. He surprised her by doing absolutely nothing. Leaning against the tiled wall, he simply stood and observed her. This made Dahlia feel as if she were on display, a sensation which she enjoyed immensely. Mentally, she chose her character, sliding into it without a hesitation. Right now, she was the type of sexy woman who could put on a heart-stopping, cock-hardening live-action show for her man.

Slowly, she rotated for him under the shower, pretending that she was standing beneath a summer rain shower or an outdoor waterfall. She could imagine that, the two of them at some tropical paradise, all alone in the wild, with the water crashing down around them.

Of course, most waterfalls didn't have tubes of conditioner on the rocky ledges, and Jason now seemed very interested in Dahlia's hair care and body wash products. What was he up to? It was her turn to stare at him, as he finally chose a slender bottle of body oil. When bathing in the tub, she always added several drops to the water to make her skin soft. While Dahlia stared, Jason poured a generous amount of the expensive liquid into the palm of one hand, and then used this oil to lube up his very erect cock.

She continued to gaze at him as he worked his hand up and down. It was intriguing to watch a man touch himself. Jason used a firmer stroke than she would have felt comfortable doing herself. The motion of his fist around his cock had the desired effect. He grew even harder after only several seconds of pumping.

The scent of roses filled the shower, and Dahlia grinned at her bathmate, watching now as he drizzled even more of the oil over himself. It glistened in the light, making his cock look as if it had been gilded in golden foil.

When Jason reached for her, she was ready, but he surprised her once again, this time turning her so that she faced away from him, telling her to put her hands flat on the tiled walls.

'Stay still for me,' Jason murmured. 'And behave.'

Dahlia did as he said, remembering in a flash how he'd created the ultimate scenario up in the Hollywood hills and again outside of Sammy's, and trusting him to come through for her again. It turned her on that he didn't talk, didn't tell her what he was going to do. Generally, she liked a bit of X-rated discussion, but she realised that being kept on edge could be even sexier. She closed her eyes as Jason moved closer, pressing his naked body to hers so that she could feel his cock pushing between her thighs. The oil was slick and slippery on her skin, and she couldn't believe that she'd never thought of doing something like this before.

But just as she was mentally congratulating Jason on surprising her, he did it once again. He wasn't going to fuck her pussy. Not all nicely lubed up like that, his cock silky with the added glistening sheen of the bath oil. No, he was going to slide his cock between her rear cheeks and probe her ass.

Dahlia had been taken this way before. She was well versed in different positions. Yet she hadn't done this in the shower before, and she was excited at the thought. More excited at the action, as Jason used his hands to part her lovely bottom cheeks and then ever so gently place the head of his cock against her rosebud opening.

Something about the heat of the water and the way the oil made his cock seem to glide inside her dulled the pain she'd felt previously in this position. She didn't mind a spark of pain with her pleasure, but this type of sex had always been slightly frightening to her. If a guy was large, as Jason was, the feeling of being stretched could be overwhelming. The body oil changed that. As Jason slipped back and forth, she didn't feel stretched. She felt opened; a different sensation entirely. With her weight against her palms on the tile walls, she leaned her head back, giving into the feelings that flooded through her. Really paying attention to them.

If Jason had been talking to her, calling her a dirty girl, nasty girl, bad girl for letting him take her like this, she would most definitely have gotten off too quickly. But because he remained silent, she could play out her own fantasies in her head.

She felt the knobby head of his cock as it rocked back and forth, and then she felt him plunge in further, and it made her breath catch in her throat. It didn't hurt, but suddenly she felt filled by him. With his cock all the way inside her, Jason's hips were sealed against her, connecting to her. Rather than thrust back and forth, he stayed that way, and she felt his cock throbbing within her. This was one of the most intense feelings she'd ever experienced. Jason moved his hands up and down her arms, creating shivers that ran through her body. Each time he did, she contracted on him, which made him throb even harder.

She was going to come from this, with nothing else necessary. She closed her eyes, waiting for it to happen; waiting for the contractions to work through her and set her free. The moment before she came was actually almost better than the orgasm itself. Yearning for it, stretching for it, she sighed and pushed back against him, and this made Jason break his silence – her taking the power away from him with a single gesture. He couldn't stay quiet any more.

'Oh, fuck,' he said, grabbing her around the waist and holding her to him. 'You are so fucking tight back there.'

His words brought her to the finish line but, as she finally climaxed, those tantalising pulses of pleasure shimmering through her body, the hot water of the shower gave out, drenching them in a chilly blast of cold.

Jason swore – 'Oh, fuck!' – the words sounding entirely different than they had a moment before, shocked by the temperature change, but unwilling to stop before he'd come. He gripped into Dahlia's skin even harder, lifting her feet right off the bottom of the tub as he climaxed inside her.

* * *

143

Carolyn, standing in the hall outside the bathroom door, listened for a moment to the sound of the lovers within. She couldn't believe that they were doing it in the shower now that she'd decided she really would climb into the closet and watch. Thwarted in her plans, she returned to the kitchen, helped herself to a bottle of beer from the refrigerator and made her way to her bedroom.

On her desk were a series of CDs as well as a copy of the interview with Zach Modine. Was it wrong that she wanted to put on her headset and listen to him talk? Back up the tape and hear it again? Analyse his voice? Had she overreacted to seeing Melody coming down the stairs like sex in motion? Couldn't she handle a sexual tango for a boy?

She didn't know. It had been so long since she'd done the flirting dance that she'd actually forgotten most of the steps. What she really didn't want to do was think about it. Instead she wanted to listen to Dahlia, and as she heard the lovers emerge from the shower and rush down the hall to Dahlia's bedroom, a smile of anticipation lit her face.

'Oh, baby, I like it when you do that.'

Dahlia moaned something soft in response, something kitten-like, and Carolyn had an instant vision of just what it was she was doing that Jason liked. It surprised Carolyn to realise that she had such a dirty mind, and could easily create pictures for all of the things she heard. Some visions were based on what Dahlia had told her in the past; things about the types of techniques she employed to drive men crazy. Dahlia had perfected several tricks, including drawing her tongue back behind a man's balls to touch that little pleasure centre of nerves. 'Drives men crazy,' she'd confided in Carolyn once, after several drinks at Sammy's.

So, yes, some of the pictures appeared to Carolyn because at one time or another Dahlia had described them for her. But other visions were simply from her own imagination working overtime.

'Your mouth is so warm and wet.'

Dahlia made that humming noise again, reminding Carolyn of a harmonica. Jason moaned at the sensation, as if the feel of those vibrations around his cock were close to driving him over the edge. That must have been it, Carolyn decided, because when Dahlia murmured something else, Jason's words became intelligible, lost in a climactic, guttural sound.

As she listened from the floor in the kitchen, Carolyn tried to get the nerve to open the grate and climb through. But she couldn't get past opening the latch on the top of the curled metal. Terrie, who seemed to have lost some of his previously bottomless faith in her mental health, regarded her bleakly from the living room. If Carolyn was away from her stereo, which he had come to recognise as a no-dog zone, then why was she not petting him, or brushing his coat, or taking him for a walk?

Carolyn mentally promised to. Later. Right now, she was simply too busy, enthralled with Dahlia's scheduling ability. Or lack thereof. Dante was due in less than an hour, and Jason simply had dropped by to say hello, catching her in the shower and joining her there, which is where the evening's activity began.

Sometimes, when things like this happened to Dahlia – and they tended to happen to her more often than they might with other, less sociable people, or with people who were not currently starring in a soap opera – Dahlia would become angry and send the man away. After that, his name was forever crossed off her list, no matter how many bouquets of expensive flowers or boxes of hand-dipped chocolate strawberries or packages of French lingerie he sent in apology. One discarded suitor had even bought her a platinum and diamond necklace. She'd thanked him politely, but did not change her 'no date' policy, would not let him back into her bed.

But Jason's risk-taking had paid off. How his heart must have pounded as he'd joined Dahlia beneath the hot spray, and how vindicated he must have been when she'd been receptive to his intrusion. Carolyn had heard their laughter all the way down the hall. It had been loud enough to pierce her headset.

From her position on the kitchen floor, Carolyn looked at the Elvis clock, those legs mesmerising as they swung back and forth, and then suddenly she remembered that Dante had a key. She'd had to let Jason in, settling him in the living room and knocking on the bathroom door to let Dahlia know she had company. He must have made himself at home in the bathroom after Carolyn had gone back to work. Dante was different. Dante could make himself at home without Dahlia being able to stop him. He had never returned his key after they'd broken up.

The moans in the next room slowly subsided, replaced by low, giggling bedroom talk. Carolyn tried to imagine what Dahlia was telling Jason. 'Thanks for the lay, honey, but you have to go now because my recently reunited ex-boyfriend and I are planning on watching a porno movie marathon.'

Without any explanation, or any warning, the door to Dahlia's room suddenly opened, and Carolyn quickly stood and reached for Terrie's leash, as if that's what she was looking for in the kitchen. Jason, his no longer crisp white shirt open and untucked, the buckle of his belt still undone, rushed past without seeming to see her, calling out to Dahlia that he'd call later.

The front door opened, then closed, and Carolyn, hand on the leash, watched as Dahlia passed by in a blur of naked flesh, entered the bathroom, and closed the door behind her. In seconds, the shower was on again. What on earth had she told Jason? He'd been in fine spirits leaving. Carolyn almost couldn't wait to get the edited update the following day, and even considered knocking on the door to ask what exactly was going on. But there was Terrie, yipping excitedly at the prospect of a walk, and Carolyn took his leash off the hook and prepared the dog for a stroll.

Chapter Thirteen

You could live your life in fear, paralysed by thoughts of things that might not even happen. Or you could do what you wanted to, buy the ticket and take your chances. Dahlia liked it the second way much better, even if it meant that the risks for disaster were higher. So Jason had surprised her – well, good for him. The boy was earning points each time she saw him. His status had risen considerably. What a tease, the way he'd entered the bathroom, then flung the curtain back *Psycho*-style before grabbing her in a slippery, soapy embrace.

She hadn't even stopped to consider what might happen if Dante arrived early. From past experience, she'd learned that it never paid to worry about things that might not actually come true. Deal with the bad when it happened. If Dante had shown up, then maybe they would have tried a threesome, like she'd fantasised about since they'd watched the porn movie. Two men vying for her attention. Now, that was something truly worth considering.

Poor Carolyn lived life the other way, lost amidst fears and worries. And look where it had gotten her. No man. No desires. Yes, she had a good gig as a DJ, but when the microphone was off, she didn't seem to have much to live for.

Yes, this evening even Dahlia would admit that she had managed to cut things pretty close. Dante had arrived practically on Jason's heels, and he probably could have seen Jason speeding around the corner in his shiny red convertible, had he thought to connect the car in some way with Dahlia. She found it extremely exciting to have two men fuck her within the same evening.

Their different techniques were more easily discernible when she was able to compare their styles back to back. Or side to side, front to ass, head to tail ... Even with his bold moves, Jason was still slightly more hesitant than Dante, but Dahlia supposed this was simply because he was a newer lover in her line-up. In time, Jason would most likely grow more confident. At the moment, Dante was easily the winner of the two. He knew exactly what to do, and exactly how to turn her on.

And, oh, did he turn her on.

So who was she tonight? She was the girl with two boyfriends, and it was a role she found that she relished.

Returning from her walk with Terrie, Carolyn was not surprised to see Dante's silver convertible parked in the driveway, or to hear noises coming from the shower – laughing voices that sounded only slightly different than they had a little over an hour before. Dante's voice was a bit deeper than Jason's. And Dahlia's laughter was richer. In Carolyn's opinion, it seemed more genuinely happy with Dante.

What did that all mean?

Could Dahlia be using Jason to get back to Dante? Was the whole thing a set-up to make Dante jealous so that the couple could permanently reunite? Carolyn couldn't guess what was going on in Dahlia's mind.

As she hung Terrie's leash back on its hook, the couple, wrapped in thick white towels, hurried down the hall. Before long, those familiar noises began again. Dante's voice, gruff and hungry-sounding, reached Carolyn in the living room. This time, she poured a drink

148

before sitting cross-legged on the floor by the vent, ear against the metal, listening.

Dante rifled through Dahlia's toy chest, a small floral-decorated box that looked frilly and innocent but was, in fact, filled with the sex toys they had collected together. Handcuffs. A silk blindfold. A Ping-Pong paddle that was black on one side and red on the other. As Dahlia watched from her position on the bed, Dante took this and twisted it in his hand. Mmm, yes, she would like that. Dante was an even better dominant than Jason. He could play at any role, and was particularly sexy when acting as the principal to her naughty schoolgirl, but Dahlia shook her head. They couldn't risk the sounds that a spanking made. Carolyn might be able to block out most of their vocals by listening to her endless supply of rock bands, but Dahlia didn't think even heavy metal could cover the noises of a rubber-coated paddle connecting with her naked ass.

Finally, Dante settled on something simple: a long, white feather. He tied Dahlia to her bed using two pairs of her stockings, just as he'd done before. Her wrists were above her head, her legs spread, ankles bound to the bedposts. It was sexy to be so well captured while knowing that there was no actual risk involved. Dante would never do anything to hurt her or to truly frighten her. It was his mission to simply make her come in the slowest most decadent manner possibly.

Like right now, as he carefully ran the feather over her body. It took incredible effort for Dahlia not to scream with laughter, and she bit her full bottom lip and turned her head back and forth, trying to compose herself. Oh, God, but it was hard. The feathers were light, tantalising bits of fluff that managed to arouse all sorts of feelings. Being tickled was such an odd type of erotic torture. It made her want to beg Dante to touch her harder. To stroke her with the palms of his hands, up and down her body, following over the places that the feather fluff had found. The two sensations would meld together in the most perfect way – the softness of the feather followed by the firm, warm touch of Dante's large hands.

But she didn't beg. Not yet. She waited, as still as she possibly could stay, in order to see what he had in mind. Sometimes their very best interactions occurred when she let Dante control the scene. He had a wicked mind, which she supposed came from being a writer. He was always able to create the most decadent scenarios.

As if to prove that she was right, Dante brought the feather along the insides of her legs, treating one side to gentle tickling circles and then the other. Dahlia couldn't take it any longer. She threw her head back against the pillow, finally letting loose with a harsh, sob-like laugh. A bark, almost. When he reached her pussy, she would melt. Just from the first touch. Ah, but Dante must have guessed that, because he didn't continue up her thighs to the split between them. Instead, teasing, he now worked the feather in circles over her breasts, touching the tips of her hard-as-rock nipples.

'Please,' she said, her voice wavering. 'Please, Dante.'

Sometimes he made her tell him what she wanted. But not tonight. It was so obvious. And rather than torment her any more, he obeyed her silent request, bringing the sweet white feather lower, to tickle the lips of her pussy.

That was divine, like a million tiny fingers stroking her. She thought of Harry and his endless supply of boas, wondering suddenly if he used them in this way. Why hadn't she thought of that before? Feathers were so intensely sexy. As Dante continued to play with his, she steeled her body, trying to stave off the orgasm. Trying to make it last. She knew that she wouldn't be able to stand much more. She'd scream. She'd laugh. She'd beg him to fuck her. Yet she did her best, body arched into a taut line of composure, reined in by pure will alone.

What were they doing in there? Carolyn could make out the little gulps of laughter, followed by the sound of Dante's sexy voice as he admonished Dahlia to behave herself. But she couldn't get a good picture of what was going on.

She closed her eyes tightly, trying to get up the nerve to open the grate. All it would take was a little pull, and then she could wriggle through and into Dahlia's closet. The large walk-in would undoubtedly provide her with an area to hide. She could get close to the door and listen better, could possibly look through the crack and see what was what. She took another sip of wine first, to steel her nerves, then gripped the curled metal edge of the grate and yanked it, just like Billy had. The small metal door came open easily, and noiselessly, and she pushed through, arriving silently in Dahlia's closet, amidst her long dresses and her Imelda Marcos-like collection of shoes.

The door to the closet was open a crack, and the candlelight from the bedroom created interesting shifting designs on the wardrobe around her. Carolyn moved forward, as stealthily as any voyeur, and peered through the opening of the doorway, holding her breath as she finally got her first glimpse into Dahlia's world.

Oh, yes, Carolyn understood now. Dahlia was being tickled. And once again, she easily found the story in her mind that went with a previous experience for Dahlia. Will Davis, the English Composition T.A., had been into tickling. And cleaning. He'd enjoyed running colourful feather dusters up and down Dahlia's body until she begged him for release. He'd even made her wet his king-sized waterbed twice with his endless tickling games. Dahlia, confessing this to Carolyn during a night of heavy tequila drinking, had said that the embarrassment combined with the arousal had been one of the most spectacular sensations she'd ever experienced.

'The relief,' Dahlia had told her roommate. 'Mingled with the release.'

'I don't get it,' Carolyn had said. She'd never considered herself a prude, and in college – before Steven – she had done many of the things that girls in her dorm

151

had done: given a blow job in a moving car, fucked outside on a balcony. But wetting the bed! Was that really sexy?

According to Dahlia it was. Anything that pushed the limits was fair play. For some reason, she always brought out the wild side in her dates. Was there anything she hadn't already tried at least twice? Not in Carolyn's collective memory of stories. She was an awful lot like Harry in that sense. But that didn't stop Carolyn from watching Dante run the long white feather all over Dahlia's curves. Up under her chin, then down the line of her throat, over her collarbone. It looked so incredibly pretty. Dahlia was nude, but Dante had his boxers on, black silk ones. Carolyn could tell from the way the candlelight made the folds of the fabric look wet.

For a moment, Carolyn focused on his body. She had seen him without a shirt before, when he'd helped rearrange furniture in their living room and stripped off his button-down Oxford. So she knew about his muscles, his washboard stomach. When Dante had writer's block, he often spent the time working out, as if pumping iron might jolt his creative side into motion. Since he was blocked a lot, he had an amazing body. Still, Carolyn had never seen him only in boxers, and she strained to make out what his cock would look like when revealed. It was definitely erect, creating a tent beneath the silky fabric. Then suddenly it was out of view as Dante moved closer to the bed, running his tongue along the same trail as the feather.

This was why Dahlia couldn't compose herself. If she could make it through the tantalising tickling torture without laughing, then Dante's tongue was sure to drive her over the edge. Carolyn watched as her roommate shifted her hips on the leopard-print sheets, shimmying her body in rhythm to the ministrations of Dante's tongue.

It was as if the couple knew someone was watching and had set up the perfect stage. But they couldn't know, Carolyn assured herself, pressing even closer to the door, one eye focused on the activity that went on only a few arm's-lengths away.

This was entirely different from listening. When she sat in the kitchen and worked to hear each word, each syllable, each moan and sigh, she also created mental images to go with the dialogue. Watching the reality of Dahlia and Dante made her suddenly want to participate.

But how?

She put her hand down, for support, coming to rest on one of Dahlia's marabou-trimmed high-heeled slippers. Taking this in hand, Carolyn ran the feathers along her arms, shuddering at the tickling sensation. Her gaze still focused on the crack of the doorway, she moved the slipper under her chin, then slid it beneath her shirt to tickle the naked skin on her flat belly. She traced the feathers everywhere that Dante traced them on Dahlia, echoing the actions of the lovers. In her mind, it was sort of a ménage à trois. The three of them were getting off together, even if the others didn't know it.

But then Dante slid his boxers off and climbed on to the bed, preparing to fuck Dahlia missionary style. With Dahlia firmly captured to the bed, it was a kinkier sort of position than most missionaries probably attempted. Dante didn't relinquish the feather, either, and as he plunged his cock between the plump lips of her pussy, he ran the feather around the tips of her nipples, then down her concave stomach to her delta of Venus.

As he withdrew, he held open her labia with two fingers and touched the feather to her waiting clit, making her moan louder than she had all night. This made Carolyn raise up on her knees, pull open her pyjama bottoms and thrust the slipper against her own pussy. She could feel what it would be like to have Dante open her like that, spreading the petal lips of her sex and tickle her with that one long feather. She knew what it would be like to look up in his eyes and see the glimmer of yearning, combined with the power that he held in this situation. It was all up to him when Dahlia would come.

Staring at the lovers, she pressed harder with the slipper against her cunt. But suddenly something stopped her. Some small voice in her head that still had the sense to know the difference between right and wrong. What was she thinking? How would she explain the damp, matted feathers of Dahlia's once-fine slipper? Another voice answered the questions quickly. Simple. She wasn't thinking. This wasn't the time to think. This was a time to come.

Carolyn pressed harder against the tip of the shoe until she climaxed, biting down on the echoing moan in her own throat that wanted so desperately to escape. What would happen if she let loose and made noise? What would Dante say if he flung open the closet and found her there, still shuddering from the power of the orgasm? It was better than any she had experienced in months. Why had it felt so good? She could answer that easily: Because she wasn't alone.

Before she could contemplate this any further, she backed out of the closet, lowered the grate, and hurried to her bedroom. She didn't notice that she still had the slipper in her hand until she'd closed the door to her room.

What the fuck was she going to do with it?

Rather than ponder that disturbing question for more than a second, she shut the shoe in her dresser drawer, hidden under several old T-shirts. Dahlia wouldn't notice, would she? The girl had so many different pairs of shoes and they were all jumbled together on the floor of her closet in a colourful pile of leather, satin and lace. There was no way she would miss one slipper, and if she did, there was no way she would pin the loss of the slipper on Carolyn.

Relieved by these thoughts, she climbed beneath the covers, still feeling pleasure pulse throughout her body, all the way to the tips of her fingers. What in the world was she doing? She wasn't sure. But she did know one thing – she simply couldn't stop.

Zach didn't understand. He'd thought that he and Carolyn had made a connection. Now she was avoiding him every time she saw him. And he had a strong feeling that Melody had something to do with it. Mel had always had a dangerous streak to her. It was one of the things that he'd found erotic at the beginning, the never knowing what was going to happen when you were with her. That feeling was a lot less appealing now that they'd broken up.

Although he tried to talk to Carolyn at the apartment, she was never available. He'd knocked, rung the bell, and even peeked through the front windows once, but he felt bad about that. He knew her history. As someone well versed in the music industry, he remembered reading about the man who had stalked her in college. The story had made all the papers because even though she was only on a university radio show, she'd already had something of a cult following at the time. He wouldn't say anything to her about it, but he guessed that the experience had left her shattered, and was one of the reasons she was tough to get to know.

It seemed the only way to reach her was to call the station – to banter with her on-air personality of Stormy Winters. To make requests that she would then answer in her own way. Tonight, he chose his favourite Stones song, 'You Can't Always Get What You Want'. That was true, he knew it. But he was bolstered by the uplifting line – 'You just might find you can get what you need.'

He thought he needed Carolyn.

Now he had to explain that to her, without scaring her away.

Chapter Fourteen

When Dahlia's date arrived the following evening, Carolyn realised that her roommate had actually taken her suggestion at the bar seriously and added a new beau to her line-up. Because here he was, standing in the foyer with a half-smile filled with anticipation on his face. A smile that made Carolyn think he'd already had Dahlia and he was excited about the prospect of having some more. Before she could answer the door, Dahlia flung open the bathroom and yelled out to her, 'Come here, Carolyn!'

Carolyn hurried down the hall as Terrie barked like crazy inside the living room, incensed by the scent of a man he didn't know.

'I'm Ariel,' Dahlia said.

Carolyn blinked hard. Dahlia had her long hair tucked into a short, black wig. The glossy cut looked good on her and made her appear exotic, like Cleopatra. Still, the shock of it, and the request to be called by a different name, made Carolyn stand and stare at her like an idiot.

'What do you mean?' she finally managed to ask.

'Ariel. I'm Ariel. He's Joe and I'm Ariel. Sorry, I meant to tell you earlier, but it's been a little crazy today.'

Carolyn nodded, as if she understood, and as Terrie continued to bark uncontrollably, she went to answer the door. In a way, she felt exactly like the dog. She hated letting strangers into the apartment, especially when she was tired, like now, after working all day. Her guard was down.

But there was nothing else to do. Dahlia was still dressing. Sometimes, Carolyn thought that Dahlia must enjoy making men wait. That it was all a part of her masterplan. She had her routine down to the second, so there was no reason for her to actually be late. Carolyn knew that she could get dressed and made up in record time. So when she was late like this, it had to be on purpose.

Putting on her most casual face, Carolyn opened the door, let the man in and, while Terrie sniffed inquisitively at his boots, offered him a drink. This particular specimen didn't seem to be Dahlia's type at all. Dahlia liked the sun-drenched beach gods, the average Ken doll. Jason was the light-brown-haired version. Dante was the brunette. Joe looked like neither. Although well built, Carolyn could tell that he was older than Dahlia's usual partner – at least 45. She kept sneaking looks as she went into the kitchen for a drink. He seemed to feel her appraisal, and met her straight on, steel blue eyes connecting with hers, as if daring her to speak.

'So what do you do?' Carolyn finally asked. It was Indian summer in LA. The apartment was hot, and poor Terrie, having given up on smelling the man's shoes, had chosen to sit on the floor under the window, panting hard. The fan in the corner did little more than stir the heat.

'I'm in the industry.'

While in other parts of the country, the words could take on a variety of meanings, in LA 'industry' could only mean movies. Carolyn looked at him more closely. He had reddish sideburns, full lips and those startling grey-blue eyes. Yet there was something slightly off about his appearance. From different angles he was either handsome or repulsive. Carolyn couldn't figure out what it was about him that made him either one.

157

When she met his eyes again, they were staring directly at her. Perhaps he was doing the same thing, she thought. Sizing her up as well.

'What type of movies?' she asked, waiting for Dahlia to come rescue her.

'Slasher films,' he said. 'The stuff the teenagers like.'

As he said it, Carolyn locked on his look – handsome monster. The type of killer in a movie who is almost good-looking, but flawed in some small aspect. To Carolyn, the flaw was in this man's eyes. Too blue. Too grey. Too something.

'How did you two meet?'

He shook his head and grinned, obviously embarrassed. Carolyn found this oddly charming, and he became instantly handsome again. 'She answered my personal ad in the *Weekly*.'

Carolyn was startled, and she knew that it must show on her face. She wondered if he was joking.

'It's not that I have a hard time meeting women,' he said, obviously thinking that's why she looked so startled, 'but I'm tired of the chase. I advertised for the specific type of girl that I was looking for. I didn't expect much, I have to tell you.' He smiled again. 'I really didn't expect someone like Ariel.'

It was the fact that Dahlia would answer an ad that confused Carolyn. Why would she need to? Her calendar was always over-booked. But then again, it was obvious, wasn't it? With the faux name, and the wig she was wearing, Dahlia was playing dress-up again. Being someone she wasn't, for a night. Like Cinderella, role-playing until midnight, when she had to turn back into the person she used to be.

'This isn't your first date?' Carolyn asked. Where was Ariel/Dahlia? Damn her roommate and her need to make an entrance.

'We met at a coffee shop last week. Nooners on Beverly.'

Carolyn nodded that she knew the place. It was a cafe located on the first floor of a motel between Fairfax and

La Cienega. An ultra-hip hangout, it boasted waitresses who wore navy-blue micro mini dresses and knee-high black combat boots, and waiters in tight jeans and ripped-sleeved T-shirts.

'Safe, neutral territory. But we clicked. Right off.'

Carolyn tried unsuccessfully to remember how many men Dahlia had been out with recently. Dante. Jason. Cancelled on Marlon. Were there other men besides Joe that Dahlia kept from her? Men she slipped out with in the middle of the day for a quickie? Did she do Chaz in the back of his big black Rolls Royce? Or maybe fuck some up-and-coming movie star in the private celebrity penthouse at the top of the salon?

'I couldn't believe it when she walked in the door,' Joe said, pulling Carolyn back into the conversation. 'I had no idea she was my date until she strolled over to my booth and sat herself down.'

He must have thought he'd hit the jackpot when he saw Dahlia/Ariel walking into the cafe, thought Carolyn. Joe looking at her and then looking away, sure that he wasn't going to end up with someone as lovely as Dahlia. At least, not on the outside.

Handsome monster. Make-believe beauty.

Weren't they perfect for each other?

It turned out that Joe was an amateur filmmaker. Yes, for his day job, he was a professional, but at night, he liked to videotape the women he was with. This wasn't exactly how he explained it, but Dahlia understood and read the message in the words he didn't say. He told her that she was so lovely that he wanted to tape her. He didn't say that he taped every girl he fucked – that was implied, but not stated. In Dahlia's mind, she recognised him quickly as a collector, someone who wanted to add a visual notch to his video library for each woman he banged. Dahlia pegged him easily. In a way, she did the same thing.

But she didn't let on.

Besides, she'd been taped several times previously,

and had no problem with this concept. Making a personal porn movie was exciting if both partners were attractive. And she found Joe more interesting-looking than most of her dates. In the past, however, she'd been videotaped only as herself. Now, as Ariel, the idea stirred her, helped her to hone her acting abilities. Because Dahlia's alter-ego was a shy and unsure girl, Joe had to convince her, to tell her repeatedly how beautiful she was, how lovely she'd be on tape.

'Perfect,' he said, looking her up and down through a square he made with his thumbs and fingers, like a pretentious movie director. 'You've got a classic face, a stunning body. You'll look killer on film. In fact,' he promised, as if this might be the number-one selling point, 'I'll bet you won't even recognise yourself.'

Ah. It was as if he had read her mind, knowing that she was playing a role. Letting her dive into it and lose herself in the lines. So Dahlia, as Ariel, let herself be convinced, but first she made sure that she got to keep the tape. That was her one sticking point. No way was she going to wake up one day to discover movies of herself for sale on the Internet. It wasn't part of her life plan.

What she most liked about the experience was that she would be able to watch herself later, see what she looked like when she was in character. So after Joe left, knowing that her roommate was doing a night show at the station, she popped the tape into the video machine, poured herself a glass of wine, and cued up the starting point.

Joe had been right. She didn't recognise herself at all. There she was, primping nervously for the camera in her blue-black wig, looking a bit like herself, but at the same time like someone else. Slowly, she slid one hand along her naked body in real time, watching as Joe touched the movie-star version of herself.

He was an adequate lover. Not as in tune with her desires as either Jason or Dante, but this was only their second time together. What could she honestly expect? Still, he knew how to do the basics. Running the tips of his fingers along the hollow of her throat. Following the line left by his fingertips with his tongue, tickling her gently to get her to move her body for him.

She did. Slowly. Shimmying her hips, closing her eyes and leaning her head back. Turning her body into one long curve. Joe sucked in his breath as she touched herself, taking over from him, stroking her body as if discovering the pleasure of it for the first time.

Her room was the ultimate boudoir setting. With the candlelight flickering on the pale blush-coloured walls, the scene reflected in the mirror over her vanity, it was as if the room had actually been dressed for a sex scene.

Although she hadn't thought that watching would get her all stirred up again, it did. She found herself breathing harder as she watched Joe part her legs and dip down between them with his tongue. As Joe spread her thighs wider on film, Dahlia got busy with her hand in present time. She made the circles that she liked best as she watched Joe work his tongue where it mattered.

He had touched her so softly at first, his spiralling designs making her heart race and moan aloud even though she was trying to stay in the role of sweet, shy and innocent. Now, she made herself come while she watched, lost in the vision of seeing herself getting fucked on the camera. It was even better than movie night with Dante. Better than almost anything she'd ever done.

Joe licked her more firmly as the tape continued to play, using the flat of his tongue to part her lips, covering the whole of her clit with each stroke. Dahlia tried to mirror his touch with her hand, licking four of her fingers and rubbing herself with her wet fingertips. She was so in tune with her movie self that she sensed that they were going to climax simultaneously – real life and on screen, mimicking each other. And as she came, for once she understood Carolyn's habits; she could figure out exactly why her roommate was so obsessed with listening . . . and watching.

Chapter Fifteen

*I*n the morning, Dahlia slipped into Carolyn's room and lay down on her bed. She took no notice of the fact that the bed was still made, the crisp white sheets pulled tight and tucked in, black duvet smoothed of any wrinkles. Carolyn hadn't gone to sleep yet. Sometimes after doing a show, she needed hours to wind down. But unlike her evening shift, she couldn't have a glass of wine after an all-night show. It just felt wrong to be drinking in the daytime.

Carolyn watched as Dahlia gathered the blankets up and around her, cocooning herself in a down nest. Dahlia liked to be comfortable. Luxuriousness was what she loved best.

'So how's Ariel?' she asked, hoping she sounded casual, but dying to know what had happened the previous evening. It killed her that she'd had to go to work and miss eavesdropping on Dahlia and Joe in assorted deviant positions.

From her smile, Dahlia seemed to like the question. But she didn't answer right away. Instead, she gave Carolyn a coy look and said, 'What do you mean?'

'Joe's not your type.'

'My type –'

'Come on, Dahlia,' Carolyn said, 'I know the guys you

like. Dante. Jason. I know the way they dress. The way they look. Joe was different.'

'That's what I liked about him,' Dahlia confessed, and Carolyn waited for a moment to see if she'd continue. If she'd give her the play-by-play. These days, she often knew when Dahlia was editing her evenings, and it intrigued her. 'I wanted a change.'

'So you changed yourself?' Carolyn asked. She wondered why Dahlia lied to her, like now, as she launched into a story about how she'd met Joe at the salon. Was she embarrassed that she'd answered an ad? Or had Joe been the one who'd lied?

'He told me,' Carolyn said, before she was even sure she was going to come clean with this bit of information. 'Told me about you and him at Nooners. About how he couldn't believe his luck.'

'Oh,' Dahlia said. That's all she said, but Carolyn could practically hear the gears shifting in Dahlia's brain as she spun some other story to share. 'I felt weird telling you I answered an ad. I mean, I've suggested that you do it so many times, but you never have.'

Go out with a total stranger? The thought was mortifying to Carolyn, but she didn't say so. She simply said again, 'But who were you last night?'

Dahlia lay on her back on the bed, lit a cigarette and blew clouds of smoke towards the ceiling fan. 'Who was I?' she repeated. 'I was this shy girl who didn't know she was pretty. It was like Halloween. Putting on a costume. More fun than simply playing with people in the bar, you know? I played someone who was attractive but had no idea. Those types of people can be so lovely. They act sweeter, nicer. Just different from the normal Hollywood starlet.'

But Dahlia knew she was pretty. Again, Carolyn didn't get it.

'Why did you answer an ad?'

'I wanted to have a little fun. Wanted to be a little wild in a way I couldn't be with Dante because he knows me too well. Joe loved it. And he was good, too.'

Ah, here it was. The juicy stuff. The dirt. What Carolyn really wanted to know.

'It was as if he'd seen that Sam Kinison show,' Dahlia said, losing her audience, and grinning when she realised that Carolyn had no idea what she was talking about.

'There was a special on cable,' she continued, 'and at the end, Kinison gave advice on cunnilingus.'

'The comedian?' Carolyn asked, to make sure she had this straight. Was there a Sam Kinison sex therapist?

'The one who died,' Dahlia said, 'in a car accident. He just ended his show with this advice to men, or lesbians, I suppose – said to make the alphabet with your tongue when going down on a woman.'

While Carolyn looked at her, Dahlia stuck out her tongue and traced a letter A then B then C in the air. Dahlia's pink tongue in sensuous motion gave Carolyn a medley of dirty thoughts. Pausing for effect, Dahlia added, 'You know what? It works.'

'Really?' Carolyn asked, trying to act nonchalant. In her mind, she could envision playing with Zach like that. Having him trace those letters over and around her clit. She wondered if he would spell out words. Lust. Sex. Sweet. Melody. There it was, the reason she wasn't going after him. Whenever she thought about Zachary, Melody was only one beat away. When she realised she'd lapsed into an odd silence, she tried to think of another question to ask Dahlia. 'And if he wants to go out with you again –'

Dahlia shrugged. 'He was good, but he's not my type. You were right about that.' A pause for effect. 'Ultimately, he was Ariel's type. But not mine.'

After Dahlia left for work, Carolyn found herself in her roommate's bedroom. She seemed drawn to the place, even when Dahlia wasn't there. She liked to look around, to test the atmosphere, seeing if maybe she could slip back into the world of sex and pleasure. It was a comforting way to spend an afternoon, imagining that she was Dahlia, getting ready for a date. Because if she really were her, she'd know how to solve the problems in her life, wouldn't she? She wouldn't ache so much at the thought of Zach and Melody being together.

On this morning, without even looking specifically, she discovered the tape. It didn't take much effort, because Dahlia had left it out on her nightstand. Carolyn hadn't been after anything in particular when she found it. She simply was doing her usual rounds of Dahlia's bedroom, touching the perfume bottles, stroking the lingerie. The tape was noticeable mostly because it hadn't been there before. Carolyn reached for it, saw that there was no label and wondered whether this was a bootleg version of the *Sinderella* flick that Dante had viewed with her.

She checked the clock and then staged her own private viewing in the living room. And as she watched her roommate playing to the camera, she had a similar reaction to the one Dahlia had during her own screening.

Magic. That's what it was. Pure and simple.

Chapter Sixteen

*H*e was getting worked up again. Getting ready. He knew how it felt inside before it happened, that urge building, that need arising, hot and powerful within him. Undeniable. For two days, he didn't go out. He paced his apartment, not sleeping, not even eating, just planning.

It was why he was so good. His total focus. Unwavering dedication to his personal cause. But in his starkly decorated apartment, he finally grew tired of the silence and put on his headset, listening to the music that he liked best. Raucous music. Noise, more than anything else. Sometimes Nine Inch Nails. Other times Marilyn Manson. The Sex Pistols when he wanted to listen to vintage – the godfathers of the genre.

The sounds helped calm the voices in his head. And finally, after blasting his eardrums with one band after another, he found the will in himself to go to sleep.

It was so important for him to have his strength together if he was going to do this right.

Chapter Seventeen

*T*hat evening, Dahlia was late coming home from the salon. When Carolyn saw her, she realised why. The team at Chez Chaz had given her a full make-over. This happened every once in a while on the rare occasions when things were slow at the salon. Today, Dahlia's lovely face was done in a rainbow of make-up, and even though Carolyn didn't usually pay much attention to the hues on the canvas of her eyelids and cheekbones, she noticed that her roommate looked different. Transformed in some way.

'Wait until you see –' Dahlia said, sounding like a game-show hostess about to reveal the fabulous prize behind door number one. Dahlia was wearing an opaque lavender scarf over her hair. Before she pulled it off, Carolyn had a fleeting suspicion that Dahlia was going to be bald, like the sexy chick in the first *Star Trek* movie.

But she was wrong.

Dahlia's hair was a glistening platinum. How odd to leave the house as a redhead and return as a blonde bombshell. She looked beautiful. But then Dahlia always looked beautiful. On her worst days, she looked better than most people did on their best. Now, with her blonde goddess appearance, she seemed more like a pin-up than ever.

'Chaz wanted to give me a new look,' Dahlia explained, spinning around so that Carolyn could see her metamorphosis from all angles. 'All the stars have been going red lately and he felt it was getting a little too much. He'd like to see a return to a more classic look. Like Marilyn. You know, fifties starlet.'

'It's great.'

'Also,' Dahlia confessed, 'he's redoing the salon. Getting rid of all the pink and changing to a pale blue, and he thought my hair should complement it.'

'What do you mean?' Carolyn wasn't sure she should ask the question.

'You know, blue and yellow are complementary colours.'

They're also Bruin colours, Carolyn thought, picturing the football uniforms of the UCLA athletes, but she didn't say anything.

'So when I'm at the front desk, I'll be complementing the whole salon.'

Had he chosen an orange theme, would she have as happily dyed her hair purple? Knowing Dahlia, Carolyn was fairly sure she would have. She didn't comment on this. Instead, she said, 'Wonderful,' as Dahlia was obviously expecting. But she wondered to herself if Dahlia minded her role at all. She was a manager at the salon, but Chaz used her as if she were some sort of fashion accessory. From the way she preened in front of the mirror, it seemed as if she didn't mind in the slightest.

'I hope Marlon likes it,' Dahlia said breathlessly, sounding just like Monroe. Was she going to act different now because of her new hair colour? That would be interesting, Carolyn realised. How would a blonde behave differently in bed from a redhead?

'And Marlon is –' Carolyn asked, momentarily forgetting that he was the boy Dahlia had cancelled on.

'A French friend of Chaz's,' Dahlia sighed. 'And he's handsome. Oh, God, Carolyn. Just wait until you see him.'

* * *

In fact, Marlon was more than handsome. With his male-model looks it was easy to imagine him on the catwalk, head up, shoulders back, hands deep in his cargo pants pockets looking ultra-casual. Somehow Dante, with all his youthful charm, looked like a schoolboy compared to Marlon. Carolyn couldn't recall ever seeing anyone so perfect-looking in person. Nobody but Dahlia. They made a good match.

Standing in the entrance of the kitchen, Carolyn checked him out. Terrie was crouched in a corner, growling angrily at Marlon, who was doing what all non-dog lovers do – nervously offering his hand up to Terrie to sniff. He stared over at Carolyn, obviously expecting to see Dahlia.

'I'm the roommate,' Carolyn explained. 'She's just finishing getting ready.'

Marlon made as if to stand, perhaps thinking he had a shot at helping her get ready. Or possibly he was simply being polite, rising when a lady entered the room. But Dahlia poked her head in from the hallway entrance, and he stopped in mid-motion.

'Five minutes,' she said, like a stage manager telling the cast when to expect the curtain call. 'I just have to put on my dress.' That made Carolyn turn as well, wondering whether Dahlia was actually naked in the doorway. She wasn't. Framed in the doorway, she had now shown her date what she looked like in her silk robe and marabou-trimmed slippers, half dressed, half undressed. It was almost sexier than if she really had been wearing nothing at all.

At the sight of the slippers, a different pair than the ones she had ruined, Carolyn felt herself flush. Dahlia didn't seem to notice. She had locked eyes with Marlon, who was observing her with a look of total lust. Dahlia in her robe was a picture he'd undoubtedly keep in his mind all the way through the evening. Carolyn could almost hear his thoughts: Will she leave her slippers on during sex? I hope she does. Those pointy high heels dragging against the backs of my legs –

Carolyn walked through the kitchen, meeting her roommate in the hallway. Dahlia half-turned to look at Carolyn, a smile on her lovely face. Then she leaned forward, as if she were going to tell Carolyn a secret. As she did, the white robe opened with the movement, pulling away from her bare skin, revealing one of her perfect breasts.

Marlon was going to be able to touch that breast later in the evening. Carolyn would bet on that. And even more certain, she was sure that she'd be able to listen to them, and watch . . .

Somehow that made everything OK.

While Dahlia was out with Marlon, Carolyn looked over her roommate's trunk of cosmetics. For a moment, she considered trying them out, changing her looks the way Dahlia did. But she didn't know how to do all those little tricks with the different tubes and powders. With the wand of mascara or pots of glosses. Instead, she chose one of Dahlia's sultry nightgowns, something expensive and silky, and she slid into it carefully so that she wouldn't spoil the lines. Dahlia had her lingerie specially cleaned, ironed and ready for the next evening's Olympic sexual event. Carolyn didn't want her to know that she'd been playing dress-up with her clothes.

On the bedside table was a make-up tip book, one of several written by Harry. Carolyn looked it over, considered her cosmetics again, but couldn't seem to make herself try them out. Instead, just as she started to think about slipping into a pair of Dahlia's high-heeled slippers, she heard the front door opening.

They were back early!

Quickly, she stripped out of the nightgown, then looked around frantically, first for her glasses, then for her clothes. She got into the closet to hang up the nightgown, putting it somewhere on the rack with others like it, sliding into her own clothes in record speed, trying desperately to open the grate from the inside, her fingers fumbling in the dark. She could hear their voices,

Dahlia calling out her name, then sounding surprised when she didn't get a response.

'Hey, Carolyn – you back there?'

She heard footsteps, her feet and then his feet, and then she heard Dahlia saying, 'She must have run out to the store.'

Why wouldn't the fucking grate work?

Dahlia was in Carolyn's room now, walking around. Carolyn could hear her saying, 'She's a DJ. That's why she has so many demos.'

What was Dahlia doing in her bedroom? Maybe she simply wanted to give Marlon a tour of the apartment. *This is where my roommate sits and listens to her music all evening. We can be as loud as we want, Marlon. Are you ready for me?*

Why couldn't Carolyn open the grate? If she could just make her way into the kitchen while they were in her bedroom, she could pretend she had just gotten back from taking out the garbage, pretend she'd used the side entrance. Finally, pushing through, pulling the gate closed after her, brushing off her hair, she realised that the couple was still in her room. What were they doing? Looking at her pictures of rock stars? Perusing her mammoth selection of CDs for some sexual background music to play?

'Don't you think she'll be back soon?' a heavily accented male voice asked.

'We'll hear her,' Dahlia said. 'She'll come in with her bags of groceries. She'll make a lot of noise. We'll have time.'

And all of a sudden Carolyn realised exactly what they were doing. But why would that excite Dahlia? Was she doing what Carolyn had been doing? Was Dahlia pretending that she was her? Carolyn leaned against the counter to think. If she came in with the garbage cans now, they would know she'd been gone too long for such a short errand and would wonder what she was up to.

Of course, she could simply burst in on them, and

171

they would have to be the ones to explain what the fuck they were doing. But Carolyn didn't want that. Didn't want Dahlia to have any idea that she listened. That she was addicted to it.

Now she could hear the couple begin their sexy pre-show talk. She could make out a bit of the man's conversation and realised that Dahlia was doing one of her patented stripteases for him. Carolyn desperately wanted to listen, but couldn't. Not without walking down the hall and pressing her ear to the bedroom door. Partially open, she could tell. If they caught her, they'd know that she'd been in the apartment all along. Dahlia would know she'd been in her room, would maybe guess that the grate served as a quick entrance and exit.

Silently, Carolyn reached for her keys and walked out of the kitchen using the back entrance. She headed down the street to the store, resolving to make plenty of noise when she got back, just like Dahlia said she would.

Dahlia adored the world of make-believe. Doing it sprawled out on Carolyn's plain white sheets was a completely different experience from being fucked on her leopard-print satin ones. But it wasn't only the sheets that altered the sensation. Her roommate's entire bed-room was totally unlike her own, and this made her feel as if she'd entered one of those theme hotels she'd recently read about. It was a new craze among the hipster set – going to a tacky motel where you could choose which type of night you wanted to have based on the decor of your room. A castle. The back seat of a T-bird. An outdoor paradise.

Dahlia had decorated her own bedroom in a highly femme style. A gilded mirror ringed with angels hung on the wall across from her bed, positioned where she'd be able to watch herself if she so desired. In one corner stood a girly dresser from the forties with a rose-coloured organza skirt around the base. Tiny French perfume bottles and little picture frames resided on all of the ledges, further enhancing the feminine touch. She had a bowl of potpourri by the bed, rose petals now faded from bright crimson to a more muted dusky red, releasing their pastel fragrance to the room.

Finally, tall candles with twisting ivory bases stood on any empty space, waiting to be lit to add a bit of mood lighting to the already sensual environment.

Carolyn's bedroom couldn't have been more different. Aside from the utilitarian bed, a simple silver frame for head and footboards, there was a fairly uncomfortable black leather couch and a once-sleek black desk that now showed scuff marks from her kicking her Doc Martens up on the surface. The floor had the same shag carpets as the rest of the house, but while they seemed lush and luxurious in Dahlia's room, they appeared lacklustre in Carolyn's. For art, she had chosen pictures of rock stars she'd interviewed. These were framed and added the only really intriguing pieces in the room. Carolyn with everyone from Bowie to Bush.

Unlike Dahlia, she didn't spend money on her surroundings. She didn't really put out cash for anything except music equipment. Her furniture was either cast-offs from friends or the type of stuff picked up at garage sales and flea markets. Still, this managed to lend the room an oddly charming air, as if the pieces were somehow embarrassed to have been thrown together in such a rag-tag manner.

Aside from the novelty of the furnishings, what Dahlia liked the most about playing in her roommate's bedroom was that she felt totally unlike herself in this environment. Carolyn always wanted to know why she played those silly games at the bar. Pretending to be someone she wasn't. Simple. There was a lot of stress that went with being Dahlia. She had an image to present that took a lot of work. Imagining that she was somebody else, *anybody* else, was freeing.

Marlon didn't seem to be aware of any of this. He just wanted to be with Dahlia. *In* Dahlia, for that matter. But he went along with her plans, humouring her, stroking

173

her lovely soft hair away from her face and promising to call her anything she wanted. These pretty girls, the really beautiful ones, always were the strangest. Especially the Americans. He'd learned that over time, having experienced a wide variety of wacky requests from various lovers. For some reason, it came with the territory.

'Carolyn,' Dahlia said. 'Call me Carolyn.'

He'd have called her George if that's what it took to get inside her. And even though he didn't understand, he did as she asked.

Instead of making noise when she re-entered the apartment, Carolyn was as silent as she'd been sneaking out. She couldn't stand the feeling of not knowing. She had to learn what Dahlia and Marlon were doing in her room. Anyone would want to know. For once she didn't feel bad about snooping.

Walking silently was easy because of their thick carpet. In a few quiet steps, she'd arrived just outside her bedroom door. It was open a crack; just enough for her to hear what was going on. In the hallway she stood totally still, listening. For a moment, there was no sound at all. Maybe they'd gone out or retreated to Dahlia's room for some 'normal' sex.

But then the noises began. They must have been on a break before, catching their breath, or lost in the silent world of kissing. Suddenly the sounds came on in earnest. For a moment, Carolyn couldn't believe what she was hearing. It startled her enough that she sucked in her own breath loudly, and then she had to hold it in, frightened that they might have heard her. They didn't. She was safe. Safe to listen to what it would sound like if someone was in her bed, making love to her.

This was the oddest thing ever, listening to Dahlia and Marlon, eavesdropping in a brand new way by standing out in the hall. It wouldn't matter if they heard her, she knew, because they were doing something much more bizarre than she was. Eavesdropping was a simple

174

crime. Pretending to be *her* ... Well, that just didn't make any fucking sense.

But still, it was arousing, listening to Dahlia as she made those crazy moans, lust-filled, energetic. And then listening harder as Marlon echoed her, and then called out her own name. Not Dahlia's, but Carolyn's.

'What a bad girl you are, Carolyn.'

Carolyn.

It had struck her as odd in the bar when Dahlia played at being her. Now she was absolutely flabbergasted. For a moment, it was as if she were in the room with the two of them. Actually in the bed with Marlon. She knew what he looked like, and could easily imagine herself with him, limbs entwined, his hands moving over her body. No, that's not what was going on at all. Carolyn suddenly heard a sound that was somewhat similar to applause. After a moment more of listening, she realised that Marlon was spanking Dahlia as he fucked her. That, she knew from Dahlia's stories, was one of her all-time favourite things. Dahlia loved being naughty. Dante had liked to play games like this as well, and Carolyn had heard afterwards of the time he'd taken her to a sex shop in Hollywood and had used a paddle on her in the store before purchasing it.

That was an image: Dante taking her over to the counter in the very centre of the store, and then hesitating as if he couldn't make up his mind. 'Not sure if this is the one for us,' he'd said.

'Try it out,' the man behind the cash register had offered, appearing generous but obviously wanting to see Dahlia's skirt raised and panties lowered. Wanting to see her haughty bottom get a serious spanking.

'Good idea,' Dante had said, as if they'd rehearsed the script ahead of time. He'd dragged Dahlia's skirt up at the back, pulled down her white panties to the tops of her thighs, and given her a brief but thorough spanking before deciding that, yes, this was the toy for them. Dahlia had told Carolyn that she'd just about come on the spot. If Dante had simply slid one finger under her and tapped it against her clit, she would have exploded. The spanking had made Dahlia so wet and excited that they hadn't even been able to wait until they got home to fuck. Instead, they'd done it in Dante's car, sliding into the back seat in the parking lot and ravishing each other.

Carolyn couldn't imagine anything like that. She thought she would simply ignite from embarrassment if anyone was to . . . to what? Spank her in public? When would something like that ever happen? Still, she couldn't even manage to work it into her fantasies. Each time she thought about it, she would stop, not understanding. Dahlia had tried to explain. Being in public, being seen, was the sexy part. And since they'd been in a sex shop, where nobody could really be shocked, it was safe.

Now Marlon brought Carolyn back to the present. The sound of him saying 'Such a bad girl, Carolyn' was somewhat unreal. The fact that he was moaning her own name, calling it out louder and louder as his excitement rose, made her feel like she was going crazy. Slowly, she slid down the wall to sit on the floor. She hoped that they would continue all night. She sat in the hallway, one hand against her mouth to keep herself from matching his moans, the other deep in her panties, squirming against her clit until she reached her climax.

Dripping and wet and all alone in the hallway.

Melody, crouched outside the DJ's apartment, listened to the raucous sounds of lovemaking with a sneer marring her exquisite face. So the girl was kinky. Well, so fucking what? She'd written the book on kinky. Christ, she and Zach had done just about everything you could think of. Her mind quickly categorised their escapades: outdoors, in public, on stage. Yes, on stage. They had fucked once after a show, when the audience had left and most of the employees were gone. Zach had known one of the owners of the club, and had asked if they could stay on after. To 'rehearse'.

Well, they'd rehearsed all right. Rehearsed him fucking her in the centre of the bare wooden stage, one lone red light focused on them. That had been killer. The only thing better would have been if the audience hadn't left. She loved the thought of all those eyes on her. It was why she liked performing so fucking much.

She knew that listening to the DJ with some other guy ought to have made her feel better. Maybe the girl really wasn't after Zachary. Maybe it was all in her own head. But somehow, knowing that Stormy was into dirty things made her feel more challenged than she had before. She tried again to see inside the room, but although the windows were open, the shades had been drawn.

Didn't really matter. She could close her eyes and see what was going on.

Spanking. Dahlia loved it. Loved being on the receiving end, that is. She'd tried the dominant role before. She would try anything once just to see if it worked for her. But that was one particular experience that hadn't turned her on. Dressed up in a vinyl catsuit, spike heels, a long, braided crop in one hand, she had done perfectly fine in her effort to subdue a naughty wannabe slave. And although he had come heartily, begging her for weeks afterwards for an encore performance, something hadn't felt right inside her. Not that there was anything wrong with his desires, it just wasn't her type of thing. The whole scenario had seemed wrong as she'd called him a bad little boy, as she'd made him do things. Grovel. Crawl around on his hands and knees. It had felt rather silly.

But being over a man's lap, for some reason was totally different. Feeling his hand drag her skirt up and back, lower her panties ... then that moment before anything happened. The waiting, while she steeled herself for the first blow. That was fantastic. Anticipation was one of her favourite emotions. There was something else, too. A moment when she had to force herself not to laugh, because even *this* was all a game. She was playing a role. When it was over, after both had come, they'd go back to being themselves.

She was testing Marlon tonight. Over drinks at the Formica, she had confessed to him that sometimes she liked to be naughty. His eyes had gleamed, just as Jason's had when she'd told him the same thing. Yet Marlon was more self-aware than Jason, and more in control of himself. Maybe he was simply more experienced. He hadn't said anything right away but he'd appeared to file that bit of information for future use. And later this evening, he had fulfilled her desire.

'So you've been naughty?' he asked, taking her over his sturdy lap and making her answer him, having her talk to the floor.

'Yes, Marlon,' she'd confessed, giving him her best bratty schoolgirl act. Just her tone of voice had made him want to spank her. She could tell. There was something in it that men liked. That taunting quality of her voice. Marlon had started right away. He'd been forced to hold her down when she started to fight him. And he'd continued to talk to her the whole time.

The man was imaginative. She gave him that. He had created a whole story to go with the spanking. Explaining exactly what she'd done to deserve it. Flirting with someone else. That's what he said. When she hadn't. That wasn't something she'd do on a first date. On a fifth, maybe; if they were at a party or a bar, she might make eyes at someone else just to see how her beau would behave in such a situation. Jealousy was another emotion she liked to play with. Some men became instantly angry, their faces going all red. Others could control themselves and use their feelings in positive ways. Dante was good at that. He would notice what she was doing but not respond. Then later, he would punish her – always in the most pleasurable ways imaginable. He had an incredible imagination. Must be the writer in him.

Marlon wasn't as capable as Dante, but he was good.

178

'You don't ever flirt with someone else while you're with me,' he said, pausing to observe the range of hues he'd brought forth on her once-pale bottom. 'Now, tell me you're sorry.'

She wouldn't. She wanted more. If he spanked her long enough, and just right, she would be able to come from it. So she tossed her white-blonde hair and tried to get away. Marlon wouldn't have any of it. He scissored her legs firmly between his, grabbed hold of her wrists in one of his hands and pinned them at the small of her back so that she could not get free.

'I can make you obey,' he said, and his voice held a dangerous sound that Dahlia adored and admired. But she wasn't finished playing. With her body, and her defiant attitude, she continued to test him.

In a flash, Marlon upped the ante. He shoved her off his lap and pulled his belt from the loops of his slacks. 'Do you need this, then?' he murmured, getting his mouth close to Dahlia's ear. 'A taste of leather against your skin?' Quickly, he pressed the belt into her hot flesh, just letting her feel it. She looked into his eyes, seeing that he was giving her an out. If she didn't want this, all she had to do was tell him that yes, she'd be a good girl in the future. She was glad that he had offered her an escape route, but she didn't take it. Instead, she remained silent. Her eyes issued the challenge, and Marlon shook his head and brought her back over his lap.

'You really need your hide tanned, do you?' he asked. 'A good-old-fashioned thrashing.'

The words did it for Dahlia as much as the actions. If he could keep talking, she wouldn't need much more. Marlon seemed to understand this, because instead of bringing the belt down against her skin, he slid it between her thighs and pressed the leather against her cunt. The sensation was almost too much. A feeling of leather slipping in her juices, the edges of the belt, and then the flat lip of it, rocking against her clit.

'Why are you such a naughty girl?' Marlon asked her,

now positioning her on the edge of the bed on all fours, her ass towards him. He took the belt and let it fall against her skin, not hard enough to hurt, but just to let her feel the weight of it. Then he undid his slacks and took out his cock, slipping it into her with one thrust. He used the belt on her thighs as he fucked her, still not swinging it, just tapping her with the leather, as if simply to hear the sound it made. A sexy, heavy sound. Dreamy and unreal.

He kept talking to her as he fucked her but Dahlia remained unusually silent. She knew that Marlon didn't need her to join in his conversation. His words were working well enough for both of them.

Why she'd pretended to be her roommate was something that Dahlia hadn't yet worked out. The only thing she could think was this: it was new. And so few things were new to Dahlia. Excitement at the danger of it had made her wetter than usual. Had fuelled her fantasies, pushing her deeper and farther when Marlon smacked her. Better not to contemplate it too seriously. Sex was supposed to be fun, and dirty, and messy. And Dahlia knew how to make it all of those things.

Part III

'Tied up and twisted the way I'd like to be.'
Dave Matthews, 'Crash'

Chapter Eighteen

*A*fter nearly a week of being able to watch Dahlia with her dates, Carolyn now had created a routine. Returning from the radio station, she would change silently into her pyjamas, feed Terrie, then climb through the little hatch into Dahlia's closet. No harm. No foul. Who could it possibly hurt?

Nobody.

Returning home at dawn one day, she found Dante and Dahlia having themselves a little wake-up sex. Good for them, and good for her. She instantly got comfortable in the closet, and was so caught up in the moment that she didn't realise that Dante had slid off the mattress and was approaching the closet door. By the time her mind registered what was happening – Dante most likely in search of one of Dahlia's sexy costumes – it was too late for her to get out of the way. Too late for her to do anything but close her eyes and wish she were in her own bed.

The wish didn't come true.

When Dante opened the closet door, there she was, sitting on the floor, one hand inside the bottom of her white pyjamas, heart racing. It was gut-wrenchingly obvious what she'd been doing. But it was only obvious to the two of them. From Dahlia's position on the bed, where she lay sighing about the sex Dante had just given her, she couldn't see the interior of the closet. Thank God for that particular small favour. Carolyn couldn't imagine such a confrontation with Dahlia.

'Dante?' Dahlia said, calling out from their nest of tangled sheets. 'Are you going to make us coffee?'

Carolyn waited for him to say something, to yell in surprise, to get Dahlia over to where she was sitting in a guilty heap. To expose her. His dark eyes took in the grate, removed so that Carolyn could wriggle through. She tried to imagine what she must look like from his perspective. She was seated amidst Dahlia's pretty shoes, her cheeks completely flushed, her fingers sticky.

Dante's face lit into a smile, lips curved upward, handsome chin jutting out at her, as if to say, 'I see you. I know what you're doing.' She'd shocked him, but then he was shocking her as well. Totally naked, he stood with his cock still hard and glistening wet. Carolyn found herself in awe of his body as he looked down at her, even though she knew that her world was about to end. That the gig was up. Still, she had the brain power to think that Dante was tremendously built. Awesomely hung. And that, in another lifetime, she would have spent hours masturbating to the thought of experiencing his attributes.

All of these thoughts flickered through her mind in rapid speed, so quickly that she didn't have time to plan her next move or to think of what to say. Finally, Dante reached for the red plaid bathrobe hanging on the back of the door, winked at Carolyn, then shut the door after him.

Carolyn couldn't believe it.

Quickly, she slid back through the grate, silently replacing it, coming to sit on the floor of the kitchen, confused and still excited. She didn't know why, but she understood what the look on his face had meant. He was not going to tell Dahlia.

*　*　*

Terrie slobbered against Carolyn's face, thrilled to have company again. He dropped his ball in front of her and waited patiently to see if she'd throw it. Carolyn heard Dante in the bedroom, through the grate, saying, 'I'm going to make coffee. You stay in bed and wait for me, you sexy thing, you.'

Carolyn jumped up, wishing there were time to hide in her bedroom before he appeared, but there wasn't. In order to reach her room, she'd have to walk by Dahlia's bedroom door, where she would come face to face with Dante. Panicked, she stood up and brushed off her pyjamas. She was smoothing her hair as he walked into the room. Dante's brown eyes gleamed at her as if something had made him terribly happy.

'Good morning, Carolyn,' he said, still smiling in that absurd way, in that we-have-a-secret way. To do something, anything, she picked up Terrie's wet green ball and tossed it into the living room. Terrie burst after it at warp speed.

'Did you have a good show?' he asked next.

If she opened her mouth, she was either going to burst out laughing or crying. Instead, she shrugged in some sort of non-response way and waited for Terrie to give her something to do again.

Bring me the ball, she willed silently. *Bring me the fucking ball.*

But Terrie took the tennis ball and walked over to the corner, deciding to chew on it for a while before giving it back to her. Now Carolyn had absolutely nothing to hide with, nothing to do with her hands but stroke them up and down her arms in that nervous way of hers.

'It went well,' she said, speaking to the floor rather than to Dante. How had she ever gotten herself into this situation? Why had she even heard Dahlia in the first place? She should have been in her room with her headset on, focused on her work, as always.

'How about you?' she finally asked. 'How'd you sleep?'

'You tell me,' he said, deftly taking control of the

185

situation. 'You tell me everything. Just how well did I sleep?'

'Oh, shit!' This came from the bedroom. Dahlia had apparently forgotten to set her clocks and had just realised how late she was. Within seconds she arrived in the kitchen in a flurry of activity. In a crunch, she could get dressed and done up in less than five minutes, still managing to look as gorgeous as ever. She took a swig of orange juice out of the carton, said both hello and goodbye to Carolyn, kissed Dante, pet Terrie, and left.

'Now,' Dante said, coming closer to Carolyn, 'spill it.'

'I don't know where to start.'

'The beginning.'

'I'm not sure what you want to know.'

'How long have you been sitting on the floor of Dahlia's closet, listening while she and I make love?'

Make love. That was a nice euphemism for the things that Dahlia and Dante did together. With feathers. And paddles. And costumes. And hot wax. And whipped cream. Still, Carolyn tried to remember the first time. She closed her eyes to bring up a picture.

'I came home from walking Terrie when you guys were making all that noise –'

She suddenly realised that the first time she'd eavesdropped on Dahlia wasn't during a date with Dante but Jason. Her brain tried to get a few steps ahead of her mouth, but it was too late. He knew, and his eyes suddenly narrowed.

'It wasn't with me, was it?'

Carolyn shook her head. Her dark hair was loose from its normal ponytail, and it momentarily covered her face. She wished she could just leave it, hanging in front of her, hiding her like a midnight curtain.

'Who else?' Dante asked, his voice serious.

Carolyn hadn't meant to rat on Dahlia, but she'd been simply too stressed to think far enough ahead to save her. And she'd been up all night, working. Fielding phone calls from people like Melody and Zach. That counted for something, didn't it?

'Who?' he demanded.

'It's not my place.' Oh, didn't *that* sound prissy?

'And Dahlia's closet is?'

OK, he had something there, and his words made Carolyn flush. No, the closet wasn't her place, either. This was no good. None of it. Why hadn't she stayed later at the station, preparing for her next show? Why hadn't she wandered through the record library, one of her favourite pastimes before she'd discovered the wonders of Dahlia's closet?

'I've got a pretty good means of blackmail, Carolyn.'

'One of her other dates,' Carolyn said softly, wishing she were anywhere but here, having this conversation.

'Shit.' He looked down at the floor, his brow furrowed. 'Plural. You mean there's more than one other guy?'

Poor Dante. The girl had a full social calendar. Carolyn, who had a lyric to fit every situation, thought of one of her favourite Leonard Cohen songs, 'Everybody Knows'. There was a line about having a meter above a bed that, Carolyn figured, would tell how many lovers a person had had. It's what Dahlia needed.

'How many?'

In a way, Carolyn found herself surprised that he didn't know about the multiple men, that he hadn't guessed, or that Dahlia hadn't told him. What in the world did he think she was doing when she said she couldn't meet him until late? That she was bringing work home from the office? Snips of hair to piece together into wigs? Dante couldn't be that fucking stupid. Or maybe he was just that stupid about fucking. Men liked to think that their women were into them more than the other way around.

He leaned against the counter. 'I know it's dumb,' he said, as if reading her mind. 'I just didn't want to see the signs.'

This conversation wasn't any fun at all. Carolyn wondered how long she was going to have to stand here consoling him. She watched him take a sip of coffee, give her a hangdog look, and then try to pull off a smile.

'But it turned you on, didn't it, Carolyn?'

That flush came back. Instantly. She felt as if she could make toast off the heat of her cheeks. Dante took this as an affirmative and he came a step closer. Carolyn moved a step back.

'You know,' he said, 'you're a funny girl.' He stared at her. She waited. It was her nature to simply wait and see how things would play out, then react to them.

'You're so pretty, but you act as if you're some sort of leper or hunchback. The way you hide yourself, flinching at every move.'

Carolyn remained silent.

'Dahlia once mentioned your –' He paused. 'Your incident in college. But you can't let that ruin your life, can you?'

How did they get here, to this conversation? Dante stared at her, waiting for a response. 'Not ruin my life,' she finally agreed, 'but change it.'

He put one hand on her shoulder. The touch was electrifying. It had been so long since a man, any man other than Harry, had touched her. She remembered a friend of Dahlia's from the salon, a masseuse, who had come over for dinner one night. She'd told them that some of her clients were never touched. Not ever. In their daily life, they moved through the hours without any human physical contact. No spouse or lover. No connection with a co-worker, no reason to shake hands, to get a pat on the back. Nothing. This woman's hands during a massage were all they got. Once a week. For 60 minutes.

Dante squeezed her shoulder. Then he took a step even closer and put his arms around her. Carolyn's brain started to whir. What was going on? Dante was feeling put out because Dahlia was cheating on him, but why did he want to hold her?

'You're so pretty,' he said again, this time into the top of her hair, and then she felt his lips on her forehead, then on her cheeks, and finally on her lips. His kiss opened something inside her, and when he motioned with his head toward the bedroom, she took his hand and followed.

Dahlia and Harry sat face to face in the little coffee room, the walls of which were now a pale sky-blue.

'I think it's going well,' Dahlia said, lifting her cup of espresso, leaving a rose-coloured lipsticked kiss on the rim when she set it back down.

'Doesn't make a lot of sense to me,' Harry said.

'She's always liked listening. Back in school, whenever she had the chance, she eavesdropped. I knew it. I've always had a sense about what turns people on. Not only men, but women too. Carolyn so obviously likes to watch. Especially since I like to *be* watched.'

'But what are you up to now?'

'Look, she's borderline ready to date again. I can tell. That's all I want for her. To get over Steven and get out there. If watching helps her out, wakes her up, then more power to her.'

'But what's up with Dante?'

Dahlia shrugged. 'You'd really have to ask him that question, Harry, if you want an honest answer.'

Carolyn had seen Dante in action. So she knew what he was capable of. But in her bedroom, she learned the difference between watching and doing. And the difference was spectacular.

Dante moved slowly, carefully undressing her, kissing her everywhere – from the nape of her neck, beneath her heavy dark hair, to the delicate indents of her collarbone. He bent on his knees to untie the tiny bow on the waistband of her pyjama bottoms and as he slid them down her thighs he left kisses in their wake. While he worked, he continued to ask her questions, and his constant conversation was what turned her on the most. Confessing to him. Who would have thought that it

189

would have been such a turn-on? To come clean about something so dirty.

Ah, Dahlia would. She'd told Carolyn often about the pleasures of confession. Now Carolyn finally understood the concept.

'You like to watch?' Dante asked, a rhetorical question, since he knew the answer already, but she nodded anyway. Nodded and then managed to part her lips and whisper 'yes'.

'Always?'

She nodded again, remembering the first time. The *real* first time. When she and Dahlia had roomed together in college. She'd hidden out in their closet, waiting for Dahlia and her English T.A. to show up. This was something she rarely thought about; rarely allowed herself to remember. But it had thrilled her, hiding out, listening. She hadn't been able to watch because of the position of the bed, but the words themselves had been enough. It had been worth it to stay there all night, waiting for the couple to leave in the morning before opening the door and freeing herself. The conversation had been fuel for months of fantasies. Dahlia playing coy and sweet, teasing him: 'Do you like it like this? Or like this?' And the man's hungry response: 'Just don't stop. Don't ever, ever stop.'

Carolyn wouldn't confess this part to Dante, but she would tell him the rest. Of how she had watched him and Dahlia. The night of the tickling, with that lovely lone white feather. The other nights after.

'Did you want to try anything that you saw?' he asked. And she realised what he was offering her. If she told him, then he would do it. He would make her the star of the show, would make her fantasies come true. She took a deep breath, and then she confessed some more.

They didn't light candles. Didn't do any of the little frilly things that Dahlia loved to do before sex; things that she said enhanced the mood. Carolyn wasn't that type of a girl. Or, if she was, then she'd forgotten. Instead, they fell together on her bed, stripping each other's clothes off in a hurry, easy enough since Dante had on only a robe. She felt his hands on her – the tips of his fingers slightly callused, which surprised her. When would Dante ever do work that would rough up his hands? As a writer, he spent all his time in front of a keyboard. Except when he was fucking off.

Or fucking, she thought, as he stroked the insides of her calves gently, so gently, that she had shivers running through her body. He looked up at her with a gaze of wonderment, and Carolyn couldn't immediately understand the expression. Then he spoke, and suddenly she understood.

'So pretty,' he murmured, 'you're so amazingly pretty, baby. And you don't even seem to know it.'

It felt good to hear, so good, but then, as Dante peeled open the top to her pyjamas, she stopped him. She couldn't do this. Couldn't go through with it. She covered her small breasts with her hands, feeling too exposed and not knowing how to recover.

He shook his head. 'You want to, Carolyn. You know you do.'

She did. He was right. But there was some part of her that couldn't go forward. Some part that wouldn't let her continue. And, when they got right down to it, there was a part that wouldn't let Dante, either. They stayed still, looking at each other, totally still for a moment. Where could they go next? Carolyn felt scared to speak first. Wished this had never happened, that they'd never started. It was crazy.

'What if we just ... touch,' Dante suggested softly. 'Just...' He grinned at her. 'Let our fingers do the walking.'

She thought about it. Touching seemed different from fucking. The concept of it was somewhat pleasing, and she was so aroused already. If he left her alone, she would definitely touch herself, recreating the image of seeing him and Dahlia together. Without speaking, she nodded, and he began. And, oh, he was good. His fingers made their way along her body, stroking her ribs, the rise of her hip bones, the gentle curve of her waist.

That was all right. She sat back against the pillows and looked at him, and her shyness started to fall away. Tentatively, she reached out and stroked his broad chest, her fingers teasing his dark, curly hair, twining in it. He leaned back and let her. He didn't offer suggestions or any encouragement except several deep moans when she made him feel good.

Then it was even better.

They moved as if dancing, skin to skin, exploring each other. It was like being in a living fantasy. No pressure, no fear. She touched him and he touched her in return, and each time they moved together she felt waves of warmth move through her. The climax built so slowly that she almost didn't see it coming.

Almost.

She could hear her heartbeat in her ears, was aware that her breathing had sped up, as if she'd just gone on a long run. All of those sensations that she'd chalked up as past history came flooding back. Being touched by someone else was so different than taking care of herself. Dante's fingers ran over the lips of her pussy, then stroked between them, finding her clit and tickling it lightly with the tips of his fingers. He knew just how to do it, and what was most amazing to her was that he played with her differently to how he played with Dahlia. As if being with her brought out a totally different side of himself.

A more gentle side.

Carolyn found that secret place, reached it with him, and for once she forgot about Dahlia, forgot about comparing herself to her roommate. She didn't need to scream, to make those wild noises; she simply gripped on to Dante's shoulders and let the power of the pleasure slam through her. Let that other side of herself loose once again to enjoy what it felt like to be with a man.

Curled up with him afterwards, naked, feeling his body against hers, Carolyn couldn't believe it had actually happened. Dante's fingers still made those magical circles over the wings of her shoulder blades, up and under her long hair. This was like a dress rehearsal for the real thing, and Carolyn loved Dante for letting her practise with him.

Although Carolyn really wanted to go to sleep, Dante wanted to talk. Talk about listening. It was obviously a turn-on to him, the thought that she'd been listening to his and Dahlia's various escapades. Carolyn remembered the way he'd been the morning after he and Dahlia had rented that porno movie. Standing in the kitchen together, asking if she'd heard them; if she'd been bothered by the noise the night before.

'Did you hope I was listening?' Carolyn asked him now, after reminding him of that time.

'Of course. It would have added to the fun. The excitement.'

'Have you ever listened to anybody?'

His head was against her chest, as if listening to her heartbeat, but he knew that's not what she meant. Finally, he sat back and looked up at her. 'Sure.'

'When?'

'Whenever I could.'

'Not good enough, Dante.'

He was silent a moment, obviously considering. Either what he wanted to tell her, or how much to reveal. Then he shrugged. 'I'm a writer. I like to watch. To listen. It's sexy. Kinky. So, whenever my old roommate brought someone home, I always stayed up late and tried to hear what I could. Or once, at a beach house in Malibu, I realised I could see into the neighbour's back yard. And I watched some stuff there.'

'Stuff?'

'Nice stuff,' he continued. 'Fucking outside. I've always liked that.'

193

Now, Carolyn rolled away from him so she wouldn't have to see his face when he answered.

'What will you do about Dahlia?'

'Do?'

'Will you tell her?' She closed her eyes, waiting.

'What for? She's telling me next to nothing. Why would I cue her in?'

Carolyn didn't have an answer for that at all.

Several hours later, Carolyn and Dante woke up simultaneously. They'd both heard a noise and had been startled awake, and were even more startled to find that they were in the same bed together. Their reflections mirrored each other – they looked immediately guilty and then embarrassed for feeling that way.

Dante recovered first, reaching his arm over her to pull her close. At least he was a gentleman about it. If he'd rather have been with Dahlia, he didn't let on. He didn't say, 'Let's keep this a secret,' or, 'There's no need to share what we did.'

But Carolyn was aware that he dressed quietly, and she did as well, slipping a robe on and tying it tightly around her slender waist. She walked Dante into the kitchen, preparing to make coffee, but he shook his head. 'I've got to run,' he said, and then took a step closer to her and kissed her.

Really kissed her.

She felt those sparkling flashes of heat in the base of her stomach and lower. The soft downy hair at the back of her neck felt suddenly electrified. He didn't do anything else. Didn't try to touch her. Didn't say he'd call. He just smiled, and then blew Carolyn a kiss as he walked down the hall to the front door. 'No time for Terrie today,' he called out, sounding apologetic.

Carolyn stood in the hall, waiting. They'd heard a noise, something that had woken both of them. Was it Dahlia coming back home? Had she forgotten something? No. It was Billy and Max. Carolyn saw their van parked outside. Dante saw it, too, because his shoulders seemed to relax.

'I have a meeting with a big shot,' Dante continued, and Carolyn noted that he looked relieved.

'You're the big shot,' Carolyn yelled to him, and he poked his head back into the apartment and gave her a thumbs-up sign. It was one of his moves. She was still staring at the doorway, grinning stupidly, relief flooding through her, as Billy and Max walked through the open door and into the living room.

'Who's that?' Billy asked, turning to look out at the landing as Dante left. They both heard the rev of his BMW engine, and then through the front windows saw the blur of silver as the car sped down the road.

'Dahlia's ex. One of them, anyway.'

'Looks like they got back together,' Billy said, and Carolyn felt her cheeks go red.

'I mean, if he's leaving now.' Billy consulted his watch. 'Were they breaking up all night? Or were they doing something else?'

Carolyn didn't want to answer, so she turned and went back to the kitchen, as if she hadn't heard.

'What's he do?' Billy wanted to know next. He'd given Terrie his standard treat. Now he followed her into the kitchen. He got the cleaning supplies out from under the sink while she started the coffee. Max seemed less than interested, strolling past them to the rear of the apartment to start with Dahlia's room as usual.

'Dante's a writer.'

'Great American novelist?'

'Not in LA, silly,' she said grinning at Billy. 'Nobody reads in LA. He's a great American screenwriter.'

'Like just about everyone I know.' Billy sighed.

'You, too?'

He nodded. 'Been writing for years, even taught for a while. Then gave that up. Hated teaching because of that saying, "Those who can't do, teach." I tried freelancing, and now I do this while I file away the pink slips.'

'Never would have guessed it,' Carolyn said honestly.

'I'm trying. I'm always trying. It seems that whenever I get an idea, someone else already has it.'

'That's standard,' Carolyn told him, trying to make him feel better. 'Remember the year that all those underwater movies came out at the same time?'

'I wouldn't mind if my movie came out at the same time as someone else's. But I hate it when I think of an idea and then someone else writes it before I can.'

'Like?'

'I had an idea for a meteor movie, and then those other two hit the box office. Literally. There won't be another movie made about meteors for a long, long time.'

'What about writing what you know?' she asked.

He stared at her.

'That's what Dante said,' she explained. 'He said that in order to be a convincing writer, you should write about things that you know.'

'Does that work for him?'

'He always seems to have work.'

Billy looked around the apartment, obviously thinking. 'Write about cleaning, you mean?' Carolyn didn't know what to say. Obviously, Dante's advice wasn't the best for this particular situation. 'Not too interesting,' Billy said, and he was smiling, 'unless you've got a bad case of obsessive-compulsive disorder.'

Carolyn thought that after being with Dante she wouldn't need to watch Dahlia any more. But for some reason she had the opposite reaction. Now that she'd been touched by a man, she wanted to watch even more. Wanted to watch Dahlia with her new favourite man of the moment, Marlon. As luck would have it, Dahlia seemed to want to showcase this particular lover, making it with him two nights in a row for Carolyn's listening and viewing pleasure.

Marlon spoke French in a fluid accent that added to the rest of his charms. '*Mon cher*,' he said in his deep voice, '*voulez-vous couchez avec moi ce soir?*'

Everyone knew how to say this. Everyone who grew up in the disco generation, anyway. Even Dahlia, who had flunked French in high school, knew what it meant, and it made her giggle. They must have gone to a bar, Carolyn realised.

'*Oui*,' she said, just as Carolyn opened the grate and climbed through. Marlon was still at it with the French talk, crooning hungrily to her.

Dahlia, sounding awed, asked, 'What did you say?'

'I want to make love to you. All night long. I want to do things to you that no man ever has. Take you places you've never been before.'

Ooh, la, la, Carolyn thought. Clichés in French. Besides, Dahlia had been everywhere. Where could Marlon possibly take her that she hadn't already been?

It didn't seem to matter. Dahlia sighed at the translation, and Marlon, realising he was having the effect he wanted, continued to speak to her in the most romantic of languages.

After a moment, Carolyn began to listen more carefully. Then she had to bite her fist, so that she wouldn't laugh out loud. Unlike Dahlia, Carolyn hadn't flunked out of French. She could speak it passably, and as each statement was duly translated for Dahlia, she realised that Marlon was mistranslating. Intentionally. He told Dahlia, in French, that she should dress up like a whore and dance on stage for a living, maybe down at Hip Huggers near the airport. He insisted that her ass was so divine it should be in magazines, and that he wished she'd let him fuck it.

In English, for Dahlia's ears, he said, 'You are so amazingly beautiful. The prettiest girl I've ever gone out with. I couldn't stop looking at you at that party.'

Dahlia shouldn't have slept through French class. If she had known how he was playing her, she'd have kicked him out of bed. Still, Carolyn was glad that Dahlia had been a F for French student because she found herself enjoying the interaction immensely.

In French, Marlon said, 'I wonder if these are real?'

Carolyn quickly understood that he was pawing at her breasts.

'What did you say?' Dahlia asked, breathless. 'Please, tell me what you said.'

'I said your breasts are amazing. They're so perfectly round. I could suck on them for hours.'

There was a muffled response, and then Marlon's words were lost. Carolyn pictured him kissing all down her body, getting to her sex, speaking directly into her. She was sad that she couldn't hear any more. Usually Dahlia's moans and sighs were enough for her, but Marlon was a pure entertainer, simply playing around with French for his own amusement.

She slowly pushed the door to see if it would open a crack without a squeak. Luck was on her side, and it did. The scene was so amazingly explicit that when Marlon started speaking again in French, Carolyn didn't really notice what he was saying. But when she did, she was shocked.

Marlon was on a mean streak now, still talking in French. 'You're a good little fuck, Dahlia.' Dahlia purred when she heard her name. 'This makes the rest of the dismal evening worthwhile. I didn't think I could bear to hear any more about your idiotic life at the salon. What is it you do all day? Answer the phone and cater to bored rich women? How do you stand your life?'

Carolyn wondered how he could keep up such a serious conversation, a dual conversation, and still remain aroused. Maybe all he required was looking at Dahlia's face, at her perfect body, while he rocked his cock in and out of her.

'Now be a good girl and come for me. Yes, that's right, come for me, baby. Then I'll come, too, and I can get the hell out of here.'

'Oh, Carolyn,' Dahlia sighed the next day as she walked into her roommate's bedroom, ready to give her the morning report. Carolyn lowered her headset and focused her attention on Dahlia. Her roommate was practically vibrating with poorly reigned-in energy.

'He spoke French,' Dahlia said, and Carolyn almost blew her cover by saying that she knew. How would she know?

'Why?' Carolyn asked. 'Is he French?'

'I told you that the other night.' Dahlia paused dramatically, then said, 'I think that he may be the one.'

'I thought you couldn't handle being with just one.'

'That was then,' Dahlia said matter of factly. 'You know I was monogamous when I was with Dante. Sometimes a girl has to blow off a little steam before she settles down again.'

'Why would you settle with Marlon?'

'Didn't you see him?'

'Other than that,' Carolyn said. 'Did you two really click?'

'Sure,' Dahlia said, smiling, 'in more ways than one.'

Carolyn found that she was torn. She knew that Marlon had no intention of being her man. For the first time since her initial wave of guilt about listening to her roommate and Jason, she considered coming clean, confessing her dirty secret.

But for some reason, she just couldn't tell Dahlia. So instead, when Harry called her late that evening, she decided to confess to him.

Harry didn't have the time to listen. He was calling to invite Carolyn to a party.

'Tell me when we get there,' he said when she told him she had something on her mind.

'Where?' she asked, twirling the phone cord around her fingers, unconsciously mimicking one of Dahlia's sexy ways of moving. Always flirting, even when nobody was there to watch.

'A party.'

'I don't think so, Harry. It's late.'

'Come on,' he urged. 'Go to your front door and look outside.'

She did as he said. Peeling back the window shade, she saw Harry standing in the centre of the lawn in a fabulous hot-pink ballgown the exact colour of the plastic flamingos congregating nearby. He was talking to her from his cell phone, spinning in circles as he spoke. Carolyn opened the window and then hit the 'hang up' button on the cordless phone. Harry came forward to talk to her through the window. It reminded her of a production of *Romeo and Juliet*, except this one would have been better labelled *Juliet and Juliet*.

'There's a party,' Harry explained, 'and I think you might like it.' Carolyn gave him a blank look, not understanding at all. With his sparkling blue eyes and cupid's bow mouth, he looked like any other starlet you'd see in Hollywood. 'And it's only late for early birds. The really good parties don't start until after the witching hour.'

'Parties,' Carolyn echoed. 'You mean, one of the *special* parties?' Suddenly, she couldn't keep the excitement out of her voice. She'd always wanted to know what went on at Harry's Hollywood hills fiestas, a behind-the-scenes look into how the kinky crowd played when no one was looking.

'You have to dress in drag, though,' Harry said, his eyes glinting. It was obvious that he was titillated by the idea of transforming her, and Carolyn was charmed with the idea herself. It would be so much easier to go out in costume. To pretend to be someone else. If Dahlia was into play-acting as Carolyn, then Carolyn could be ... well, anyone, couldn't she?

Carolyn went around to the front door and opened it up for Harry. He took a minute, having to go to his car to get his trunk of cosmetics, and while she was waiting, she heard the door open to the apartment upstairs. Oh, God, it would have to be Zach, coming downstairs now just as Harry poofed in through the front.

'Carolyn,' Zach said coming towards her. 'I've been wanting to talk to you, but you're never home.'

Terrie loped through the door in the entryway where

the trio was congregating. Carolyn was surprised again to see that the dog didn't bark. Terrie knew Harry, but he didn't really know Zach. Dahlia and Jason emerged right then, in a whirlwind of unco-ordinated clothing, as if they'd just picked up whatever had been lying on the floor after their fuck fest, which was most likely what had happened. Carolyn realised that Dahlia had already gotten over her sole desire for Marlon because here she was, out with another soldier in her army of men.

Carolyn saw Zach look over Dahlia, now clad in a skin-tight polka-dotted outfit. What was she trying to be now? A slut? She felt something fall in her stomach, and she said, 'Sorry, busy right now. We're going out to a party.'

Zach glanced at Harry, then looked at her and nodded. 'Another time,' he said, slipping into his coat and then walking out the door.

'What was that about?' Harry wanted to know. 'Why were you so cold to him?'

She didn't answer, and wasn't up for explaining about seeing Melody emerging like some floozie from his apartment. The make-up artist just shrugged, then sighed and explained the rules of the party. After that, he waited in the living room for Carolyn to choose her clothes. The outfit was simple. To dress like a man wasn't any more difficult than finding a pair of black pants, a white shirt, tie, and black suit jacket. Carolyn had all the components. It was the rest of the look that Harry helped with.

Sitting on the edge of the tub, she put her faith, and face, in his hands. Harry pulled her hair back into a ponytail then tucked it up into a dark brown wig. He was silent as he did the rest, shading, sculpting, adding a hint of a goatee. Harry's daily life had prepared him for this. He was constantly fiddling with people's features. For his most famous cosmetic book, he had transformed women into men, men into women, just to show he could. Now, he added the finishing touches, then stood back, admiring.

'No, not right.' He shook his head. 'Something's missing.' After a moment of walking all around Carolyn, checking her out from every angle, he disappeared into her bedroom, and emerged with a sock rolled tightly and stuffed into a second sock.

'Stick this down your pants.'

Carolyn's eyes widened, but she did as Harry said. Then she posed for him, striking what she hoped was a masculine stance. He nodded. 'Perfect. You're so handsome, even I want to do you.'

The party was held at a mansion once owned by two movie stars from the twenties, long-dead celebrities who Carolyn had never heard of. But Harry explained that very few people were ever invited to view the place, and that Carolyn was getting a true backstage Hollywood experience. One that she should appreciate. She could tell her children about it someday, minus certain sexy details.

A winding tree-lined driveway led into a palatial entrance where attractive young valet attendants dressed in silver lamé took the cars. Carolyn slid on a pair of prescription tortoiseshell wayfarer sunglasses as she and Harry entered beneath the domed doorway and into the mammoth building. She didn't want her wide-eyed expression to give her away as a novice to this type of scene.

'Gorgeous,' Harry said, 'you look like someone famous incognito.' It was just the thing to say to calm Carolyn's nerves.

Inside, the mansion was all marble and gilt-edged, with pillars and urns that appeared as if they'd been spirited away from some crumbling Greek ruin. Sunken living rooms filled with sumptuous velvet pillows looked as if they were waiting to cushion someone's swan dive. Carolyn was busy drinking in all the decor, so busy that she didn't immediately notice the naked people. When they were almost on top of the medley of nude bodies, she suddenly sucked in her breath, making her pretty date for the evening laugh in spite of himself.

'Good Lord, Harry,' Carolyn murmured as they approached the orgy. 'Why did we even bother with costumes? Nobody's wearing anything.'

In the centre of the largest room, on a bed of pure white fur rugs, several guests were already entwined. All men, Carolyn realised as she made out several limbs, strong backs, muscular thighs. But she wouldn't have been able to untangle the partners if she'd been paid. She couldn't tell which part belonged to which person, so tightly connected were the revellers.

'They're starting early,' Harry explained, steering Carolyn towards a towering fountain created from crystal champagne glasses. He snagged two and handed one over, watching with a look of pleasure as Carolyn downed hers and took another. She was most definitely not concerned about herself or her own appearance, focused intently on the bevy of beautiful creatures around them.

'Most likely, they are part of the waitstaff,' Harry continued.

'What do you mean?'

'The hosts hired them to get the rest of the crowd into the mood. It's always difficult to be the first person to disrobe.' Harry said this with the sound of experience in his voice. Had he ever been the one to take off his clothes first? Carolyn could imagine it easily, but she didn't have time to quiz him because Harry was on the move. Quickly, on something of a mission, he led Carolyn down a long black marble hallway to the rear of the building. A set of French doors opened on to the gardens, and from the top of the stairs, they could see a sprawling swimming pool lit from beneath the water, a large gazebo and a gigantic white tent.

'You choose your pleasure,' Harry said, pointing out the different locations. On the gazebo, Carolyn made out several slim figures in suits. Were they the musicians? She knew that in general, musicians usually ignored the guests during their break. Although, at this particular fiesta, the guests were admittedly difficult to ignore. In the curving, turquoise pool, naked people swam and lazed about on colourful inflatable rafts. The weather was just warm enough for this type of decadence, and Carolyn noticed that the kind host, whomever he might be, had positioned heaters on the patio, where guests might dry themselves after a dip.

It was impossible to see inside the tent, but Harry told her that this was where the food was. Carolyn couldn't imagine eating right now. She was too enthralled with watching, her stomach doing flip-flops as she gazed in various directions, unable to choose one particular view to focus upon.

Harry gently took her wrist and led her down the steps. At the edge of the pool, he slipped off one high-heel and dipped his toes in the water. A handsome youth with wet blond ringlets swam to the side. His face was clean of make-up, but his lips looked stained, as if someone had kissed away a dark, cherry lipstick. Kissed him hard. With clear, blue eyes, he looked up incitingly at Harry.

'It's delightful,' he said, indicating the temperature. 'Join us?'

Harry gave Carolyn a questioning stare. Was she ready to go on her own, or did she need him to stay with her? She needed him, but she wouldn't say so.

'I'm fine,' she said, hoping that she sounded as if she meant it. 'Go on.'

Harry didn't need any further words of encouragement. He quickly stripped down to his pale rose-coloured lingerie and dove gracefully into the pool, looking like a nubile extra from an Esther Williams movie. Carolyn watched for a moment, but then started to feel like an extra herself – an extra wheel. The men in the pool didn't want to be with her, and they might not want her to watch, either. Why had she agreed to come to the party? She'd only wanted to see what happened behind closed doors, but now that she'd seen, she didn't know what to do with herself. This wasn't her type of place.

Carolyn shut her eyes for a moment and tried to imagine what her roommate would do if she were here. Dahlia would know exactly how to behave, always able to find the right mood, to join a situation and make it seem as if she were an integral part. Carolyn didn't have the same ability, but she wouldn't flee. She would not leave without Harry. This decided, she started to walk along a stone path through the manicured gardens in the direction of the gazebo. If this was where the musicians were, she would feel most comfortable here. She could talk about any type of music.

But when she reached the white-framed trellis structure, she realised that this was simply another gathering of guests ... the *female* guests. All in drag similar to hers. Elegantly cut suits, men's wigs, or their own short, sleek hair. No, this wasn't right. She couldn't talk to them, could she? She started to walk away, but one called out to her.

'Join us?' An echo of the invitation posed by Harry's swimming friend. Carolyn, biting her bottom lip in thought, hesitated only a moment before slowly climbing up the white wooden steps.

Dahlia had found her true calling. Being in a sandwich between two men, their bodies on either side of hers, their hands roaming over her naked skin. She'd planned dates with both Marlon and Jason, intentionally over-booking her schedule in the hope that the men would be willing to play roles in her fantasy. Harry had asked Carolyn out for the evening, and Dahlia had known that this would be the perfect time. She had the apartment to herself.

But creating a comfortable situation for all present was more difficult. She'd told Jason that they would be meeting a friend for drinks at Sammy's, told Marlon to meet them there, and then proceeded to get both men tipsy. Maybe this was more normally a man's role, but ever since watching the various co-minglings on the X-rated movie with Dante, she'd been unable to get the image from her mind.

She simply had to try it.

By the third round of tequila shooters, the men were talking louder, seeming to get along well. Dahlia thought it was time to bring up her suggested activities for the evening. Now or never.

'I had this idea –' she started.

'I was guessing you had something up your sleeve,' Jason said, grinning.

'Really?' Dahlia asked. Was she that transparent?

'Why else would you ask another man on our date?'

'*Your* date?' Marlon said, challenging Jason. 'Why isn't it *our* date?'

Before they could get into that, Dahlia interrupted. 'It is our date,' she said sweetly. 'The three of us.'

Now there was a charged silence, as she waited to see if the men would get it. And, then, as she realised from their expressions that they did, she waited breathless for their responses. When had she last been so turned on? She couldn't remember.

Chapter Nineteen

*T*he entire evening was unlike anything Carolyn had ever experienced before, either in reality or in her fantasies. Yes, in her fantasies, she had definitely thought about making love to a woman. She understood that picturing things that she wasn't even sure she wanted to try was exactly what fantasies were about – exploring the unknown. Exploring *Dahlia's* unknown, if she were going to be honest with herself. And why wouldn't anyone want to be honest with him or herself? But, truly, the actual act of being with another woman was something she'd never done.

And at Harry's party, she found that she couldn't make herself do it, either. Instead, she watched, which was something she found very comforting. She was accustomed to watching Dahlia, and now watching this other group of beautiful women turned out to be so pleasurable that she couldn't make herself look away. It didn't hurt that the other female guests all seemed to be clones of Marlene Dietrich, or that none of them had taken the costume to the extremes that she and Harry had. The women were in suits, yes, but they hadn't tried at all to look like men. In fact, if anything, the cut of their outfits was intended to show off their womanly curves.

They didn't seem at all offended by having her as an audience, either. Her favourite to look at, a sleek young beauty with golden-streaked brown hair, even came up to Carolyn and whispered, 'It's fine to take things slowly. I spent my first three parties without lifting a finger.' She waggled her pinkie in Carolyn's face . . . 'But if you do want to play, simply take a step forward.'

Carolyn nodded and then perched on the edge of the gazebo to watch. There were three other women, and it seemed as if they'd simply been waiting for her to arrive before getting started. Now that she had joined them, they quickly got down to the business at hand. Which meant that while Carolyn observed, they peeled off their suit coats, removed their pressed white shirts, shoes and crisp slacks, revealing lingerie similar to what Harry had on: lacy, frivolous confections that looked as if they'd been created in a different time.

With nimble fingers, they assisted each other in the removal of their foundation attire, until soon they were all naked and entwined in a similar fashion to the men Carolyn had seen when she'd first arrived.

It was lovely; as if this had been what women were created for. To be pretty and curvy and made to fit together in such extraordinary ways. Sexual puzzle pieces that worked even when the interlocking male parts were missing.

Dahlia was a fan of those interlocking male parts. Back at the apartment, with Jason and Marlon working her in a team effort, she could not control her excitement. The threesome had chosen her king-sized bed as their playground, and after quickly stripping out of their clothes, had embarked on this new journey together.

At the start, Dahlia had set out a few ground rules. 'If anyone feels uncomfortable –' Both men had shaken their heads, but she'd continued, 'We can stop at any time.'

'But when can we start?' Jason had asked, and Marlon had laughed at his eagerness. Then they'd all laughed, because it was such a thrill – the way Dahlia's naked body looked in candlelight, the way Jason took a step forward and cradled her chin in one hand, staring into her green eyes, holding her for a second with his gaze.

Then things began to move more quickly, and smoothly, as if they had rehearsed their roles ahead of time. Marlon lifting Dahlia from behind and carrying her to the bed, stroking her body with the tips of his fingers while Jason moved to the foot of the bed and began to tickle her toes with his tongue. Dahlia couldn't believe how decadent it felt, and also couldn't believe she'd waited this long to try it.

For someone who loved sex as much as she did, why hadn't she thought to incorporate a second lover? Marlon and Jason seemed at ease with each other, showing no signs of jealousy as they rotated positions on the bed, licking along Dahlia's body, making her arch her hips and beg wordlessly.

And when they got in deeper, got into the actual act, they continued to move in synchronicity. The men seemed to have made silent agreements as to who was going to do what to whom. Turning Dahlia on her side, they took her in a spoon embrace, Jason working her from the front, Marlon taking up the rear. Everything went slowly, languidly, so that by the time the men were ready, Dahlia was desperate, her lips parted to beg for more.

Wasn't that what Dahlia always wanted? Forget what she'd told Carolyn about Marlon being right for her. She couldn't honestly choose one man, could she? Because over everything else in the world, what Dahlia always wanted was one thing: more.

Carolyn couldn't believe that this was really her. She felt transformed, transported, but after several minutes she forced her eyes away from the throng, needing a breather. Quietly, she walked away from the gazebo, looking out at the lawn, twinkling with a drapery of fairy lights hung from the low branches of the jacaranda

209

trees. She could make out other groupings, couples entwined, but she couldn't see where Harry had got himself to.

Wrapping her coat around her, she continued walking towards where she'd last seen him, at the pool. When she reached the tiled edge, she stopped. Not because she'd found him, but because she'd found someone else she knew.

Dante.

His eyes were as wide as hers as they stared at each other, but his mouth was too busy around the throbbing member of his playtime partner for him to murmur anything other than a mumbled 'Oh'.

Carolyn was shocked. But she knew she shouldn't stand there, transfixed, watching, and she quickly made her way to another part of the yard, shaking beneath her black jacket. What was going on? Did everyone participate in these hedonistic gatherings? Everyone but her? Was she the only person who didn't know what was going on in the city after hours?

Suddenly she felt a hand on her shoulder, and she turned to find Harry smiling at her. He was wearing someone else's long white robe, and his mascara was smudged around his eyes from playing in the pool.

'OK?' he asked, staring into her eyes, seeming to honestly want the answer.

'Dante's here,' Carolyn said.

He nodded, as if to say, 'Of course,' then added, 'Dante's often here.'

Carolyn shook her head. She didn't get it.

'I introduced Dante to Dahlia,' he explained. 'At the salon. He swings both ways.' There was a pause while Carolyn soaked up this information. 'But, oh, how he swings,' Harry sighed, as if reliving a happy memory.

'So Dahlia knows?'

'It's why they broke up.' More revelations that Carolyn hadn't expected. Again, Dahlia had kept a secret to herself. 'She knew from the start. I wouldn't have let her date him without knowing the truth. For a while she was fine with it. But when she started to fall for him, that made things more difficult.'

'But you've been with him –'

Harry nodded.

'Were you jealous at all?'

Harry steered Carolyn slowly towards a table filled with fantastic arrays of desserts – strawberries dipped in chocolate, huge silver bowls of fresh whipped cream and other decadent creations to eat or feed to a hungry lover. Or possibly spread along the naked skin of one.

'Jealousy is fleeting,' he said, but Carolyn thought she caught a different look in Harry's eyes. One she hadn't seen before – a darker, pained look.

'So you didn't introduce them intentionally.'

Harry shrugged. 'He was with her for a while, then back with me, and now he's with –' Harry spread his arms magnanimously. 'With the world.'

Carolyn didn't understand. But then, there were so many things she didn't get, so many new things for her to process. Finally, she simply let Harry sit her down and feed her grapes while her mind whirred with visions of Harry and Dante and Dante and Dahlia and all the different groupings that those three players might include. But mostly she wondered where she, herself, fit into all this.

Dahlia had no such questions in her mind. She knew exactly where she fit: between Jason and Marlon. One of her lovers had entered her pussy, was thrusting in and out in a slow, decadent manner. The other was taking her ass, working equally slowly, making the ride last. Dahlia knew which man was where, but when she closed her eyes, she could pretend that she didn't. That added to her excitement, the anonymous feeling of the men in her bed, as if they were simply tools to bring her pleasure.

And, oh, did they ever do their jobs. She couldn't remember a time when she'd felt sexier or more cared for. These two had been well chosen; hand-picked for the private party. She knew that Dante would have loved to be in the scene, but it was harder for her when he was involved. She loved Dante. Yet she understood she could never have him, only him, without him looking for boys on the side.

She could play that way, too. Could play the field, sample the selection. It was easier than giving her heart. In bed with Jason and Marlon, all she was required to give was pleasure, and she got it back in return.

The three of them moved together easily, glistening with the lightest foil of sweat, making soft noises, the type of uncontained moans and sighs that simply couldn't be helped. Dahlia's lovely hair, spread over her shoulders in a golden mane, made her seem even more wild, more animalistic. The men, as if they thought that speaking might make the vision disappear, kept almost silent, their bodies talking for them.

'I'm going to come,' Dahlia announced seconds before it happened. The words brought them all to the same place, the same page, and hands gripping into each other, fingers overlapping, the threesome merged even more tightly together, climaxing as if the three had become one entity.

Things had changed. Carolyn couldn't pretend that they hadn't. At work, she did her best to focus on the music. But every song she played reminded her of the night with Harry. Mercy Playground's 'Sex and Candy'. The Eurythmics' 'Sweet Dreams Are Made of These'. Prince's 'Little Red Corvette'. Everything she listened to seemed super-charged with sex. So when Zach called to make a request, she was already heated up, her body ready from hours of lyrical foreplay.

'You're mad at me,' he said.

She checked the clock. She was playing a raunchy number from LL Cool J that gave her four minutes to chat.

'I just don't like playing games,' she said.

'I'm not. I like you.'

'And you like Melody.'

'We've broken up,' he said. 'I told you that when we met.'

Carolyn sighed. This was such a difficult thing for her to do. By letting herself care about him, she was opening herself up for heartbreak, for messy involvement. But she couldn't pretend that she didn't care. 'Maybe,' she finally said, 'you ought to tell that to Melody.'

Now Zach was the one who seemed confused, but Carolyn wasn't going to spell it out. There was no way she was going to tell him who he could fuck or not. Still, she owned the mental image of Melody leaving Zach's apartment, and she simply couldn't get that out of her mind.

'Did you want to hear a song?' she asked. It was the one thing she could safely offer him.

'Yeah,' he said, 'but it's odd.'

'Anything for a fan.'

'Play "Back-stabbing Baby",' he said, choosing his own song, 'and dedicate it to Mel.'

He came for Carolyn when she slept. That was the only time he could still get her. He said, 'Hey, Carolyn, over here!'

She looked around, trying to place the voice, and then saw Steven, standing there. Waiting. He called out, 'I need to talk to you.' And every night, she went to him, like a zombie, even though she knew what was going to happen. Recurring nightmares are like that. You see the next step, but you can't stop yourself from taking it. You're on an automated track that pushes you forward, with walls that close in around you and only one exit. The worst way out.

'Just for a second,' Steven said, and she walked even closer, away from the safe, bright lights lining the pathway, into the darkness between two hulking lecture halls.

Terrie whimpered when she kicked out in the night. The dog licked her face until she opened her eyes, until

213

she stroked his silky, golden fur and whispered to him that everything was fine. 'Ssh, baby,' she murmured, 'it's all right.'

This was a lie. But then, she thought it was OK to lie to dogs.

'I want you to tell me what Marlon is saying,' Dahlia said midweek. Following her decadent night of two lovers, she had spent a one-on-one evening with her French-speaking beau.

'What do you mean?' Carolyn asked.

'He talks French to me when we're in bed, and he translates each line for me, but –' Dahlia hesitated. 'I think he's lying.'

This caught Carolyn completely by surprise. How would Dahlia know? Dahlia didn't speak any French. Nothing aside from the 'chez' at Chez Chaz, and Carolyn didn't think she knew what that meant, either. Before she could ask how Dahlia knew, her roommate answered the question for her.

'There's something sarcastic in the way he says the words in French. I can tell from the tone. When he gives me the translation, it always sounds different.'

'They're two different languages,' Carolyn said. 'He may simply be accentuating different words in French.' Why was she defending him? She didn't know. Dahlia was right. She should confirm her feelings.

Dahlia shook her head so violently, a sparkling diamond clip flew across the room. 'No, it's something else. He's playing me.'

'How do you want me to tell?' Would she have her hide in the closet? The idea almost managed to make Carolyn smile.

'You can tape us. You've got all the equipment here. Next time, put a tape recorder in the drawer of my night table and then I'll turn it on right when we start. Then I'll give you the tape and you can translate for me what it says. That way I'll know if he's really saying what he says he's saying.'

The thought of transcribing a tape of their lovemaking brought a quick blush to Carolyn's pale cheeks. Dahlia read the look easily.

'I know it might be embarrassing, but it shouldn't be. Not really. I mean, I tell you everything already.' They both knew that this was a lie, but neither one would confess to that fact. Carolyn could go around in endless circles trying to make sense of what Dahlia was thinking. 'I really hope you'll do this for me,' she added.

'If you think he's playing with you, why even go out with him again?'

'Didn't you see him?' Dahlia asked.

Carolyn shrugged.

'Besides,' she said more seriously, 'I like him. He listens to me talk about the salon. He asks me my opinion of current events. He seems so perfect. Outside of bed, anyway.'

She waited, silent, and Carolyn realised she wanted to know the answer.

'Sure,' Carolyn said, finally. 'I'll do it. Just bring me the tape.'

Chapter Twenty

*O*n Saturday night, Carolyn prepared to wait for her entertainment of the evening: Dahlia and Marlon. This time would be even more exciting because she was going to have a tape of the evidence afterwards. She'd just finished setting up her equipment in the drawer by Dahlia's bed when the bell rang. Making sure that the sound-sensitive device was ready, she hurried down the hall to look outside, careful as always not to make any noise.

Through the peephole she saw that Harry was outside. He was pacing back and forth beneath the light that hung over the entryway, and he looked upset, his dark brows furrowed low over his lovely blue eyes. Carolyn quickly opened the door, thinking he must be on the outs again with Jake.

She was wrong.

'What the fuck are you doing here?' Harry asked immediately, stepping into the room and backing her up with his body. Even though he was only her height, just a bit taller in his high-heeled suede boots, he had a definite presence. One that was suddenly forceful. He sounded angry, and she didn't know why. Although she'd seen him distraught before, generally about the state of his extremely complicated love life, she'd never seen him look like this. Carolyn stood back and stared at him.

'I'm not doing anything,' she admitted, feeling totally confused and more than mildly guilty. Could he possibly know that she'd been planning on watching Dahlia?

'That's exactly what I'm talking about,' Harry said, not making anything clearer. 'You've got a date tonight.' He separated the words with little spaces, as if talking to someone who didn't possess a firm grasp of the English language.

Carolyn simply stared at him. Harry had obviously been doing drugs. Because Carolyn *never* had a date, and Harry knew this.

'Zach. Saturday night. Putting you on the list.' Again, he took a break between each statement, as if patiently trying to jog the memory of an amnesiac. His brilliant blue eyes flashed coldly at Carolyn, reminding her of a mentholated flame. Chilling, yet oddly mesmerising.

'There's no way I'm going to that club.'

'You go to clubs all the time,' Harry sighed dramatically.

'For work,' she explained. 'That's different.' When she went for the station, she was Stormy Winters. She'd never go as Carolyn. Why didn't Harry understand that? Why was he pressing this issue?

'He likes you. It was obvious. You should go see him play. You can't stay home moping.'

'I wasn't moping. I was . . .' Well, she couldn't really answer that one. She was preparing for a night of listening in on her roommate, and although she'd planned on telling him only days before, now it was something she just wasn't about to confess to.

'I'll go with you.'

Carolyn refused to listen. Instead, she walked down the hall to the bathroom. Harry was unconcerned with politeness. He followed her into the tiny room and sat on the edge of the tub, watching her, studying her. When she met his eyes in the mirror, Carolyn realised that he was looking at her from a professional angle,

217

head tilted, as if trying to figure out what he'd do with the blank canvas of her face. She'd seen him with that look before, but it wasn't going to work with her.

'He likes you, Carolyn,' Harry said forcefully. Then he shook his head. 'It's been so long since you went out that you don't remember what guys look like when they flirt.'

Harry was wrong on that. Carolyn remembered. She knew the feeling she got in the bottom of her stomach whenever Zach smiled at her – a flurry of excitement she hadn't felt in ages. Not since before Steven. Tears blurred her vision, and she suddenly couldn't see anything but a wash of colour as she buried her face in one of Dahlia's bright red washcloths.

'You're going to that club,' Harry said, his voice holding a tone she'd never heard before from him, but she recognised easily from herself. Stubborn determination. 'You're going,' he repeated, 'and I'm going to make you up.'

Harry's work had been featured on the covers of all of the hip magazines. His books were best-sellers, the latest one a coffee-table photograph book filled with models made up to look like movie stars of another era. But he'd never managed a transformation like the one he did with Carolyn. He started with her hair, turning her wash-and-wear style into a masterpiece, a sleek mane that perfectly framed her face.

'*Voila*,' Harry said, obviously pleased with his own work. Carolyn stared at her reflection, unused to wearing her hair down.

'You like?' Harry asked, when she remained silent.

Carolyn nodded, and she felt a wave of excitement at what else would happen this evening. How might Harry further transform her? She was quick to find out. At his insistence, the two went into Dahlia's bedroom, where Harry was sure he'd find all the cosmetics required to turn her from an ugly duckling into a swan.

'I don't know,' Carolyn protested under her breath. 'I don't think I can –'

'I'm going with you,' he repeated forcefully. 'It's not like you're Cinderella, sent out to the ball all alone, except for your dog, a pumpkin, and some mice. What kind of a mean trick is that? I'll be standing right next to you, holding your hand, doing your touch-ups. You'll be ready for that close-up all night long.'

This said, he came around to perch on the edge of Dahlia's frilly vanity, facing Carolyn and making her meet his eyes. He took one of her hands between both of his, holding steady. 'It won't be scary if I'm there,' he assured her. When he let go of her hand, he rolled back his sleeves, just the edges, but enough so that Carolyn could see the scars – thin bands of faded red that criss-crossed the insides of both of his slender wrists. He caught her looking, but didn't stop rummaging through Dahlia's toys.

'You know about my "incident", don't you?' he asked, his voice utterly casual.

Carolyn didn't. Dahlia had been a true pal to Harry. She'd never shared this particular secret with Carolyn. As Carolyn shook her head, she realised that she was more impressed with Dahlia sometimes by the things she didn't do or didn't say. Harry shrugged, as if it was all in the past, then muttered to himself about blushes, chiding Dahlia for not having the colour he wanted to use, something called 'Tawny Sunset'.

'It was a long time ago,' he said, 'before I was the worldly wise and infinitely stable creature you see before you today. Usually at work, I wear long sleeves. When I go out, I cover up easily with bracelets. Nobody ever notices.'

Carolyn smiled, but it was all in her lips, not in her eyes. She thought about the type of pain Harry must have been going through to try and take his own life. Whatever it was that drove him to that black point, she was glad he hadn't succeeded. When he looked up and saw that she was still staring at his wrists, he said kindly, 'I understand fear, kiddo. I've been there.'

Now, Carolyn looked into the mirror, locking on her own reflected gaze.

Fear, she thought. Is that what this is all about?

Steven hadn't really known her. When she closed her eyes as Harry painted on the eye shadow, she could see each step of that night, each frame as if it happened only yesterday.

Harry said, 'Tell me about it, Carolyn. If you do, it will go away.'

She opened her eyes, surprised.

'I swear. The more people I told about my situation, the less I could understand why I'd even tried it. After a while, I couldn't even remember how bad I'd felt. It was like I was someone else back then. When I think about it now, I feel as if I'm remembering somebody else's past. Some poor sucker who was actually going to off himself when a romance didn't work out. Can you believe it? Me? Distraught over some boy?' He laughed because they both knew that generally he *was* distraught over some boy – but never seriously.

Now he paused to blow a bit of blush from the puff of a round, black make-up brush. 'Close your eyes again,' he said.

Carolyn remembered the night perfectly. After doing her show on the college radio station, she'd said good-bye to the station manager and started walking down the hill towards the dorms from the student union. There was a space between two buildings, and that's where Steven had stood, watching. When she got close enough, he'd called out to her. Just her name.

'Dahlia told me that someone was obsessed with you,' Harry said when Carolyn didn't offer any information, and Carolyn opened her eyes again as he now brushed a cinnamon-coloured mascara on to her lashes. The feeling of the lengthening liquid was alien, and she

220

blinked rapidly, creating racoon-like smears so that Harry had to start again.

Obsessed.

Carolyn had looked up, seen who it was, and walked towards him. Steven had actually waved at her, a friendly 'come here' sort of gesture. She'd always felt a little sorry for him. He was cute, in a nerdy way, but such a loner. She had tried to be his friend, to give him an outlet, a girl to talk to.

'Hey, Carolyn,' he'd called, as she got closer. 'Come over here a second.'

The space where he stood was dark, in shadows, and she had felt the slightest pull of fear inside of her as she took a step away from the well-lit walkway and towards where he stood. But it was just Steven. Nothing to be afraid of here.

'Purse your lips,' Harry said, demonstrating for Carolyn what he wanted her to do. When Harry did it, his mouth looked perfectly feminine. He seemed much more at ease wearing lipstick than Carolyn ever would. Yet she followed the instruction, still seeing that night in her mind.

The next part of the movie was blurry, out of focus. Steven got close enough to grab her and he slashed out at her with something sharp and silver. Later, the police told her that he'd used a huge kitchen knife. He'd been carrying it in a home-made sheath for weeks, watching her movements, waiting for the right time. He slashed once, and she actually looked to him for protection. Something hurt, hot like fire, but she didn't link the pain to him. How could her friend be capable of hurting her? It wasn't possible. At least, not until she saw his eyes. They were focused on her, watching intently, and the silver blade cut out at her again, this time connecting with her shoulder. She screamed. She knew she did. But it was like a dream, where she was trying to talk, trying to beg him not to hurt her, trying to call for help, all at once. Instead of a massive, Fay Wray type of shout, her voice was garbled, useless.

Where were the rest of the students? The 40,000 kids who made up the college body? College campuses can be surprisingly deserted late on Sunday nights. Especially the Sundays before a holiday. Three-day weekends mean ski trips or drunken ventures to Palm Springs.

Why had she gone to him, gone to this no-man's land between the two huge lecture halls? How had he planned it so well, catching her when the campus was practically abandoned?

She'd been running since high school, and at some point, some burst of energy helped her untangle herself from him and sprint back on to the lit walkway, screaming, until a security guard heard her and caught her in his arms as she flailed down the hill. He had carried her to the medical centre around the corner.

Steven was gone by the time she was coherent enough for the doctors to understand what she was telling them. But they found him easily enough, barricaded in his apartment, naked, and one of the police officers told her later what it was like to take Steven away.

'He didn't struggle,' the man said, 'but he wanted to tell us why he had done it. Insisted that we listen. At first, we were just concerned with getting him out of the place, worried he'd pick up one of those little paring knives and slice his wrists. But over and over he asked if he could tell us. My partner wanted to know if you were an ex-girlfriend. I mean, the pictures he had of you framed and displayed around the apartment didn't look like the types of photos that psychos generally take. They weren't the kind taken with a telephoto lens. They looked like nice family-style pictures. The kind you would give to a boyfriend.'

Carolyn shuddered when he'd said that. Several of her friends had been robbed in the months before Steven got her. Nothing big had been taken. A little money. Some jewellery. And their photos. They realised later that all the pictures were ones that Carolyn was in.

* * *

Harry said, 'OK, darling, you're finished. You can look now.' Carolyn turned to the mirror and saw. Harry's eyes shined behind her, as if he was going to cry.

'You're beautiful,' he said. He was right. She was. 'You know you are, anyway, don't you?' he asked, sounding concerned. 'Even without all this shit.'

She couldn't believe it. She brought her hand up to stroke her hair, but he caught her, not willing to let her mess with his look. 'You're beautiful, anyway,' he said again. 'I just helped bring it up to the surface.'

Melody had her panties off and her feet up near her ears. It was an awkward position for anything other than getting fucked. But that was OK, because that's exactly what she was doing. Getting fucked by Zorg. If Zach wouldn't make love to her, then she was forced to go elsewhere. And she'd always liked a good fuck before a show. Something to release the tension.

'Come on, baby,' she purred. 'Do me harder.'

She knew that some people liked to save the energy, conserve it before going up on stage. Freddy, for one, never made love until after a gig. He was worried that he'd simply want to curl up on the floor and go to sleep. But Melody found that doing it made her even more wired. When she hit the drums, she was invigorated, and a hot, sweaty screw session ahead of time revved her up even more.

Because Zorg wasn't much of a talker, they hadn't ever lost themselves in sweet nothings afterwards. With his shaved head and starkly structured face, he showed no signs of softness or weakness. No feminine side interested in cuddling and caressing. Fine with Melody. As long as his cock was as hard as his expression, she didn't need to mix words with him.

Still, he made up for his silence with his moves. Hard and powerful, he took her to the edge of orgasm several times before helping her over it. His bareback cock slid in her juices, slamming to the hilt so that his balls slapped against her. Right before he came, he slid one hand along her throat, pressing there lightly, as if to feel her pulse beneath his fingertips. That made her come. The power of it; the fact that he was in control.

She climaxed hard, and as she came she thought of Zach and wished, more than anything else, that it was his cock inside her, his hands caressing her, his lips against her ear, whispering her name.

What was Dahlia up to now?

Jason just didn't get it. She wanted to see him, then she didn't. She wanted to fuck him with another guy in her bed, then for two days she wouldn't return his calls. He got the feeling that she was the type of person who got bored easily.

The fucking cunt.

He still wanted her, though. Even after she'd turned out to be exactly the type of aloof and difficult girl he'd pegged her for from the first sight. That didn't make it any less difficult to stop thinking about her, to stop wanting her.

Sighing, he left another message on her machine, a light-hearted query about whether she would meet him for lunch the next day. Or the day after. Didn't he sound desperate? He hated himself for getting like this. It was why he had stopped caring so long ago.

If only he could feel that same hard-hearted way again.

Chapter Twenty-One

*T*wo Moons was located on a side street, near the very end of Melrose Avenue, directly off Santa Monica Boulevard. The club was located in a two-storey black building with a bright gold neon sign out front. During the day it didn't look like much more than a hulking warehouse. But at night a transformation took place. The yellow neon magically flickered over the line of people waiting to get inside, the illumination turning their faces golden in the darkness.

There was already a crowd outside, waiting to get in, and all of the parking spaces in the back lot were taken. Harry wasn't concerned in the slightest. He simply manoeuvred his little black Morris Minor until he'd gotten it situated illegally on the curb. It was a parking ticket waiting to happen.

'Don't worry,' Harry said when Carolyn raised her eyebrows at the parking job. 'I know all the meter maids in this neighbourhood.' That made sense. Harry knew everyone. And, more importantly, everyone knew Harry.

Although she would have been more comfortable taking her place at the end of the line, Carolyn let Harry press them through the crowd to the burly bouncer holding a sheet. While they waited behind another couple for their turn to try and get in free, Carolyn looked at the various outfits on the girls in line behind them – short halter-style dresses worn over baby T-shirts. Tight black skirts and tops made of a shiny material. Harry noticed her staring at the women, and he shook his head. 'You look better than all of them put together,' he whispered kindly.

At the front of the line, the bouncer looked them over for only a millisecond before giving Harry a broad smile. 'On the list tonight, huh, doll?' he asked, his voice almost a falsetto, which was strange to hear from a man so big.

'Yeah, Dameron,' Harry said, then nudged Carolyn to speak up. In a tiny, unrecognisable voice, she heard herself say, 'Carolyn Winters.'

'Stormy,' Harry said, pointing to the place where her name appeared. Dameron made a check-mark, ignored their IDs, and let them through. Before she could put her ID away, Harry reached for it. On her driver's licence, Carolyn was wearing her heavy frames, no make-up, and a severe ponytail – very different from the smouldering seductress standing on the steps.

Inside Moons, she felt instantly more at ease. Like most LA clubs, it was dark, like the inside of a bat cave. It would have been helpful to be bats, Carolyn thought. At least then they would have had some sort of sonar abilities to find where they wanted to go and avoid bumping into people, tables and the odd set of stairs.

Holding hands tightly so that they wouldn't be separated by the throng, Harry and Carolyn made their way up to the second floor to find a place by the wooden railing. From there, they both scanned the rowdy audience from above, Carolyn surreptitiously slipping her specs on, even though Harry didn't want her to muss her make-up. She just couldn't see a thing without them. Carolyn knew that Harry was looking for young blood – as always. And she was looking for Zach.

'He'll be backstage, getting ready,' Harry said, loud enough to be heard over the bad music being blasted at them from a set of gigantic speakers. He didn't look over at Carolyn as he spoke, obviously trying to make eye contact with a studly blond sun god in the arena below. The muscled Adonis apparently felt Harry's eyes on him and glanced upwards. He winked at Harry, and Carolyn was surprised when her date for the evening stayed at her side rather than going down to make himself better acquainted. It was against Harry's nature not to walk down the stairs and continue to flirt, or at least to get a phone number for a post-concert connection.

'Go on,' Carolyn said, now feeling much more comfortable than she had earlier in the evening. She had been to concerts like this thousands of times. The only difference was that she wasn't at Moons in a DJ capacity. She was here as an actual member of the audience. Instead of abandoning her, Harry turned and looked directly into her eyes. 'He's warming up in the dressing room. He'll be on stage in a minute. Stop touching your face.'

Carolyn couldn't help herself from scanning the crowd anyway. Harry grabbed hold of one of her hands and held it tightly as the room continued to fill up. Then the lights dimmed even more until the room was almost black and the band took the stage. For a moment, Carolyn actually forgot where she was. Zach was transcendent, one of those performers who changed when he got on the stage. A light seemed to emanate from him as he grabbed hold of the microphone and started to sing. And then, it was as if he was singing directly to her, giving a private concert for her own listening pleasure:

> Back-stabbing baby keeps me up 'til sunlight
> Streams across our empty bed.
> Back-stabbing baby fills my mind with worry,
> While she's fucking with my head.
>
> I am not the one you're missing.
> Who is it you're out there kissing?

Don't forget how much I loved you.
Baby, be true.

'Wow, he looks different on stage,' Harry whispered.

She nodded because she couldn't talk. Zach had the aura that only the really great rock 'n' rollers have: Jim Morrison at his prime in leather pants and no shirt; Mick Jagger in body-hugging T-shirts and spidery black leggings; Bowie, perfection at each stage of his career. Dressed less noticeably in faded jeans and a white tank-top, Zach's hair was loose, a gold wave waterfalling over his shoulders. He had a braided leather choker around his neck. It was all he needed. His music dressed him up and wrapped him around with a mystique that made the girls in the front row squeal.

Looking at him, Carolyn found that she couldn't manage to turn off the professional side of herself. The appraiser. In her mind, she knew that he was going to be famous. Someday, there would be arenas of people coming to watch him. She stared as he blended one song into the next, then gripped into Harry's hand so hard that he tried to extract himself from her claws.

She and Harry stayed through the main band, Magic, a nothing outfit that was going nowhere fast. Carolyn mentally predicted the reviews that would be written about the show. 'Switch the headliner and the warm-up band,' Michael Evan Smith from the *View* would undoubtedly write. 'Look out for the illustrious Zachary Modine and Zoom Box.'

When the houselights came on, a group of girls were still there in the front, armed with phone numbers written on slips of paper that they handed to the roadies. One even held a tiny teddy bear dressed in a leather jacket, obviously wanting to give it to one of the musicians.

'Get this to Zachary Modine,' a pretty brunette begged. Harry, who had found his golden boy from downstairs, didn't mind the fact that Carolyn wanted to wait. It gave him time to engage in small talk with this latest object of lust in his life. The three of them sat on the balcony as the rest of the crowd filtered outside or to the bar. Carolyn wanted to know if the gorgeous girl downstairs, or any of her girlfriends, would be invited backstage.

When a beefy roadie nodded to the teenyboppers, Carolyn reached for Harry's hand and they walked towards the stairs.

'You don't know that she's going to get to see him. Lots of girls will do anybody backstage.'

But then, as if he had actually heard the words, the roadie looked up at them.

'Stormy?' he called out.

Carolyn nodded. The man smiled and waved them backstage.

A warm rush flooded through Carolyn's body. When had she last been so on edge about seeing a guy? That was a silly question. It had been over six years. She knew that without thinking hard.

'This way,' Harry said, sounding as excited as she felt.

Just as they approached the dressing-room door, it opened, and Melody Jones appeared, closing the door behind her. The drummer was already cleaned up after sweating her ass off during the show, now clad in head-to-toe red leather, boots, pants, and a jacket that was only zipped halfway up, revealing her pale skin beneath and the lush curve of her breasts. She looked like the human equivalent of a Pashmina shawl, luxurious and soft, and Carolyn could easily envision her with her limbs wrapped around Zachary.

'So glad you could make it, Stormy,' Melody purred. 'Zach said you were coming. That you might do another piece on us.'

Things clicked into place for Carolyn. Had she only been invited as a DJ? Had Zachary been teasing her this entire time with his requests, calling her at the station only in hopes of getting more air time? Her heart fell, but she didn't let it show in her face. Instead, she slid into the Stormy role, climbing inside as if it were a pair of worn-in jeans.

'You never know,' she said, smiling her fake, radio smile that put a sound of warm, rich pleasure in her voice. There was a difference when you smiled. Listeners could tell.

Melody grinned at her. 'Come on,' she said, slipping into a sexy drawl. 'We were good. Admit it.'

'That's why I'm here,' Carolyn said, keeping the same stupid fake grin on her face. 'Checking you guys out.'

'Did you want to see Zach?' Melody asked. 'I can just check, to make sure he's ... decent.' The way she said the words made Carolyn think that she'd just been fucking him, and from the way Melody was speaking, languid and relaxed, in control, it sounded as if she'd won. But Carolyn had never really been competing, had she?

'That's OK,' Carolyn said. 'Just thank him for getting me on the list, if you would.' She could get on any list she wanted. That's not why she'd come here at all.

'There's a party –' Melody started, and she said it in exactly the same tone of voice that Dahlia used when she knew Carolyn wasn't going to do something. That sympathetic manner that made Carolyn want to kick something. Instead, she shook her head. 'Harry and I have plans,' she lied. Then before she was forced to say anything else, she made her way back down the stairs. Distraught, she moved more quickly now, pulling Harry out of the club after her.

As soon as they were in motion, Harry informed her, 'We're not going home.'

'No?' Tears streaked her make-up, and Harry again warned her not to touch her face, that he'd take care of it when they got there. It was obvious that he didn't like his masterpiece getting all smudged.

'Get where?' Carolyn asked, her voice hoarse.

'Sammy's Mango Hut. We're going to get you drunk.'

* * *

Melody had won. At least, that's what she thought as she watched Zach moping backstage after the show, not interested at all in the party or any of the girls who had snuck their way back to see him. Interested in nothing but staring forlornly at the door. When Melody asked him what was wrong, he just shook his head.

'You waiting for Stormy?'

He gave her a look, and the disgust in his eyes momentarily froze her. But she forced herself to go on speaking. 'She's not interested, Zach. She's just playing with you.' As she spoke, she came closer to where he sat on a leather stool, then straddled him, her body facing his, and kissed him hard before he could stop her.

'You're the one who's playing,' he said, roughly pushing her away from him. 'I know what you've been doing. Up to your old tricks again. We're not going to get back together, Mel. It just isn't going to happen.'

She shrugged as if she didn't know what he was talking about. As if she didn't want to get back with him, either. But her act fooled neither one of them.

'I know about you and Zorg, and I know about you and the others. And I'm guessing that the reason Carolyn isn't here has something to do with you. Let me spell this out, Melody. If you don't back the fuck off then I'm going to quit the band. It'll be you and Freddy and Roger, having one big fuck fest. And –' He paused and got close to her face so that she could see the hatred in his eyes '– if you ever try to kiss me again, let me promise you, it'll be the last thing you ever do with that filthy tongue of yours.'

Before Melody could say anything else, he was gone.

At Sammy's, for the first time ever, the handsome bartender did a double-take when Carolyn sat down. She could almost hear the hinges in his neck move as he swung around to look at her. Although she still felt lousy, Chester's attention managed to lift her spirits. Usually, he fawned only for Dahlia, making sure that she had everything she needed, all the accoutrements that went with her infamous shot of golden-hued tequila. When Carolyn placed her order, Chester generally set the beer bottle down, not even bothering to offer up a glass. For Dahlia, he flirted in the most obnoxious of ways.

Carolyn found that flirting less undesirable now that it was aimed in her direction. Chester, breaking her thoughts, said, 'What would you – Wow!' Obviously realising it was her in mid-sentence.

Harry grinned broadly. This reaction was caused by his own magic fingers, his ability to trick the eye with well-placed cosmetics. He stood at Carolyn's side, beaming, like Dr Frankenstein, proud of his monster.

'She'd like a shot of tequila,' Harry ordered for her. 'And so would I.'

While Harry went to the men's room to 'freshen up', Carolyn caught a flicker of her reflection in the mirror behind the bar. Was the pretty girl really her? The pale-skinned brunette with the shining eyes. Could a little mascara and lipgloss make that much difference? Apparently so. Chester moved to block her reflection, coming in for a closer look.

'I can't believe –' he said, but stopped himself. Although young, he knew a lot about women and he didn't want to offend her with his compliments. If he said he couldn't believe how much better she looked, wouldn't that be the same thing as telling her she looked hideous before?

'You look so different,' Chester said softly. 'Why –'

'Harry and I were playing around with Dahlia's cosmetics.'

'Just girls having fun,' Harry added, returning from the men's room. 'You know how it is. You put on a little blusher and you just can't stop.' He widened his eyes dramatically at Chester, who seemed to find the open flirtation a bit disconcerting. Harry knew exactly how to interact with straight men. A little batting of the eyelashes, if only to let them know what they were missing by not opening themselves up to his game.

232

'You look real nice,' Chester said, settling on a mid-way statement. 'I didn't recognise you right off.' The tequila bottle came out. Then the lime. Then the salt. Then the inevitable question.

'Body shot?'

Carolyn could feel something fluttering in her chest, a feeling that spread through her body to her fingertips. It was the way she had felt at a high-school dance when a cute boy had looked her way.

'Thanks.' She grinned, just like Dahlia did, but unlike Dahlia, Carolyn didn't shake her head no. Chester waited, as if he thought she might be teasing him. But she wasn't. This was what normal people did when they went out and drank. They had fun. They were risqué. It had been years since Carolyn had let herself feel like this, on the verge of being out of control without any true danger. Now was the time to start. With the mask of Harry's make-up on her face, she could do what Dahlia liked to do: pretend to be someone else.

And who was she this evening? Simple answer to a stupid question. She was Dahlia. Because Dahlia always got what she wanted.

'Really?' Chester asked.

'I've never done one before,' she confessed, toying with a strand of hair in the way that Dahlia liked to do. Harry didn't even bother her for touching his master-piece. He seemed to understand that she was being a girl. That she was interacting, and that this was a good thing. 'What do I have to do?'

Chester moved more quickly than Carolyn had ever seen him: salt on the back of his tanned hand, lime face-out in his boyish grin. He motioned with his head for her to down the shot. She did, with only the slightest of shudders, a metallic flavour lingering for a moment on the back of her tongue. Then, when he put out his hand, she licked off the salt, savouring the way his skin tasted beneath it. He leaned forward, over the bar, offering her the lime wedge from between his lips. She sucked the juice from it and then collapsed back against the chair, laughing. Chester spat out the lime and laughed, too. He seemed pleased with himself, and a little bit giddy.

For another moment, Chester leaned forward towards her, over the bar, so close that she could smell the subtle scent of his spicy aftershave. He tilted his head to the side, admiring her from this distance and seeming pleased with what he saw. Then he whispered, 'Next time, let's do that without the lime.'

Carolyn shifted on the bar seat, understanding what he meant. He wanted to kiss her. Did she want to kiss him back? He was cute. Even Dahlia had said that. Cute, in a dishevelled, surfer-boy kind of way. And the women who came to the bar, like the one on the end in a sapphire blue halter dress who was shooting daggers at her, definitely flirted with him. Maybe she should give in. Get over her sexual anorexia.

Forget Zachary.

Dahlia arrived with her date at this precise moment. She looked at Chester, with his wild grin, then at Carolyn, leaning helpless against the wooden railing of the chair.

Harry mouthed, 'Body shot,' by way of explanation, but Dahlia already seemed to understand. She took another glance at Carolyn, and a gaze passed between the roommates. *You play at being me,* Carolyn seemed to say with her expression, *and I can play at being you. Fair is fucking fair.*

For a moment, Dahlia didn't move, didn't say a word. Marlon, apparently feeling the tension in the air but not understanding it, asked, 'Isn't that your roommate?' and Dahlia nodded, but still didn't seem completely sure that it was Carolyn.

Harry piped in next, asking, 'Doesn't she look great?'

When Carolyn glanced up at her roommate, she couldn't immediately translate the expression on Dahlia's face: displeased; uncomfortable. Then she got it. Chester was looking at her, paying attention to her instead of Dahlia. Her roommate was actually jealous. First time ever.

Carolyn tilted her head, acting more drunk than she actually was. 'Next one's on me,' she offered.

Dahlia, always quick to recover, settled herself on the open stool next to Carolyn's. She took her time, artfully arranging her clothes, crossing her legs and then sliding the hem of her mini-skirt a tiny bit higher on her thigh. This drew the approving stare of a man approaching the bar, waiting to order.

'That'd bring a crowd,' Dahlia finally said. Marlon sat himself on the other side of her. He seemed captivated by the concept as well.

Chester, understanding the dare, quickly cut another wedge of lime, handed over the salt shaker, and poured a fresh shot. It was easy to tell from his expression that he thought he'd died and gone to heaven. First, he'd found a girl willing to do a body shot with him. Now, his favourite patron was going to kiss a girl in front of him. Tonight would be ripe with fantasies that could take him through future slow times. Memories that would accompany his hand on solo nights.

Carolyn sprinkled the salt on the back of her wrist and got the lime ready between her lips. The citrus flavour was sharp and brought her back to reality. Was this really going to happen? Dahlia took her time. She made sure the men in the bar were very aware of the scene they were about to be given. Harry, always the showman, started a steady drumbeat with his fingertips on the counter, setting the mood. Girls kissing didn't affect his own libido, but the excitement that seemed to swirl all around their little fivesome was heady, none the less. As intoxicating as the tequila.

With finesse, Dahlia swallowed the golden liquid, then licked the salt from the back of Carolyn's hand. Her tongue sent a pulse of heat radiating through Carolyn's body. It felt like a feline's tongue, a hungry cat, lapping at her. The back of her neck, beneath her hair, felt warm and wet, and the place between her legs suddenly woke up as waves of anticipation rolled through her. She knew instantly what it would feel like to make love to

Dahlia, to climb on to her roommate's animal-print satin sheets and slide into a silky 69.

Carolyn held perfectly still, looking into Dahlia's eyes, waiting with her breath held for what was to come. Dahlia, like a trained actress controlling a scene, moved in for the kiss.

Or the kill.

She wasn't at home. He'd looked in the windows and banged on the door until her dog, Terrie, had started barking ferociously inside.

Why hadn't he seen what was going on before? Why hadn't he known that Melody wouldn't stop at simply phoning in song requests? The girl had always been hardcore; demented when she set her sights on something. He'd let himself believe that she was just playing. The fact that she was so obviously still after him should have alerted him to what she was up to.

Carolyn must be out somewhere with her drag-queen friend, and he hadn't been able to explain. There wasn't going to be any more of this confusion between them. He assured himself of that. If he had to wait all night on her doorstep, that was exactly what he would do.

Sticking his hands in the deep pockets of his well-worn leather jacket, Zachary took up position on Carolyn's mat and got ready for a potentially long, lonely night.

There was actually a round of applause from the customers when the women parted. Carolyn dropped the lime wedge into her hand and blushed, feeling all those eyes on her: Harry's eyes, Chester's eyes, Marlon's eyes. She couldn't believe this was her, at the bar, kissing Dahlia. Couldn't believe that a night which had started with her planning on eavesdropping was ending like this.

Thanks to Harry, she thought. He was the one, her fairy godfather, who had taken her by the hand and led her, like Cinderella, into a whole new world. Now she understood a little bit better why Dahlia always wanted to get dressed and go out. You never knew what would happen. That was exciting, energising, a reason to enjoy life.

But the night wasn't actually over.

What was going to happen next?

She looked into Dahlia's eyes, but got no answers there. Dahlia was already motioning to Chester that she wanted another shot, and the way she was moving on the bar stool made Carolyn think that she was putting on a show for Marlon and had dismissed the kiss already. Something juvenile but fun. A little bit of theatre in an otherwise normal evening.

Next, Carolyn looked over at Harry. He seemed pleased with the way things had progressed. He was now standing by the jukebox, arguing in a flirtatious way with a young man wearing an open Hawaiian shirt. 'It's "take your pants off",' Carolyn heard Harry say. 'I know it. That's what she says.'

The man Harry was talking with disagreed, but he looked as if he might be ready to take his own pants off if the conversation went on long enough. To her right, Marlon and Dahlia were having a discussion about the movie they had seen. Marlon was trying to include Carolyn, every few seconds nodding to her so that she would feel a part of their little group. Dahlia didn't seem to mind this, but she wasn't actively directing her comments to her roommate.

Carolyn herself felt as if she were floating. She rarely did tequila shots, so she knew the feeling was probably from the alcohol. But it might also have come from the way Chester continued to smile at her whenever he walked by. He kept raising up one eyebrow at her and giving her a sexy little smirk, as if he knew her better than anyone else did.

As if they shared some sort of secret bond.

Carolyn could hear Harry move on to another one of his misheard lyrics. She understood now that he was being intentionally obtuse, if only to talk sex with his new friend. 'Let's ask Carolyn,' he finally said. 'She's a DJ. She'll know.' But Carolyn wasn't in the mood to play judge. So, as Harry made his way towards her with his new friend, she slipped off the bar stool and found her way to the ladies room.

At least, she almost found it, but Chester stopped her.

'Do you want to do another?'

Carolyn looked at Chester, confused.

'Body shot?' he asked, and she saw that he was holding a shot of tequila in one hand, a lime in the other.

'Two's my limit.'

They were in the hallway behind the bar, a dark wooden corridor lined with black and white photographs from beach movies: Gidget. Annette and Frankie. Elvis doing some make-believe surf moves on a soundstage filled with sand.

Carolyn thought for a moment about what Dahlia would do in this situation. If she were really going to pretend to be her roommate, than she might as well take it to the limits. Realising immediately, she grinned in what felt like a suggestive way. 'But why don't you do that one?' She could hear the way her voice sounded in her ears. Sexy. Husky. Not like her at all, except when she was on air.

'I'm working,' Chester said, but he didn't sound totally sure. Or, rather, he sounded as if she might be able to convince him otherwise. Like Harry's new date. Convince me that it's 'take your pants off' and I'll believe you.

'I won't tell,' she promised, reaching for the sliver of lime.

Chester nodded, but he didn't hand over the wedge of fruit. Instead, he downed the shot in a single swallow, then pulled Carolyn close to his body and kissed her. She could feel his strong chest against hers, his muscular arms holding her close. She could taste the flavour of the smooth, expensive tequila on his tongue. For a moment, she closed her eyes and let herself remember what excitement was like. The flush of pleasure that vibrated throughout her body as Chester pulled her bottom lip into his mouth and bit it gently before releasing her.

Bite me, she thought. Bite me, hard.

Only then was she aware that it was just the two of them in the hall. That she didn't really know Chester, and that the music from the jukebox was blaring so loudly other people might not hear her if she decided to call for help. She pulled out of his embrace, her face flushed, heart pounding. Her eyes must have told Chester of her concern because he backed away.

'I'm sorry,' he said, confusion on his handsome face.

No, it was fine. Her heart was beating faster than normal, but that was because she was turned on. She took a step back towards him, shaking her head. 'I wanted it,' she said, her voice low, coming even closer so she wouldn't have to yell. 'And I'd like another . . . this time without the liquor.'

Now he smiled, and his arms came around her again, and she could feel his hard-on throbbing with promise against her thigh. As usual, Harry was right. It was all going to work out. She just had to have faith, and to take a step in a positive direction. This evening, that direction was the ladies' room, one step after Chester.

Dahlia was getting bored with Marlon. Anyone else would have seen her kiss with Carolyn for what it was. An invitation. Look at me, she was saying. I can kiss women. I can kiss men. What do you want to do about it?

Marlon didn't seem to want to do anything. Dante would have understood immediately, and for a moment she thought of calling his cell and ditching Marlon right there. Because Dante would have taken one look at the two women together and whispered something sexy to her. Perhaps he would have taken it on himself to invite Carolyn to join them.

Did she want that? She wasn't altogether sure. But she

239

did know one thing. Static disgusted her. And she was feeling static with Marlon. Yes, he was handsome. And, yes, he'd figured out that she liked playing dirty and had been willing to go along with everything so far, including her threesome with Jason. But what else did he have going for him?

It was time to take action – the only type of action that Dahlia knew how to handle. She had a wicked smile in her dark green eyes as she planned the next stage of her evening. Silently, she took Marlon's hand and led him from the bar.

Zach, tired of pacing the foyer and listening to Terrie barking inside the apartment, finally decided to go out again, looking for Carolyn. Maybe she would be down the block at the bar on the corner. Sammy's. He'd seen her and Dahlia enter the bar once before. Perhaps it was their hang-out. He'd look there, then come right back if he couldn't find her.

When Carolyn got home, she felt like a different person. There was Harry's magnificent transformation of her. A transformation that she felt on the inside as much as on the outside. And then, at the bar, there was the body shot and the kiss. And the rest of the kissing with Chester in the bathroom, before she'd put a stop to it.

Yes, he was sexy. And young. And suddenly into her. But she'd realised that being with him was not what she wanted. She wanted more, something deeper. If she were going to finally have sex again, to truly get over the past, then she wanted to do it right. She thought about the first time she'd ever made love, and she'd waited then, too. Not lost it in the back of some high-school boy's car, like Dahlia had, but waited until she was in a proper relationship, albeit one that didn't last much longer than the sex had.

All of these thoughts came jumbling through Carolyn's mind, helped along, she supposed, by the shots she'd done. Tequila had a way of affecting her that no other liquor did. Something in the burn of it; the way it seemed to make her very fingertips tingle. She spun around in the centre of the living room, feeling giddy and light headed, and that's when she heard the noise.

Dahlia, going at it once again.

Well, she was over Dahlia. She'd play-acted at being her roommate, and this had helped her to discover that there was nothing special about her. Not really. Her roommate was just a bunch of sexual tricks tied together with a fancy ribbon. Yes, the outside of the package was pretty. But what did Dahlia have inside if she kept having to pretend that she was someone else? Carolyn felt that she understood her now and that she could actually compete if she wanted to. Could even win. It was with relief that she realised she didn't need to listen any more.

But as she walked by the kitchen, she heard something that stopped her. Something that changed her mind and made her resolve – and her knees – weaken. Dahlia was calling out someone's name as she came. And she wasn't yelling for Joe. Or Marlon. Or Dante. Or Jason. She was moaning, 'Zach, oh, yes, Zachary.'

Zachary.

For a second, Carolyn was scared that she'd said it out loud, too. 'Zachary!' Her tone of voice accusatory. Tears started immediately, and she reached for the door handle to hold herself upright, feeling instantly transformed back into her old self. All the magic of the evening wearing off in a heartbeat.

Why? she wondered.

Slowly, Carolyn walked down the hall to her bedroom. Terrie, always believing that if she were home then she should be with him, pushed her door open with his head. He looked at her with those big, questioning brown eyes, and she petted him with one hand absentmindedly.

For a moment, she considered calling Harry, but he was probably out with the kid from Sammy's. Next to her phone was Dante's number. She picked up the receiver and dialled, and by the time he answered, her voice was normal sounding.

'Sorry it's so late.'

'Carolyn,' he said, knowing her voice instantly. It sounded as if he were smiling. 'It's not too late. I was writing. What's up?' She rocked herself on the bed, and as she did, the tears threatened to start again. 'What's wrong?' he asked into her silence. When she still didn't respond, he said, 'I'll be right there.'

Not the best idea. 'Dahlia's here,' she whispered. Then after a beat, 'There's someone over with her.'

'It's your house, too.'

She shook her head, but he couldn't see that. It was not Dahlia's fault that Zach had chosen her, and Carolyn was not ready to confront her with Dante.

'Tomorrow,' she whispered, hanging up the phone instead of listening to Dante's rationale. She was worried that he wanted to be with her to get back at Dahlia. It was way too confusing. But then, as she heard the noises start up again, she realised that she simply couldn't stay in the house.

Chapter Twenty-Two

'You stupid fucking bitch.'

Melody turned around, stunned. Zorg had followed her to Zachary's apartment. But more striking than that was the fact that he was actually speaking to her. The silent mountain could talk.

'You got to stop doing this crazy fucking shit.'

'What do you mean?' Melody asked, unconcerned with the obscenities. She spoke like a trucker, too. X-rated words didn't even register with her. 'Stop what?'

'This psycho stalking thing you're doing. It's fucking over between you and Zach. It doesn't matter whether he's with some other bitch or not. You need to get the fuck over it. Move on.'

So he'd been paying attention when she'd made those phone requests; understood what it had all been about. She'd assumed he was stupid because he was silent.

'What's it to you?' she managed to ask, staring into his surprisingly animated face. For the first time ever, he seemed alive to her. His eyes glowed with a fire that Melody found both frightening and strangely enticing.

'Come on, you're not that fucking thick, are you?' he asked, taking her by her slender wrist and leading her away from the window. 'It matters to me because I fucking love you, you fucking idiot.'

Melody couldn't believe it. Not only was he speaking, but he was speaking in words that she understood. Words that actually made sense. She let him lead her to his Indian motorcycle, let him put her arms around his waist, and felt transported as he drove her back to his place, everything changing for her in a heartbeat.

Marlon didn't have any idea who this Zachary person was or why Dahlia was calling out his name. The crazy girl never made any sense when it came to sex. First, she'd wanted him to call her by her roommate's name. Then she'd wanted him to dominate her. And then she'd cajoled him into the threesome with some other guy she was dating. All of these situations had turned him on, and he'd gone with it. As he was going with it now. Because the sex with her made him come harder than he ever had, so he didn't fight it. Simply lost himself in the moment, in the fantasy, inside her. Closed his eyes and let her call him anything she wanted to.

Dahlia didn't know why she was doing it at first. All she'd ever wanted was for her roommate to get back into the game of life. So why would she do something that would hurt her? Well, maybe it wouldn't. Maybe Carolyn would be forced into action and stop pussyfooting around. Just because Zach had a tough-talking ex-girlfriend didn't mean that Carolyn shouldn't fight a good fight.

Besides, it was fun. Pretending that Marlon was the hot musician from upstairs made the evening more spectacular than Dahlia had imagined. And fun was always very important to Dahlia.

For the first time, Carolyn didn't bother to listen; didn't even stop long enough to think how it might have happened. She simply assumed that Dahlia must have ditched Marlon and run into Zach back at the apartment and then just been herself. How had Carolyn thought she could compete with that? Without even knowing where she was going, she grabbed her keys and left the apartment. Adrenalin rushed through her. She didn't know what she wanted at all, except that she wanted to get drunk. Really drunk.

Although there were a plethora of cool bars lining Melrose, only several blocks from her house, she didn't go to any of them. She didn't want to try to blend in with the Hollywood crowd, looking for a good time. So, after a brief consideration of her options, she ended up at the grocery store on Melrose and Vine, purchasing a large bottle of tequila. She ignored the comments of the pimply faced checker who asked if she were having a party.

Sure she was. A solo party. She opened the bottle and drank heartily while standing in the parking lot. Then she walked back to her apartment with one goal on her mind: to work on drinking herself into oblivion. She'd drained a quarter of the bottle within two blocks. The burn of it felt good. Forget the lime chaser. The salt from a shaker. She didn't have anyone's hand to lick now. Didn't have someone's mouth to suck the lime from.

Back at her apartment, with great effort, she tried to make the keys work in the door, but failed and dropped them. As she bent to pick them up, the foyer door opened. Zach stood inside, several daisies in one hand that Carolyn recognised as having been plucked from one of the neighbour's gardens.

'Mrs Zimmerman is going to be pissed,' she slurred. 'She'll call the cops on you. She's done it before.'

'I was stealthy,' he said. 'She'll never know.'

'You want to give them to Dahlia? I'm sure she's still inside.'

'Why would I care what Dahlia's doing?'

Carolyn stared at him, confused. 'Don't you like her?'

'Of course I like her,' he said. 'I mean,' he stumbled, 'I guess I like her. I just really met her the one time.'

'One plus one,' Carolyn corrected.

Zach tilted his head at her.

'The one time in the hall, and the one time just now in her bed.'

'What are you talking about?' Zach asked, sounding totally confused.

Now Carolyn didn't know what to say. Was he the type of fuck 'em and leave 'em musician that she'd met so often? The kind of notch-on-his-guitar guy who made his way through the pretty girl circuit of Hollywood hangers-on? And if so, did he think he would be able to get next to her now that he'd successfully screwed her roommate?

'Look, I heard you,' Carolyn confessed, even though it brought a flush to her cheeks. He didn't have to know about her listening. Eavesdropping. She could have simply heard in passing.

Zach looked even more confused than he had before. 'I know you did. I saw you at the club with your friend Harry.' Now he stared at her, as if she might be on some sort of drug. His gaze wandered down to her hand, which still held the tequila bottle by the neck. He nodded, as if this bit of information was helping him to put the puzzle pieces together.

'No,' Carolyn said, ignoring the fact that he thought she was drunk. He was right about that. She was drunk. But that's not what this discussion was about. Still, was he cruel enough to make her spell it out?

'I heard you and Dahlia.' She stared at him, pointedly, waiting.

He gave her a look that she read as: 'Carolyn, I really don't know what you're talking about.'

'Fucking,' she said, and now Zach took a step back and started laughing. He laughed so hard that he had to sit down on the edge of the stairs. Looking up at her, still half-giggling, he said, 'Her? You're kidding, right? You *have* to be kidding.'

She didn't know what to say, and Zach seemed to understand that. Standing again, he took her hand and led her into the entryway. 'Come on,' he said. 'I was going to ask you up to my apartment to talk about

Melody and explain that we really are through, that she's been pulling a head trip on you. I thought we might have a drink together, but I can tell now that you've –' He paused '– you've had a couple. So maybe you'd like to come up for a cup of coffee.'

Carolyn let herself be led away. Her mind was spinning. Was he lying to her? Was he that type of person?

By the time they'd climbed the stairs, with great difficulty because her feet wouldn't obey her mental commands, she thought she understood. Dahlia had been playing games. And, as usual, Carolyn had fallen for them.

Upstairs in Zach's apartment, Carolyn's buzz faded quickly. As she stood next to him in his kitchen, drinking the coffee he'd made for her, she started to get her bearings. Things were falling into place, suddenly making sense. And the most important thing that she understood was this – Zach wanted to have sex with her. Now.

He didn't rush her though. He simply eyed her, letting her make the first move. He seemed to understand that this experience was something totally unique for Carolyn. If Dahlia were in this same situation, it would be progressing differently. For once, that thought didn't bother her. She was tired of wishing she were Dahlia. Instead, she took a deep breath and let things happen. Let her arms fall open, welcoming Zach forward.

It had been so long, she was frightened for a second that she wouldn't know what to do. Then everything came back to her as Zach slowly and sensually lifted her dress, slid her panties down her thighs and slipped his middle finger between her lips to feel for wetness.

'Oh, you're ready,' he sighed, and it sounded beautiful the way he said it. Sounded hungry and excited, and she had a hard time believing for a moment that he was talking that way about her. Excited to be with her. Then, again, those thoughts dissipated, like smoke caught in one of the rotating fans over the bar at Sammy's, and she reached out to help him undo his slacks. This was easy. This was just how it was supposed to happen. She felt him spin her, so that her hands were against the cool wall, his warm body on hers from behind.

His cock between her legs was a welcomed intrusion. From the first pump of it inside her, all those good feelings came flooding back. In a flash, she remembered that *this* was why people had sex. The connection she felt to him, the pleasure.

'You're different tonight,' he whispered, his breath hot against her skin. He hadn't asked a question, so she didn't have to respond. Yet she felt like answering him.

'I'm different always,' she said, trying to explain that what he saw on the outside wasn't simply a reflection of the way she was on the inside.

He made a moan low in his throat. And then his hands worked their way up her body, touching her breasts through her dress, slipping into the opening and feeling her naked body, skin on skin. He murmured something to her, something that sounded like an apology. For what? For not getting her before? For not trying to see beneath the surface?

She found that she didn't care what he was saying, consumed, instead, by what he was doing. Zach knew how to make love, how to make it last, and he teased her, played with her, until her legs felt as if they would give out and she would melt into a sticky pool of pleasure.

'You're so good,' he said, surprising her. 'You feel so good on me.'

It was what she wanted to hear, and the words made her forget about eavesdropping on Dahlia. Made her forget that she was shy, that she hadn't had sex in years. That Steven had ruined it all for her.

And by forgetting, she found a peace inside herself that she'd believed was gone for ever. Her last thought before coming was that she was tired of being a pawn in

248

the game plan of Dahlia's life. Wasn't it about fucking time for her to become a player?

The next day all the rules changed once again.
But wasn't that to be expected in any game that Dahlia was a part of?

Part IV

'What a wicked game you play.'
Chris Isaak, 'Wicked Game'

Chapter Twenty-Three

When Carolyn woke up in Zach's bed, she couldn't keep the smile off her face. After having sex, she and Zach had fallen asleep together, like puppies curled up on the sofa. Early, they had woken up and gone out on the rooftop to talk some more. Or, *not* talk so much, but stay together, watching as the sun came up.

She was accustomed to being awake at odd hours, so as the sun rose and as she and Zach leaned against each other drinking more coffee, she found that she felt rested. Secure. Perfect. She felt even more perfect when he undressed her and made love to her again, under the morning sky, as the golden light shone down on their bodies. This time was slower and more careful, face to face. She put her arms around him, held him to her, saw that same energy in his eyes that he had when he was playing on stage.

'You like that?' he asked, and she remembered hearing the way Jason had asked the same question to Dahlia, following it up with the answer, 'I can feel for myself how much you like that.' But Carolyn answered for herself.

'I love it,' she said, hearing the words in her head right before she said them out loud. 'Your cock inside me –'

It was easy to talk like that with him. It seemed right to speak dirty, because his lips curved into a smile, as if he had known she had it in her the whole time.

'You said something about leashes,' he reminded her, keeping that grin on his face as he worked his hard cock back and forth, touching and teasing her with the head then the shaft. 'Collars and leashes.'

Oh, it was going to be wonderful. They'd play all the different games that lovers could, without any of the falseness that accompanied Dahlia's trysts. Because this was real. Carolyn knew it. Understood it. And as she came in Zachary's arms, she felt that she'd somehow come home.

How it had happened after one night, she wasn't sure. And how it had happened when they hadn't really spoken to each other – sure, they'd talked, but what had they really talked about? – she also wasn't sure. All she knew was that she felt better. Maybe this was the day that she would confront Dahlia. Would tell her about Dante. About listening. About the grate. Would apologise and try to make a fresh start.

But not right now. Carolyn was startled to see that it was already after ten. Zach had a meeting with his agent, something important that he couldn't reschedule.

'You stay here,' he said, smiling at her.

'No.' She shook her head. 'I'll go downstairs. I don't want to bother you.'

'I'll be back in a few hours. I like the thought of you sleeping in my bed.'

She liked the thought of it, too. Liked it a lot. Sleeping in his sheets. Sheets that the two of them had rumpled together. It was a good feeling to be in a bed that had been warmed by both of their bodies. So she stayed, sprawled naked on his black cotton sheets, ignoring the sounds that spilled in from the outdoors. She could tune out just about any noise. Construction work on the street. Dahlia's three alarms. The sound of Marlon's engine revving.

* * *

When Carolyn woke at four, she headed downstairs to shower. Dahlia's door was partly open. Carolyn looked through and realised that the cleaners had come and gone while she'd been at Zach's. The cheque she'd left stuck to the refrigerator with a magnet was gone, replaced with a note stating the next time the magic duo would be back – a week from Monday at 11:00 a.m. Carolyn marked the date on the kitchen calendar and then walked back down the hall to her bedroom.

But then she remembered the tape. Dahlia had wanted her to translate what Marlon was saying. And she'd promised to leave the tape for her. Carolyn looked around her room, but didn't find it. She then went into Dahlia's room and opened the drawer by the bed. There was the recorder, with a special extra-long tape inside. She snagged it and slipped it into her pocket to listen to during her first break at work.

Standing in the middle of Dahlia's bedroom, she realised that something seemed different. Not just that the room was clean – Max and Billy must have hung up Dahlia's clothing in order to get to the basics of straightening up – but something else nagged at her. She spun around and saw that the windows were gleaming. They'd promised to wash them the last time. Then she shrugged, unsure of what was bothering her, and left the bedroom and the apartment.

Chapter Twenty-Four

*T*he first call came at a quarter to four.

'Personal call for you,' her producer said. It must be Zach. Carolyn felt her heart race. He was calling at work, probably to make some goofy personal request. Stevie Wonder's 'I Just Called to Say I Love You'. No, that was too sappy. But something good. Then her producer continued, 'Says his name is Chaz. Line one.'

She pushed the button and took the call over her headset. 'Stairway to Heaven' was on. She had time to talk.

'I can't believe it,' Chaz was saying in his thick, French accent. 'How can you be working?'

She didn't know what he meant, and she told him so. She only knew him through Dahlia and, had only met him at Christmas parties and on the rare occasions when she visited Dahlia at work.

'I was sure you'd have a substitute. Or, at least, that they'd play an old show. When I heard you say the date, then I knew you were really there.'

'What are you talking about?'

Now, he was the one to hesitate. 'You don't know, do you?'

'I've got four minutes,' she said, watching the clock.

'Christ, Carolyn. Dahlia's missing. She never showed

up at work. They found her car parked at the salon, but nobody knows where she is. Didn't they call you?'

Carolyn thought of her phone, with the ringer off, lights blinking on the answering machine that she'd ignored. She thought of staying at Zach's all day, crashed in his bed while he was out with his agent and then at rehearsal, enjoying the sensation of being in someone else's world. Now, a rush of fear, one that was more than familiar, flooded through her.

'She's *missing*,' Chaz said again, more urgently, 'and I don't know what to do.'

She heard the way the statement sounded. *He* didn't know what to do. As usual, in Chaz's world everything revolved around him and his salon. Now, Carolyn's producer was waving to her and pointing to the clock. She put her roommate's boss on hold, cued up the next cut, gave a brief intro, and then picked up the line again.

'Chaz, I've got another call.'

The second call was from the police. They were downstairs. And they wanted to talk to Carolyn. In person.

Back at home, Carolyn walked through the apartment, not able to process the information that the police had given her. It was all happening so fast. They'd found Dahlia's body up in the hills, close by the famous Hollywood sign. Carolyn couldn't believe this. She walked into Dahlia's room, drawn despite herself to all of her pretty things. How could her roommate be dead? Her bedroom was all ready for her. Waiting for Dahlia and her next beau.

Carolyn's head hurt but she forced herself to think. After a drink, at least. Swiftly, she walked to the kitchen where she poured white wine into a goblet, and then sat on the sofa in the dark. She drained half the glass and started to think about getting the bottle from the kitchen and bringing it to the living room, where it would be nice and close. Save her a few trips. But just as she stood up, there was a knock on the door.

Too numb to be startled, she was careful. Silently, she

peeked out the hole to see Jason, holding flowers. At first, she couldn't fathom what he was doing. It was too early for anyone to send flowers. Information about the death wouldn't be in the papers until tomorrow. Besides, people didn't deliver condolence cards themselves – they sent them through the mail.

Finally, Carolyn understood. Dahlia had a date. It was only day one. Less than 24 hours after her death. There was no reason why Jason would know. Police were still filing reports. The newspapers tomorrow would carry a feature. Her salon would only do dark rinses in honour of her death.

God, I'm sick, Carolyn thought. And now Jason was knocking again.

She put her hands through her hair, smoothing it back, then looked down at her dishevelled clothes and caught a glimpse of the complete disarray reflected in the window. Who the fuck cared what she looked like? Not Jason.

Carolyn shrugged and started to unlock the door. And then suddenly she thought, Was it him? Dahlia had been playing hard to get with him lately, refusing his calls, refusing his dates. Had he killed her? Carolyn had given his name to the cops, just like she'd recited the name of every other one of Dahlia's amours. Why hadn't they contacted him yet? Why should she open the door to him?

'You there, Dahlia?' Jason called out. Through the hole, Carolyn watched as he arranged the flowers.

Why flowers?

She found herself wondering whether this evening was some special occasion for the couple? Were they marking their three-week anniversary? Despite her fears, she opened the door, and his swagger slipped a notch when he saw that it was her.

'Hey, Carolyn,' he said, waiting for her to step aside and let him in. 'Is Dahlia almost ready?'

'She's –' Carolyn started, but then she realised that she was not yet rehearsed enough, or drunk enough, to tell him exactly what Dahlia was. Not able to spill all the brutal details.

'Not yet, huh?' he asked, now pushing past her to sit on the sofa. Finally, Carolyn sat across from him, perching on the coffee table.

'Bad news,' she said softly, just like she'd heard the inspector on the phone with Dahlia's mom. 'There's been an . . . accident.' She chose the word carefully, deciding against 'incident', the name for what Steve had done to her. There. That sounded good. Like TV. She was used to hearing these sorts of statements on the stupid made-for-TV-movies she occasionally watched, the ones that Dante often wrote.

'Accident?' he asked, concerned, following his lines in the script precisely. 'Was she in a car wreck?' That was the normal first guess for anyone living in LA.

'I'm not sure how to tell you this.' Exactly on cue. She knew her part well. The grieving friend, confused roommate, prepared to console the boyfriend. The first in a line of boyfriends who would need to be consoled. Did Jason have any idea that his girl had been with another man last night?

'What are you saying?'

'She's . . .' A nice pause here for effect '. . . dead.'

Dahlia, even in memory, seemed too alive to relegate to past tense. Carolyn had to force herself to continue, to tell Jason that she'd been murdered. He smiled, and for a moment she thought that she'd gotten this all wrong. That he was the killer, and that she was about to be his next victim.

'Sick joke,' he said, and she came back to reality. He was not the killer. He just didn't believe her. Carolyn knew that she wouldn't have, either, if someone else had told her the news. Someone like Chaz, or Zach, or any of Dahlia's admirers. Any, she thought again. Any of her many boyfriends. Joe. Marlon. Dante. And all the many exes.

'Not a joke,' she said, her face in the mask of sadness. Inside, it was actually shock. Numbed disbelief. But she knew this role. She was good at it. She'd watched people put on these sad mask faces for her after Steven, and when Jason lowered his head suddenly, bit his lip, and made those manly noises that grown men make when they don't want to cry in front of a woman, Carolyn went to sit by his side on the sofa and put her hand on his shoulder.

'When did it happen?'

'Last night.' She told him that she was surprised the police hadn't spoken with him yet.

'I was out all day looking for new locations. I was borrowing a buddy's cell phone because mine was ripped off. Nobody got in touch with me.'

'Not at your house?'

He shook his head.

She realised the police were probably working through the list of people, of possibilities she'd given them, and the fact that she'd told them that Dahlia wasn't with Jason the night before may have helped him. But she suggested that he call them anyway, just to clear his name.

'Sure,' he said, nodding, standing suddenly. 'You OK?'

Carolyn nodded, even though she wasn't. Not by a long shot. Jason looked around and spotted Terrie in the corner, asleep. 'At least you've got your dog for company. And security.'

Carolyn nodded again, walked him to the door, and watched him walk away.

In the morning, Carolyn was not at all surprised to hear the coffee pot going. It just made her secure in the thought that this whole awful experience had been another bad dream, different from her normal nightmares, but hideous none the less. She and Terrie happily walked into the kitchen, both of them most likely expecting to find the same thing: Dahlia in one of her silk robes, barefoot on the lino, pouring half a cup of coffee into her favourite floral-patterned mug and then adding a generous helping of milk.

Instead, she found Dante, standing in the kitchen in a grey T-shirt and faded jeans, smiling and offering a cup of java.

'How'd you get in?' Carolyn asked, pulling her robe tightly closed, backing up a step and placing a protective hand on Terrie's head.

'Key,' he said, as if it was obvious. As he spoke, Carolyn remembered that he'd never given his back to Dahlia. 'Has she already left for work? Her car's gone.'

Carolyn's mind tried to catch up with the situation. If he had a key, why wouldn't he simply go and try to wake her up the way he liked to – climbing into her bed and slipping inside her from behind? 'The most seductive wake-up call,' Dahlia liked to say. 'Imagine opening your eyes just as you start to come.'

Carolyn took the offered coffee and tried to wake herself up. If he were the killer, then this would be a great way to hide it – to act all surprised when she told him, so that later she might go to the police and say, 'It couldn't be Dante. He showed up the next day, made coffee for us, was ready to take her out to breakfast. No way it could be him.' But if it wasn't him, then she had to break the news. Again.

'Where'd she go? The gym?' He stared at her, watching as carefully as she was watching him. 'Dahlia never gets up before seven.'

Before Carolyn could answer, he had another question.

'Is she with another guy?'

That's what he was worried about, why he hadn't simply entered her room. He sounded hurt, slightly angry, but not guilty. He was no actor. Carolyn had caught Dante in lies before. She was always aware of it when he fibbed. But this meant she had to tell him that Dahlia was dead.

Slowly, she walked into the living room and he followed her.

261

'Is she with that guy Jason?'

'No,' Carolyn said quietly, sitting on the sofa. Dante sat on the table. They were in the reverse position that she'd been in with Jason last night. 'No,' she repeated. 'She's not with Zach. She's not with Joe. She's not with Jason. She's not with anyone.'

After he left, Carolyn found herself walking through the apartment without thinking, when suddenly she remembered the tape. She'd had it for two days but hadn't remembered its existence until now. She grabbed it from her jacket pocket and held it in her hands, not wanting to listen. But finally, she slid the tape into her fancy machine and pressed 'play'.

Right away, she had to stop. Listening to the sexed-up sounds of Dahlia's vocals were too much. What had she been thinking? That was easy. She'd been thinking that maybe the tape held a clue. If Marlon really hadn't been there the entire evening, then someone else had. Someone else was on the tape.

First, she listened just to get a feel of the whole thing. An overview. And right away, she realised something she'd missed before. Terrie hadn't barked. Terrie *always* barked. When Jason showed up, the dog went crazy. When the newest beau, Joe, had shown up, the dog had literally freaked out.

So who didn't Terrie bark for? Carolyn considered it. Harry. Dante. Zach. ... Who else? Nobody that she could immediately remember. But she knew it wasn't any of those people. She'd been with Zach and she couldn't believe it was Harry, even if he had been jealous of Dante's affection. She was also sure that Dante was innocent.

Next, Carolyn listened to the way Dahlia behaved, to the way she talked. And she really talked on this one.

'It's been so long,' Dahlia said. 'I missed you.'

The man made a muffled noise. A moan.

'Too long,' Dahlia crooned next, and the man now made an assent, but still didn't speak. Odd, thought

262

Carolyn. It really couldn't be Jason. Jason was a motor-mouth, and liked to keep a steady conversation going, even a one-sided conversation. And then the words stopped Carolyn and made her heart pound.

'Don't stop. Don't ever, ever stop.'

She closed her eyes, remembering. Then shook her head as the image came quickly, almost unbidden, to the front of her mind. It was Dahlia's ex-boyfriend. The one from college. Will, the one she'd heard while listening in the closet of their dorm room. Carolyn had never gotten a great look at him. But now she knew, and she was about to call the police and tell them – at least tell them what she had figured out – when the phone rang.

He had a key. She'd given him one. That made it much easier for Billy to sneak into the apartment. Carolyn was on the phone, which helped as well. And Terrie didn't bark, because he never barked at Billy. This was because Billy always remembered to give him a little snack each time, so that the dog remembered him and liked him. Dogs were easy to trick. Only a little easier than people.

Through the hallway on the carpet that hid any sound, he stepped into Dahlia's room and waited for her to hang up the phone. When she finally set the receiver in the cradle, he was right there. Waiting.

Chapter Twenty-Five

'Write about what you know,' Billy sneered, throwing that particular piece of advice back at Carolyn. 'Isn't that what you said?'

'I didn't mean that about killing people.' Carolyn was stating the obvious, but this guy was a sicko. Maybe he truly hadn't understood that she never meant for him to commit murders.

'Doesn't matter. Nobody would have wanted to read about me cleaning places, would they? And besides, I wasn't writing about the killings, at first. I was just killing for the taste of it. And what a taste.' He licked his lips, looking suddenly even more evil than before. He had a vampirish quality to him that Carolyn had never noticed. '*You're* the one who gave me the idea to put it to good use.'

She looked at Billy from the bed. Something was still nagging at her, confusing her. 'But what does it have to do with me?' she asked. Maybe if she could stall for time she would be able to get one of her wrists free. She tried to picture how Dante had tied the knots when she had watched him and Dahlia engage in bedroom bondage play.

'You just make it easier for me to get away. Pin the

crime on the jealous roommate. Then, overcome with remorse, you kill yourself.'

'I wasn't jealous of her,' Carolyn lied. 'She was my friend.'

'She was a cunt,' he spat, spacing the words apart for emphasis. 'Turned me on with her little outfits and her sexy ways then dumped me for some other guy, a stupid frat boy, and then moved on from him to someone else. She was never satisfied. I saved a lot of men a fuck-load of heartache.'

'And the rest of women? The girls? That young kid?'

'Practice. For her. I wanted to do it right, you know. And I could tell that they were all headed in the same direction as Dahlia. The same slippery road to being a ball-breaker.'

'The young mother,' Carolyn said, her voice almost a whisper. She knew that it was probably not the smartest move for her to antagonise him, but she guessed that she had more of a chance of surviving the longer she kept him talking. Her hands were sweaty now and she slid them back and forth over her head, feeling the ropes gently to see if they'd given up any slack.

'She was having an affair.'

Carolyn looked at him blankly.

'A cleaner always knows these things. Her husband worked out of town quite a bit, but there were always men's boxers in her bed. Kinky flavoured gels on her nightstand. Pornos in the video machine. She was just like Dahlia.' Now he paused and looked Carolyn over. 'You were different.' He smiled so nicely that she found herself momentarily disarmed. 'You actually liked me. I had fun talking to you. You're pretty, but you don't know it. That's the difference. Girls who know it use it.'

'But what are you going to do with me?'

'I'm not going to waste your death, if that's what you're worried about. I never waste anything. Comes from being a cleaner. You see the stuff people throw away and it makes you sick. Rich people, discarding things that have only been used one time, or that've never been used at all. Bored before they've even taken it out of the package. So don't worry, I won't waste you. I've got this new scene I'm writing.' As he explained, a different look came over his face, an intense expression that was the most frightening she'd seen yet. But mixed with the violence in his features was a look that she understood. His expression was like Dante's when he was working on a story. 'I tried to workshop it, you know, in one of those writers' chat rooms on the Internet, but the people in my group just couldn't help me out. They thought I was being intentionally gross.'

He laughed to himself as he polished the knife on the bottom of his shirt tails. It glinted in the light, and Carolyn felt herself start to tremble. She closed her eyes, but that was somehow worse. When she opened them, something in the room had changed. She couldn't tell what at first. Then, from the corner of her eye, she saw that the closet door was open a crack. It had been shut tightly before. A shimmer of metallic magenta fabric sparkled. She recognised it as a discarded dress that Dahlia had given to Harry. Carolyn couldn't believe what she was seeing, but she now worked to keep her eyes on Billy and not to give anything away.

'Why would I be intentionally gross?' Billy asked, coming closer. 'I'd rather be real. Spell it out exactly as it happens. The drip-drop sound of the blood as it pools on a hardwood floor. The squeal of the knife when you pull it out of a deep wound.' He stared at Carolyn. 'I mean, it squeals. This intense sound, as if it doesn't want to let go. You can't make that shit up.'

The tinkle of Harry's shoulder-length faux crystal earrings suddenly caught Billy's attention, but it was too late. Even though Billy turned around quickly, Harry had already pushed the closet door the rest of the way open and was standing right behind him. Billy lunged forward with the knife, but Harry was slim and fast. With a move that would have pleased any choreographer, Harry pirouetted to the left, stepped right, and then, rising up on tiptoes in decadently towering stilettos, hit Billy over the head with one of Dahlia's clunky high-heeled clogs, the new-wave shoes from Europe that hadn't caught on in the States yet. Each shoe must have weighed as much as a sack of potatoes.

Billy was momentarily stunned, still standing, but barely. Harry used that moment wisely, throwing his boa around Billy's neck and pulling it taut. While Billy now brought his hands up to fight Harry, Carolyn continued working on the knots that bound her to the bed, moving frantically now. But despite her added struggles, she simply couldn't get free.

Harry had his boa wrapped even tighter around Billy's neck, and while Billy dug his hands beneath the blue-dyed ostrich feathers to get some space to breathe, Harry reached into his quilted handbag and pulled out a pair of shining silver handcuffs.

'Never go anywhere without handcuffs,' was one of Harry's favourite sayings. He quickly slid them on to Billy's wrists, looped a second set through the first, and locked him to the foot of the bed. Then he hurried to Carolyn's side to help her get loose.

'Ever think you'd be saved by a drag queen brandishing a feather boa?' Harry wanted to know as he sliced through the ropes with a rhinestone-studded Swiss army knife. 'Did you, Carolyn?'

She was too grateful to respond.

Chapter Twenty-Six

'You know,' Harry said softly, 'she knew.'

'I know she knew,' Carolyn repeated, confused. Then she turned the words into a question. 'I know she knew what?' she asked, the sentence sounding like a tongue-twister. Still, as she looked at him, startled, a prickle of understanding tricked its way up her spine. She thought that she understood exactly what he was saying, but to be totally sure, she needed him to explain further. Yet he didn't say a word, choosing instead to simply offer her a sympathetic look, one that was mixed with an endless supply of sadness.

'Harry,' she urged, 'come on. What did she know?' Carolyn's voice was just as low as his, even though there was no reason to whisper. They were sitting in her kitchen, staring at each other over tiny, steaming cups of espresso. It was nearly 6 a.m. They'd been at the police station for hours, and now, although both were tired, it was clear that neither could imagine going to sleep.

'About you.'

He was going to make her continue to ask him questions. Sometimes Harry was like that, needing everything to be pulled from him, bit by bit. Dahlia had complained about that occasionally. 'Harry wanted to tell me about him and Jake, but it took hours for me to drag all the dirty details out of him.'

'About me *what*, Harry?'

'About you and the closet –'

Carolyn felt her cheeks redden in their normal and vibrant response to embarrassing news. But at least that explained a little more about how Harry had been in the closet at the right time. She waited for him to continue, sipping too much from the little cup and burning her tongue.

'It turned her on, you know,' Harry said. 'I mean, she always knew you were a voyeur. That was just your personality. And she was the exhibitionist queen. What a pair you two made. The thought that you were getting turned on by watching her perform ... well, that just sort of turned her on all the more. Made her want to be wilder, to go further. And in a way she thought it might help you get better. You'd see all this cool stuff, and then maybe you'd want to do some of it on your own.'

Once again, when it came to matters of the heart and the loins Dahlia had been right. That's exactly what had happened. She'd seen it. And she'd wanted to do it. With Zach. 'But how do you know all this?'

'Dahlia and I didn't have any secrets from each other. She knew all about my little indiscretions, and I knew about hers. And, I guess, about most of yours. We just chit-chatted all the time about stuff like that at work. But afterwards, when she was killed –' He hesitated as he said that, and Carolyn realised that Dahlia's death had probably affected Harry the most of all. 'Well, I just wanted to keep an eye on you. I was driving by your apartment. I wanted to check on you, to stay close.'

'In the closet close?'

'That was sort of unintentional. I came by to keep you company and then heard the noises from outside the apartment, and I was worried. But I didn't know if you were recreating some sort of Dahlia scene, or if you were really in trouble. Then I saw the van outside, "The Confidential Cleaners", and I got extra concerned. What were they doing here at night? So I followed your method of sneaking a peak. Just to be sure.'

And thank God, he had, Carolyn realised. This wasn't the time to be embarrassed, it was the time to be grateful. Still, she had more questions to ask.

'How long had she known?'

'Since college,' Harry said, and he gave her a small smile. 'You might have envisioned yourself to be quite the clever peeping Tom, but I guess you're not all that quiet after all.' He put one hand on hers and sighed, 'You know that there's still one thing that hasn't been cleared up.'

Carolyn shook her head, her thick dark hair swishing around her face. She didn't know what he was talking about.

'Zach's waiting for you. He's been waiting all night. I saw him on the landing. Told him I'd send you up when you were ready. So here's the big question, Carolyn.'

She waited, and he gave her a look that asked her if he really needed to spell this out. She opened her blue eyes wide, nodding.

'Are you ready?'

'Ready?' Her voice trembled as she said it.

'To stop watching and start doing?' He paused again, holding her hand in both of his. 'For real, this time, Carolyn.'

That was the question, wasn't it?

Epilogue

When Zach said he loved her, it took Carolyn by surprise. She understood that this was where he was supposed to say it. She'd listened to every love song ever made, knew all of the lyrics by heart. This particular melody featured her, wrapped in Zach's strong arms, under the sheets of his bed. His chin rested on her shoulder, and she could feel his warm breath on her skin. They were naked together in a spooning embrace, his body pressed firmly against hers.

'Carolyn, look at me,' he said softly, his voice as low and soothing as when he was speaking into a microphone in the middle of a stage. Slowly, she slid out of his embrace, then rolled over to face him, to meet his gaze. His hand came up and she closed her eyes as he traced his fingertips over the lines in her face. The bones of her cheeks, her strong chin, her nose. His fingers moved lower, to touch the faded designs of the scar on her shoulder, the last remnant of Steven.

She kept her eyes closed as Zach called her beautiful. When she didn't respond, he said it again, said it just as he had the first time they'd met. As if he was in some way naming her, discovering her.

'You *are* beautiful, Carolyn.'

Dahlia had said that she would meet someone. She'd

told her over and over that if Carolyn went out and gave life a chance again, she would meet the right man. Someone who didn't know the person she'd been before. Who didn't have a need to judge her or compare her with who she used to be, or with anyone else. Dahlia had promised that Carolyn would meet a man who would love her for who she was, not who she'd been.

It had sounded too much like a greeting card at the time. Carolyn hadn't believed her, had chalked the words up to someone trying to give her a boost, trying to help her regain her lost confidence. She should have realised that Dahlia wasn't that type of person. In their years as friends, she had never tried to make Carolyn feel as if she should have been different, as if she would have been a better person if she were someone else. It's why Carolyn had liked her. With her, Dahlia was always fair.

Zach said, 'I love you.'

And Carolyn looked into his eyes as she decided to believe.

BLACK LACE NEW BOOKS

Published in May

PLAYING HARD
Tina Troy
£6.99

Lili wrestles men for money. And they pay well. She's the best in the business and her powerful body and stunning looks have her gentlemen visitors begging for more rough treatment. Her golden rule is never to date a client, but when James Travers starts using her services she relents and accepts a date.

An unusual and powerfully sexy story of male/female wrestling.

ISBN 0 352 33617 X

HIGHLAND FLING
Jane Justine
£6.99

Writer Charlotte Harvey is researching the mysterious legend of the Highland Ruby pendant for an antiques magazine – a ruby that is said to sexually enslave any woman to the man who places the pendant round her neck. Charlotte's quest leads her to a remote Scottish island where the pendant's owner – the dark and charismatic Andrew Alexander – is keen to test its powers on his guest.

A cracking tale of wild sex in the Highlands of Scotland.

ISBN 0 352 33616 1

CIRCO EROTICA
Mercedes Kelley
£6.99

Flora is a lion-tamer in a Mexican circus. She inhabits a curious and colourful world of trapeze artists, snake charmers and hypnotists. When her father dies owing a lot of money to the circus owner, the dastardly Lorenzo, Flora's life is set to change. Lorenzo and his accomplice – the perverse Salome – share a powerful sexual hunger, a taste for bizarre adult fun and an interest in Flora.

This is a Black Lace special reprint of one of our most unusual and perverse titles!

IBSN 0 352 33257 3

SUMMER FEVER
Anna Ricci
£6.99

Lara Mcintyre has lusted after artist Jake Fitzgerald for almost two decades. As a warm, dazzling summer unfolds, she makes the journey back to her student summer-house where they first met, determined to satisfy her physical craving somehow. And then, ensconced in Old Beach House once more, she discovers her true sexual self – but not without complications.

Beautifully written story of extreme passion.

ISBN 0 352 33625 0

STRICTLY CONFIDENTIAL
Alison Tyler
£6.99

Carolyn Winters is a smooth-talking disc jockey at a hip LA radio station. Although known for her sexy banter over the airwaves, she leads a reclusive life, despite the urging of her flirtatious roommate, Dahlia. Carolyn grows dependent on living vicariously through Dahlia, eavesdropping and then covertly watching as her roommate's sexual behaviour becomes more and more bizarre. But then Dahlia is murdered, and Carolyn must overcome her fears in order to bring the killer to justice.

A tense dark thriller for those who like their erotica on the forbidden side.

ISBN 0 352 33624 2

CONTINUUM
Portia Da Costa
£6.99

Joanna Darrell is something in the city. When she takes a break from her high-powered job she is drawn into a continuum of strange experiences and bizarre coincidences. Like Alice in a decadent Wonderland, she enters a parallel world of perversity and unusual pleasure. She's attracted to fetishism and discipline and her new friends make sure she gets more than a taste of erotic punishment.

This is a reprint of one of our best-selling and kinkiest titles ever!

ISBN 0 352 33120 8

To be published in July

SYMPHONY X
Jasmine Stone
£6.99

Katie is a viola player running away from her cheating husband. The tour of Symphony Xeverts not only takes her to Europe but also to the realm of deep sexual satisfaction. She is joined by a dominatrix diva and a bass singer whose voice is so low he's known as the Human Vibrator. After distractions like these, how will Katie be able to maintain her serious music career *and* allow herself to fall in love again?

Immensely funny journal of a sassy woman's sexual adventures.

ISBN 0 352 33629 3

OPENING ACTS
Suki Cunningham
£6.99

When London actress Holly Parker arrives in a remote Cornish village to begin rehearsing a new play, everyone there – from her landlord to her theatre director – seems to have an earthier attitude towards sex. Brought to a state of constant sexual arousal and confusion, Holly seeks guidance in the form of local therapist, Joshua Delaney. He is the one man who can't touch her – but he is the only one she truly desires. Will she be able to use her new-found sense of adventure to seduce him?

Wonderfully horny action in the Cornish countryside. Oooh arrgh!

ISBN 0 352 33630 7

THE SEVEN-YEAR LIST
Zoe le Verdier
£6.99

Julia is an ambitious young photographer who's about to marry her trustworthy but dull fiancé. Then an invitation to a college reunion arrives. Old rivalries, jealousies and flirtations are picked up where they were left off and sexual tensions run high. Soon Julia finds herself caught between two men but neither of them are her fiancé.

How will she explain herself to her friends? And what decisions will she make?

This is a Black Lace special reprint of a very popular title.

ISBN 0 352 33254 9

If you would like a complete list of plot summaries of Black Lace titles, or would like to receive information on other publications available, please send a stamped addressed envelope to:

Black Lace, Thames Wharf Studios,
Rainville Road, London W6 9HA

BLACK LACE BOOKLIST

Information is correct at time of printing. To check availability go to www.blacklace-books.co.uk

All books are priced £5.99 unless another price is given.

Black Lace books with a contemporary setting

THE TOP OF HER GAME	Emma Holly ISBN 0 352 33337 5	☐
LIKE MOTHER, LIKE DAUGHTER	Georgina Brown ISBN 0 352 33422 3	☐
IN THE FLESH	Emma Holly ISBN 0 352 33498 3	☐
SHAMELESS	Stella Black ISBN 0 352 33485 1	☐
TONGUE IN CHEEK	Tabitha Flyte ISBN 0 352 33484 3	☐
FIRE AND ICE	Laura Hamilton ISBN 0 352 33486 X	☐
SAUCE FOR THE GOOSE	Mary Rose Maxwell ISBN 0 352 33492 4	☐
INTENSE BLUE	Lyn Wood ISBN 0 352 33496 7	☐
THE NAKED TRUTH	Natasha Rostova ISBN 0 352 33497 5	☐
A SPORTING CHANCE	Susie Raymond ISBN 0 352 33501 7	☐
TAKING LIBERTIES	Susie Raymond ISBN 0 352 33357 X	☐
A SCANDALOUS AFFAIR	Holly Graham ISBN 0 352 33523 8	☐
THE NAKED FLAME	Crystalle Valentino ISBN 0 352 33528 9	☐
CRASH COURSE	Juliet Hastings ISBN 0 352 33018 X	☐
ON THE EDGE	Laura Hamilton ISBN 0 352 33534 3	☐

LURED BY LUST	Tania Picarda ISBN 0 352 33533 5	☐
LEARNING TO LOVE IT	Alison Tyler ISBN 0 352 33535 1	☐
THE HOTTEST PLACE	Tabitha Flyte ISBN 0 352 33536 X	☐
THE NINETY DAYS OF GENEVIEVE	Lucinda Carrington ISBN 0 352 33070 8	☐
EARTHY DELIGHTS	Tesni Morgan ISBN 0 352 33548 3	☐
MAN HUNT £6.99	Cathleen Ross ISBN 0 352 33583 1	☐
MÉNAGE £6.99	Emma Holly ISBN 0 352 33231 X	☐
DREAMING SPIRES £6.99	Juliet Hastings ISBN 0 352 33584 X	☐
THE TRANSFORMATION £6.99	Natasha Rostova ISBN 0 352 33311 1	☐
STELLA DOES HOLLYWOOD £6.99	Stella Black ISBN 0 352 33588 2	☐
UP TO NO GOOD £6.99	Karen S. Smith ISBN 0 352 33589 0	☐
SIN.NET £6.99	Helena Ravenscroft ISBN 0 352 33598 X	☐
HOTBED £6.99	Portia Da Costa ISBN 0 352 33614 5	☐
TWO WEEKS IN TANGIER £6.99	Annabel Lee ISBN 0 352 33599 8	☐
HIGHLAND FLING £6.99	Jane Justine ISBN 0 352 33616 1	☐
PLAYING HARD £6.99	Tina Troy ISBN 0 352 33617 X	☐
SUMMER FEVER £6.99	Anna Ricci ISBN 0 352 33625 0	☐
CONTINUUM £6.99	Portia Da Costa ISBN 0 352 33120 8	☐

Black Lace books with an historical setting

INVITATION TO SIN £6.99	Charlotte Royal ISBN 0 352 33217 4	☐
PRIMAL SKIN	Leona Benkt Rhys ISBN 0 352 33500 9	☐
DEVIL'S FIRE	Melissa MacNeal ISBN 0 352 33527 0	☐

WILD KINGDOM	Deanna Ashford ISBN 0 352 33549 1	☐
DARKER THAN LOVE	Kristina Lloyd ISBN 0 352 33279 4	☐
STAND AND DELIVER	Helena Ravenscroft ISBN 0 352 33340 5	☐
THE CAPTIVATION £6.99	Natasha Rostova ISBN 0 352 33234 4	☐
CIRCO EROTICA £6.99	Mercedes Kelley ISBN 0 352 33257 3	☐

Black Lace anthologies

CRUEL ENCHANTMENT Erotic Fairy Stories	Janine Ashbless ISBN 0 352 33483 5	☐
MORE WICKED WORDS	Various ISBN 0 352 33487 8	☐
WICKED WORDS 4	Various ISBN 0 352 33603 X	☐

Black Lace non-fiction

THE BLACK LACE BOOK OF WOMEN'S SEXUAL FANTASIES	Ed. Kerri Sharp ISBN 0 352 33346 4	☐

—————✂—————————————————

Please send me the books I have ticked above.

Name   ....

Address   ....

              ....

              ....

              .... Post Code ....

Send to: **Cash Sales, Black Lace Books, Thames Wharf Studios, Rainville Road, London W6 9HA.**

US customers: for prices and details of how to order books for delivery by mail, call 1-800-805-1083.

Please enclose a cheque or postal order, made payable to **Virgin Publishing Ltd**, to the value of the books you have ordered plus postage and packing costs as follows:

  UK and BFPO – £1.00 for the first book, 50p for each subsequent book.

  Overseas (including Republic of Ireland) – £2.00 for the first book, £1.00 for each subsequent book.

If you would prefer to pay by VISA, ACCESS/MASTER-CARD, DINERS CLUB, AMEX or SWITCH, please write your card number and expiry date here:

....

Please allow up to 28 days for delivery.

Signature ....

—————✂—————————————————